As the Black School Sings

AS THE BLACK SCHOOL SINGS

Black Music Collections
At Black Universities and Colleges
With a Union List of Book Holdings

Jon Michael Spencer

Music Reference Collection, Number 13

GREENWOOD PRESS
New York • Westport, Connecticut • London

Library of Congress Cataloging-in-Publication Data

Spencer, Jon Michael.
 As the Black school sings.

 (Music reference collection, ISSN 0736-7740 ; no. 13)
 Bibliography: p.
 Includes index.
 1. Afro-Americans—Music—History and criticism—
Bibliography—Catalogs. 2. Afro-Americans—Music—
Bibliography—Catalogs. 3. Afro-Americans—Music—
History and criticism—Bibliography—Union lists.
4. Afro-Americans—Music—Bibliography—Union lists.
5. Catalogs, Union—United States. I. Title. II. Series.
ML128.B45S7 1987 016.78'08996073 87-8412
ISBN 0-313-25859-7 (lib. bdg. : alk. paper)

Library of Congress Catalog Card Number: 87-8412
ISBN: 0-313-25859-7
ISSN: 0736-7740

First published in 1987

Greenwood Press, Inc.
88 Post Road West, Westport, Connecticut 06881

Printed in the United States of America

The paper used in this book complies with the
Permanent Paper Standard issued by the National
Information Standards Organization (Z39.48-1984).

10 9 8 7 6 5 4 3 2 1

*To the patriarchs and progeny of Hampton University, particularly Professor
R. Nathaniel Dett (1882–1943)*

CONTENTS

Contents

Preface

The Impetus

It was R. Nathaniel Dett's scholarly work under the auspices of Black academe and his potent two-page editorial, "As the Negro School Sings," that brought to my attention the essentiality of the Black educational institution participating in the sustentation of Black musical heritage. Declared Dett in his commentary:

> Negro music, even now, is in danger of running on the rocks. Here is where the Negro educational institution has its great opportunity.
>
> It is in the Negro school for the most part that the songs of the race have been most carefully preserved. It is in the Negro school that these folk songs, especially the "spirituals" have been used to create and intensify the atmosphere of religion.... It is in the Negro school that music directors have led Negro songs with no idea other than to produce the effect of beauty and naturalness; so it is that now only in the Negro school is the ideal presentation of Negro music to be found....
>
> So it is the various Negro schools which have the great opportunity of exerting a steadying influence on the development of Negro music. It is doubtful whether these institutions realize the chance which is theirs.[1]

Dett, through his performing, composing, arranging, choral directing, teaching, and scholarly writing, was emblematic of Black academe in action.

The impetus to develop Dett's "preservation" model into more than just a journal publication and series of lectures,[2] came only after reading a newspaper article about a retired history professor of the university at which I taught. The article, "Dr. Edmonds' Dream: A Hub of Black Study," brought the Dett concept closer to home:

> Dr. Edmonds has a dream of N. C. Central University's becoming a center for the study of blacks and black culture.
>
> Dr. Edmonds...says NCCU could develop a contemporary version of the sociological repositories developed earlier in the century at Atlanta University under W. E. B. DuBois and at Fisk University under Charles S. Johnson....
>
> "We should become, first for North Carolina and then for the entire South, a master center for information about black history, economics, sociology—everything."

[1]R. Nathaniel Dett, "As the Negro School Sings," *Southern Workman*, 56 (July 1927), 304–05.

[2]Jon Michael Spencer, "R. Nathaniel Dett's Views on the Preservation of Black Music," *The Black Perspective in Music*, 10, No. 2 (Fall 1982), 133-46.

Having such a center, Dr. Edmonds said, would make NCCU unique and perhaps provide it with "the vital link" it has long sought with the Research Triangle Park and the Triangle universities....

To explore the possibility of establishing such a center, she said, NCCU would have to send people to Fisk and Atlanta universities to study the background of these institutions' work in black sociology.

She said the exploratory work would also include the writing of proposals to determine whether foundations are interested in helping to finance a center.[3]

The Project

Endeavoring to actualize Dr. Edmonds' dream, I wrote a proposal to the Mary Duke Biddle Foundation of Durham, North Carolina. In 1984 I received the grant to pursue my research on the participative part Black colleges play in the preservation of Black music and to initiate an archival collection of Black music at North Carolina Central University (NCCU). It was my "dream" that the archive would burgeon into what Dr. Edmonds envisioned as a "center for the study of blacks and black culture."

My research entailed visiting, not just Atlanta and Fisk universities, but 17 select Black universities and colleges throughout the United States, principally during the Summer of 1985. In assessing the involvement of these colleges in the conduct of Black music conservation, I inquired into the artistic and scholastic productivity of their faculty composers, choral directors, ethnomusicologists, and performers, into their curricula and degree programs in the area of Black music, and particularly into their special research collections. Secondly, the project aimed to develop an archival collection of Black music in the Fine Arts Library at NCCU, that it might become, "first for North Carolina and then for the entire South, a master center for information about black history." After visiting the special research collections at Black colleges across the country and discerning their past and present work as well as projections for the future, I am better prepared to manage the archive at NCCU and to make recommendations as to how the university might maximize efforts in the overall scheme of Black cultural conservation.

While visiting the 17 schools, it was also my intention to solicit and collect for the archive as much music by Black faculty composers and arrangers as possible. In so doing, I was able to return with nearly a dozen of the unpublished orchestral and chamber compositions of John E. Price (Tuskegee Institute). And during my interviews with such other distinguished Black composers as Undine Smith Moore (Professor Emeritus, Virginia State University), William Dawson (Professor Emeritus, Tuskegee Institute), Alvin Batiste (Southern University), Roland Carter (Hampton University), and Wendell Whalum (Morehouse College),

[3] "Dr. Edmonds' Dream: A Hub of Black History," *Durham, [North Carolina] Morning Herald*, p. 6A, November 18, 1983.

I was able to request that they support our effort by sending us representative works from among their compositions.

During my research travel, I also made it a point to search through rare and out-of-print book stores in the various cities visited in order to purchase sheet music by historic Black composers. A number of pieces were retrieved for our collection by this means.

The Schools

The 17 universities and colleges visited during the Summer of 1985 (in chronological order) were South Carolina State, Savannah State, Morris-Brown, Clark, Morehouse, Spelman, Atlanta, Tuskegee, Dillard, Xavier, Southern, Jackson State, Fisk, Virginia State, Hampton, Howard, and Lincoln (Pennsylvania). Additionally, since this project was linked to the establishment of a Black music archive at NCCU, this book offers me the opportunity to introduce its expanding collection.

While NCCU has been added to this study, Dillard University has been deleted, for the Amistad Research Center, once located there, outgrew its library facility. Temporarily relocating to the Old U.S. Mint Building in the French Quarter of New Orleans, it finally settled at Tulane University. Had the Amistad remained at Dillard, it would have been a relevant part of this study on research collections at Black colleges, for among its holdings are the papers of composer Howard Swanson and jazz arranger Fletcher Henderson.

Each of the ten schools owning manuscript collections containing Black musical materials has a chapter devoted to its inventory in Part I of this volume. The collections are essentially ordered chronologically; however, personal papers precede general collections, precedence is given to historically prominent figures, and lengthy bibliographies and discographies are situated at the close of a chapter. The three schools without music-related manuscripts (South Carolina, Savannah, and Xavier) are nonetheless represented, along with the others, in the Bibliography and Union List in Part II. Containing 1,135 volumes on Black and African music and musicians, published in 33 countries in a half-dozen or so languages, the Bibliography opens with a table of symbols denoting which of the thirteen schools hold specific publications; appropriate symbols are appended to each citation. The subject matter in Part II is indexed, along with Part I, in the general index.

The Need

As I procured a detailed inventory of pertinent miscellanea in the research collectanea of the Black colleges visited and interviewed their archivists and librarians regarding their goals and methods, the necessity for this study became ever so evident. Aside from the recognized and utilized collections at Howard, Fisk, and Atlanta universities, scholars have been largely unaware of the reservoir of Black musical resources amassed at these other schools. Furthermore, curators have had to be involved with the larger concerns of archival management and thus have gleaned only a general idea of what specific musical materials have been accumulated. Having been funded by a foundation, this study fulfills the tedious task of cataloging for these institutions. It lists in detail published and unpublished musical compositions, hymnals and songbooks, phonograph and tape recordings, related correspondences, photographs, programs, broadsides, as well as newspaper, magazine, and journal clippings. As a general rule, the smaller the collection, the more detailed its description; but even the extensive collections are treated more closely here than in any other available source, including institutional shelf-lists.

This compiled catalogue-raisonné is multifunctional. First, it enables students and faculty to know what specific Black musical resources are readily available at their own institutions. Secondly, a researcher can refer to this volume to determine the source of needed information; and since the 17 schools represent a broad geographic area, the nearest repository holding the requisite material can be identified. Thirdly, this book can generate fresh ideas for research and publication, in that the papers of obscure historic Black musicians are here disclosed and significant musicological discoveries are revealed to the researcher for further attention. Fourthly, because biographical data is provided on persons noted within an inventory, this encyclopedic volume is of additional research value.

Just as vital to this work as the manuscript and bibliographic inventories in Parts I and II is the Introduction, in which I extrapolate and systemize the "preservation" motif posed in R. Nathaniel Dett's "As the Negro School Sings." The resultant history enumerates the conservation efforts of individual schools and music faculty whose academic, scholastic, and artistic activities deserve greater recognition. The contributions of contemporary choral directors, composers, performers, and ethnomusicologists are considered, as are such related aspects or activities of campus chapels, music curriculums, library programs, and institutional publications. The latter section completes the Introduction with a valuable bibliography of articles on Black music in non-music journals published by Black schools.

The Goal

If this encyclopedic catalog accomplishes its goals, then two developments ought to occur initially. First, there should be induced a keener awareness of the continuous need for the preservation of Black musical heritage within the superstratum of Black cultural sustentation, realized in the related productivity of Black academe. Second, there should be an increased usage of the collections described herein, culminating in the scholarly disbursement of research findings for the intellectual and cultural prosperity of the public and progeny.

If these two objectives are achieved, then a third resolve, the improvement of institutional image, should follow. A college archive avails scholastic self-image, for when faculty and students apprehend their institutional and racial heritage, they can be inspired to work as diligently as their accomplished predecessors. A viable and variegated curriculum contributes to this dynamic academic visage. And the involvement of faculty composers, ethnomusicologists, choir directors, and performers in their respective professions gives their audiences a positive perception of the universities and colleges for which they work. In short, if Black academe manifests the methods of sustentation systemized in the Introduction—that is, if *Black schools sing*—then their self-confidence and national image would be enhanced, and the essentiality of their subsistence would be better understood. Hence, visible academic distinction is "the vital link." To apply Dett's dictum, "Here is where the Negro educational institution has its great opportunity."

Acknowledgments

For their instructive and inspiring interaction and overall assistance in my research, I am grateful to the archivists, librarians, and music faculty at the schools visited: at South Carolina State Dr. Barbara Jenkins, Library Director, and Mary Smalls, Assistant Library Director; at Savannah State, Dr. Christine Oliver, Professor of Music; at Morehouse, Dr. Wendell Whalum, Music Department Chairman; at Spelman, Dr. Roland Allison, Music Department Chairman; at Atlanta, Minnie Clayton, Director of the Division of Special Collections; at Tuskegee, Daniel Williams, Archivist, John Price, Music Professor, and William Dawson, Music Professor Emeritus; at Southern, Dr. Aldrich Adkins, Music Department Chairman, Alvin Batiste, Director of Jazz Studies, Georgia Brown, Library Director, Ladell Smith, Archivist, and Janice Bell, Black Heritage Collection Librarian; at Jackson State, Dr. Jimmie James, Music Department Chairman, Bernice Bell, Assistant Library Director; at Dillard, Dr. Carole Taylor, Library Director; at Xavier, Leslie Morris, Library Director; at Fisk, Dr. Jessie Carney Smith, Library Director, and Beth House, Special Collections Librarian; at Virginia State, Catherine Bland, Library Director, Lucius Edwards, Archivist, Buckner Gamby, Music Professor, Undine Smith Moore, Music Professor Emeritus; at Hampton, Fritz Malval, Archivist, Donzella Willford and Cynthia Poston, Assistants to the Archivist, Georgia Cross, Peabody Room Librarian, Roland Carter, Music Department Chairman, Dr. Willia Daughtry and Dr. Enid Housty, Music Professors; at Howard (Moorland-Spingarn Research Center), Deborra Richardson, Music Librarian, James Johnson, Reference Librarian, Elinor Sinnette, Oral History Librarian, Marcia Bracey, Prints and Photographs Librarian; at Lincoln, Sophy Cornwell, Special Collections Librarian; and at North Carolina Central University, Gene Leonardi, Music Librarian, Debora Hazel, Head of Reference, and Reference staff Marilyn Griffin, Bennie Daye, and Veola Williams.

I am especially grateful to Saundra Russ Chambers who, during her tenure as a reference librarian at North Carolina Central University, verified entries in the Bibliography and Union List (Part II) on the Online Computer Library Center (OCLC), proofread the bibliography, and advised me on alphabetization. Ms.

Chambers is presently a reference librarian at the Twin Forks Library, a branch of the Wake County Department of the Public Library.

Above all I am grateful to the Mary Duke Biddle Foundation for funding this project at its inception and to Duke University for providing me with a grant toward its completion.

As the Black School Sings

INTRODUCTION
UNSUNG PROPONENTS OF PRESERVATION

Choir Directors

Choral Directors on faculty at historically Black universities and colleges have customarily been the ones revered as bearers of Black sacred song tradition, for their concerted spirituals have been performed by choirs in churches and concert halls throughout the United States and the world. William Dawson of Tuskegee Institute, John Wesley Work III of Fisk University, and R. Nathaniel Dett of Hampton University are among the historic figures whose work under the auspices of the Black college has inspired many unsung proponents of preservation. Roland Carter at Hampton University, Wendell Whalum at Morehouse College, Nathan Carter at Morgan State University, Samuel Barber at North Carolina A & T State University, and Robert Leigh Morris at Jackson State University currently perpetuate the practice their venerable forerunners traditionalized.

Roland Carter, for over two decades at Hampton, has been an avid enthusiast of the spiritual. In addition to the European classics, the concerted spirituals of early connoisseurs, and his own meritorious arrangements, Carter's Hampton choir also performs the choral works of such contemporary Black composers as Ulysses Kay, Hale Smith, Julius Williams, and Adolphus Hailstork.

As is the custom among Black college choirs, the Hampton choir has toured extensively, thereby exposing Black music to the nation and the world. Just as Dett's Hampton choir performed in New York's Carnegie Hall and Boston's Symphony Hall respectively in 1928 and 1929; so has Carter's choir performed at Carnegie Hall, the Kennedy Center, and at Philharmonic Hall in the Lincoln Center. And just as Dett's choir toured Europe in 1930, following the epochal lead of the Fisk Jubilee Singers a half-century earlier, so has Carter's choir toured the Scandinavian countries and the Virgin Islands respectively in 1970 and 1975. Under the direction of Carter, the Hampton choir has also produced three LP phonograph recordings, bequeathing an inheritance which shall allow heirs of Hampton to hear their ancestors sing Black spiritual songs.

In the 1970's gospel music secured a niche beside European classics and concerted spirituals in the repertoire of Black college choirs. Separate gospel ensembles also developed and became approved extracurricular activities. At North Carolina Central University, for instance, there are two gospel choirs under the auspices of the university's United Christian Campus Ministries (UCCM). From two of UCCM's constituents, the Pentecostal Fellowship Organization and the Baptist Student Union, evolved the Pentecostal Fellowship Choir in 1971 and the Baptist Student Union Choir in 1980.

Although a commonality in the 1980's, the existence of gospel choirs on Black college campuses in the seventies was still considered rather liberal, for during the fifties and sixties the "educated" refused to sanction gospel. Today its absence from a Black college campus is a conspicuity.

Composers

Black composers on faculty at Black schools are typically unable to teach composition due to the dearth of interested students at the undergraduate level and the paucity of students at the graduate level. However, the lack of a provocative commutation of creative ideas between teacher and student is partly compensated for by the ethnicity of the Black educational environment. Mark Fax (1911–1974) of Howard University, Noah Ryder (1914–1964) of Norfolk State University, and John Duncan (1908–1975) of Alabama State University were Black composers on the faculty of Black schools who were inspired to perpetuate the indigenous music of their ancestors with a continuity of new creations. These composers would have gratified Thomas P. Fenner who, in 1874, expressed the yearning that "this people which [had] developed such a wonderful musical sense in its degradation [would] in its maturity produce a composer who [could] bring a music of the future out of the music of the past."[1]

The music of Dr. Adolphus Hailstork is partly inspired by his Black college experience as an undergraduate composition student of Mark Fax at Howard University and his professorship at Norfolk State University, where he has been Composer-in-Residence since 1976. Among his compositions which assimilate elements of the blues are *American Landscape No. 2* for violin and cello (1978), *Suite* for violin and piano (1979), *Sport of Strings* for strings orchestra (1982), and *Trio* for violin, cello, and piano (1985). He synthesizes quotations, paraphrases, or imitations of the Black spiritual with blues tonalities and expressions in *Sonata* for piano (1980) and *I've Seen the Day* for soprano and string bass (1983). Blues, jazz, and the spiritual are fused in his *American Landscape No. 3* for orchestra (1982) and his *Two Struts with Blues* for strings, winds, and jazz quartet (1985). Traces of the gospel idiom can be heard in his *American Guernica* for concert band and piano soloist (1983) and gospel interspersed with quotations from Black spirituals in *Psalm 72* for choir, brass, and organ (1981). Two of his choral compositions pay tribute to the paradigmatic Black preacher and poet, *Epitaph for a Man Who Dreamed* (1979) and *In Memoriam: Langston Hughes* (1968).

Dr. Hailstork is beneficiary of the finest compositional training and recipient of innumerable compositional commissions and awards. His works have been published, recorded, and performed by symphony orchestras, instrumental en-

---

[1] Thomas P. Fenner, ed. *Religious Folk Songs of the Negroes Sung on the Plantations* (Hampton, Virginia: Hampton Institute Press, 1874), p. iv.

sembles, and choirs throughout the United States, including a quantum of performances abroad.

Composer John E. Price also serves as a commissure between the historic and the contemporary. A product of the ethnic environment of Lincoln University (Missouri) where he was an undergraduate student of composition, Price maintains an inspirational symbiosis with the Black college experience at historic Tuskegee Institute, where he has been a music professor since 1982. Utilizing scales, rhythms, and harmonies endemic to African and Black American music, he has composed such works as *A Langston Hughes Song Book* (1952/55), *Blues and Dance I* for clarinet and piano (1955), *Prayer: Martin Luther King* for choir and baritone soloist, and *Spirituals for the Young Pianist* (1979). In 1985 he received a grant from the Alabama State Arts Council to set Booker T. Washington's speech memorializing Harriet Tubman which was delivered in Auburn, New York the year of her death. The composition, for soloist, choir, and orchestra, is titled *Harriet Tubman: Booker T. Washington Speech, 1913*.[2]

Performers

The music of Black composers has been immortalized by recitalists who have performed throughout the nation and the world. One emanating soprano steadily approaching the accomplishments of Camilla Williams and Dorothy Maynor is Marilyn Thompson, who, like the latter two sopranos, is a product of the Black school. As Williams under the tutelage of Undine Smith Moore at Virginia State University and Maynor under the tutelage of R. Nathaniel Dett at Hampton University, Thompson under Roland Carter's instruction at Hampton acquired an aesthetic appreciation for the indigenous music of her heritage. In addition to performing classic and contemporary repertoire throughout the country and abroad, she brings the music of Black composers back to the Black school where a colligation of Black students can be informed and inspired by their musical history. The works of R. Nathaniel Dett, Hall Johnson, Howard Swanson, Margaret Bonds, Julia Perry, Leslie Adams, Leo Edwards, Charles Lloyd, Jr., Roland Carter, Jon Michael Spencer, Cecil Cohen, and many others have been performed in her recitals at such schools as Bowie State College, Morehouse College, Hampton University, and North Carolina Central University.

A counterpart of Marilyn Thompson in the field of instrumental music is Raymond Jackson, a music professor at Howard University who enjoys performing the piano works of Black composers. For instance, on May 5, 1985 at the National Gallery of Art's American Music Festival Series in Washington, D.C., he gave a recital consisting of Adolphus Hailstork's *Sonata*, John Child's *Choreographic Impressions*, Mark Fax's *Prelude, Fugue and Toccata*, R. Nathaniel Dett's *In the Bottoms*, and Samuel Coleridge-Taylor's *Toccata*.

---

[2] See the works of Hailstork and Price in the holdings of North Carolina Central University's Black Music Archive (Chapter 7).

The principal medium for the performance of opera by Black composers during the 1970's was Opera/South, a Black company founded by a white Catholic nun, Sister Mary Elise, former music director at Xavier University. Organized by Jackson State University, Tougaloo College, and Utica Junior College, it opened with the 1969-70 season. Although it staged operas of the standard German and Italian repertoire, it is perhaps best remembered for its premier of William Grant Still's *A Bayou Legend* on November 15, 1974. That performance garnered even more attention when aired on Mississippi Public Television on June 15, 1981. Opera/South also performed Still's *Highway #1, U.S.A.* and Ulysses Kay's *The Jougler of Our Lady*. Kay's *Jubilee*, based on Margaret Walker's novel of the same title, was premiered on November 20, 1976.[3]

On the jazz circuit is clarinetist and recording artist Alvin Batiste, an alumnus of Southern University where he is now director of the jazz studies program. Born in New Orleans and brought up amidst its jazz culture, Batiste has performed with such renowned musicians as Ray Charles, Cannonball Adderley, Billy Cobham, and Mercer Ellington's Band, and has been recording professionally since 1969. Albums featuring his own jazz quartet and compositions are *Clarinet Summit I* (1983), *Musique d'Afrique Nouvelle Orleans* (1984), and *Clarinet Summit II* (1986), produced by India Navigations in New York City.

Ethnomusicologists

The research of ethnomusicologists is fundamental to the preservation process. Entrenched in its hands-on application, they are the custodians who tap the oral tradition. Their scholarly retrieval is executed with the precise intention of documenting and dispersing ethnomusical culture in publications and lectures.

Among the contributions of ethnomusicologists around the turn of the century was the recording, transcribing, and publishing of Black folk song. In this regard, the historic faculty of Hampton University played a distinctive part. *Religious Folk Songs of the Negroes* was published in 1874 by Thomas P. Fenner, the first choral director at Hampton. The 1891 volume was edited by Helen Ludlow, the 1909 one by Robert Russa Moton, and the 1927 collection by R. Nathaniel Dett. In 1927 Natalie Curtis-Burlin produced a similar work, *Hampton Series Negro Folk Songs*.

Current work in ethnomusicology at Hampton includes that of Dr. Enid Housty, professor of music. On a 1982 Fulbright Scholarship she returned to her country, Guiana, South America, and conducted research on the pre-nuptial ritual, the Quey-Quey Ceremony. Dr. Housty has given several lectures on this Guianese ring-dance of African descent.

Dr. Roland Braithwaite, the Buell Gordon Gallagher Professor of Humanities at Talladega College, received a 1986 grant from the National Endowment for the

---

[3] See the Opera/South Collection in the holdings of Jackson State University (Chapter 5).

Humanities (NEH) for a Summer's study with Dr. Eileen Southern of Harvard University. This opportunity allowed him to further pursue his research on Black sacred music. Of specific interest to him is the first Black denominational hymnal to be published in the United States, *A Collection of Spiritual Songs and Hymns* (1801) compiled by the Rt. Rev. Richard Allen, founder and first bishop of the African Methodist Episcopal Church. On June 7, 1986, Dr. Braithwaite lectured on the subject at the National Museum of American History, Smithsonian Institution.

Dr. Aldrich Adkins, music department chairman at Southern University, has made a seminal contribution to Black music preservation. Since 1983 he has been writing a weekly article on the subject for the Baton Rouge *Weekly Press*. He has published over 100 newspaper articles covering virtually every Black musical genre, as well as a plenitude of performers from Thomas Tabb, a local blues artist, to Billy Taylor, an internationally acclaimed jazz pianist. He hopes to devote a series of publications to Zydeco music, an ethnic folk song created by Blacks who live in Cajun country around Lafayette and Opelousas, Louisiana.

Dr. Christine E. Oliver, professor of music at Savannah State University, carried out a project based on her 1978 doctoral dissertation on the orchestral works of T. J. Anderson, Arthur Cunningham, Talib Rasun Hakim, and Ollie Wilson. With a grant from NEH, awarded through the Georgia Endowment for the Humanities (GEH), Dr. Oliver produced a biographical documentary (1983–85) on these four distinguished Black composers. Each one was brought to the Savannah college campus where they delivered lecture-demonstrations and were interviewed, all of which was video-taped and photographed. The original video-tapes have been deposited in the library's audio visual department, and the finished biographical documentaries in the GEH Media Resources Center at Georgia Southern College.

Campus Chapels

Black college chapels as, for example, those maintained at Hampton, Tuskegee, Fisk, Howard, Morehouse, Spelman, and Talladega, are especial entities in the matrix of Black music preservation; for wherever Blacks gather to worship, there too is Black song. For instance, the worship music for Sunday morning services at Spelman College chapel is directed by Dr. Roland Allison, chairman of the school's music department. In addition to rendering Euro-American anthems and hymns, he says it is tradition at Spelman for a spiritual to be sung congregationally following the sermon.

Hampton University is fortunate to have preserved its red-brick Memorial Church since 1886. As a result of chapel attendance, Black students are able to retain an awareness of the various types of Black sacred music in their natural context of worship. The late Charles Flax, former chapel choir director at Hampton, facilitated this cultural experience through the programming of spirituals. And Roland Carter, chairman of the university's music department and present chapel choir director, also programs concerted spirituals as well as gospel songs, often of his own arrangement.[4]

A component of this religio-cultural substructure within Hampton's educational structure is the Hampton University Ministers Conference, founded in 1914. An annual confluence of over 1,800 clergy, lectures on various factions of the church are given and Black folk preaching is rendered. The traditional chanted declamation characteristic of climactic proclamation in Black homiletics is itself a folk song perpetuated through the oral tradition.

A constituent of the Ministers Conference is the Choir Directors-Organists Guild. With over 800 participants, this group convenes to perform and discuss Black sacred music. Presently headed by Roland Carter, the guild was established in 1934 by Madonia Porter-Owens, says Carter, "to aid in the quality of performance in churches, work of church choirs, and the quality of literature." Dr. Wyatt T. Walker lectured in 1983 on "The Soul of Black Worship—Singing," and Dr. Wendell Whalum, chairman of the music department at Morehouse, lectured on Black hymnody. Each year the week of worshipful deliberations concludes with the evening Sacred Concert of the Choir Directors-Organists Guild. The choir of approximately 1,000 voices, under Roland Carter's direction, performs a variety of sacred music by Black composers.

Music Curriculums

A sustained interest in the perpetuation of Black musical heritage is contingent upon pertinent music curricula at Black colleges and universities where there is a concentration of Black students. However, most Black schools erroneously attempt to teach all there is to know about Black music in a one, or sometimes two semester course. The critical assessment of Carter G. Woodson over a half-century ago is perhaps as poignantly valid today:

Most of these colleges do not even direct special attention to Negro music in which the Negro has made his outstanding contribution to America. The unreasonable attitude is that because the whites do not have these things in their schools the Negroes must not have them in theirs.[5]

The solution is to make further course divisions in the study of Black musical history, just as some Black schools now offer separate courses in the various European musical periods.

Before focusing on Jackson State's model curriculum in Black music, it is timely to consider one of the earliest efforts to build a Black music program at a Black school. This occured at Virginia State University in 1967 under Undine

---

[4] See the Flax and Carter papers in the archival holdings of Hampton University (Chapter 3), and the complete choral works of Carter in the Black Music Archive at North Carolina Central University (Chapter 7).

[5] Carter G. Woodson, *Mis-Education of the Negro* (Washington: Associated Press, 1933), p. 137.

Smith Moore (now Professor Emeritus) and the late Altona Trent-Johns. The intention was to disarm the dearth of knowledge Blacks had regarding their own culture. Stated Dr. Moore, "Our young people and older ones know a good deal of the music presently, but they do not know how it relates to the culture as a whole; and most of all, they do not know how much has been taken from them."

The Virginia State program, entitled "The Black Man in American Music," received funding from the National Endowment for the Humanities, the Southern Education Foundation, and Title III College Development. Although the constituent undergraduate course (titled after the project) was and remains only one semester, during the height of the program (1967–1972) it was supplemented with the lectures, performances, and seminars of such renowned Black musicians as Fela Sowande, Billy Taylor, Pearl Williams Jones, Brownie McGhee, Sonny Terry, Frederick Hall, and Robert Fryson; and concerts were given of works by such composers as William Grant Still, William Dawson, Ulysses Kay, George Walker, and Hale Smith. In addition, a Black music research center was established which housed among its materials the recordings, photographs, and printed programs of these presentations.[6]

Of the 17 universities and colleges represented in this study, Jackson State has the most developed curriculum in Black music. Their variegation of courses includes (1) Roots of Music which Spring from Africa, (2) Contributions of Black Americans to Western Music: The Influence of Africa, (3) Folk Music of Black People in the United States, Latin America, South America, and the Caribbean, (4) Folk Music of Mississippi Blues Workshop, (5) Jazz Music Workshop, (6) Introduction to Ethnomusicology, (7) Seminar in Church Music, and (8) Church Music Workshop.

The last Folk Music of Mississippi Blues Workshop, held June 17–21, 1985 at Jackson State, was directed by Dr. Joe Goree, a professor of music there. Scholarly papers were delivered on such topics as "The Ethnomusicological Approach to Blues," "The African Roots of Blues," and "Blues Guitar and Singing Styles." Also featured were the lecture-demonstrations of blues artists "King" Edwards Antoine, Jessie Mae Hemphill, Walter "Big Daddy" Hood, and James "Son" Thomas.

The Tenth Anniversary Church Music Workshop, held from June 26 to July 1, 1986 at Jackson State, was directed by music department chairman Dr. Jimmie James. Featured were the papers and lecture-demonstrations of such scholars as Dr. Wendell Whalum (Morehouse College), Dr. Kay Pace (Alabama State University), Dr. Ben Bailey (Tougaloo College), Dr. Robert Leigh Morris (Jackson State University), Dr. Jimmie James (Jackson State University), and Dr. Jon Michael Spencer (North Carolina Central University). Among the topics covered

---

[6] In 1972 Undine Smith Moore and Altona Trent-Johns retired from Virginia State University and the center was disbanded by an unsympathetic administration. Some of the holdings once located therein are now housed in the Special Collections division of the university library. See the Audio Tape Collection and Records of the Music Department in Chapter 10.

were "Black Gospel Music Performance Styles," "Spirituals, Hymns, and Anthems of the Black Church," "Shape Note Singing," and "The Role of Music in Black Worship."

Of the 17 schools studied, it is North Carolina Central University, rather than Jackson State, which offers a degree in sacred music. The two Black music courses in the curriculum that leads to the Bachelor of Music degree are (1) Gospel Music and (2) Afro-American Music: Vocal.

The jazz program at Southern University which commenced under the direction of jazz clarinetist and recording artist Alvin Batiste, is one of the largest to be found at a Black school. It was implemented in 1969 with fundamental courses in jazz history, improvisation, and jazz ensemble, and gradually developed into a degree-offering curriculum. Granting a Bachelor of Music degree in jazz studies, it is now the nucleus of the instrumental program at Southern. With an annual enrollment of approximately 50 jazz majors, many of its graduates have gone on to perform and record with leading jazz artists.

During the 1972–73 year, Southern's jazz band went on an eight week State Department tour of Africa. Batiste said the tour established the basis for his pedagogy: "It verified that African music is the center of what we are about."

Complemental to the music curricula at Southern, Howard, Jackson, Fisk, Norfolk State, Tennessee State, South Carolina State, North Carolina A & T State, North Carolina Central, and Clark is the Black College Jazz Network Project. Under the programming of Clark College, the project evolved to promote leading jazz performers in the country and to make their music accessible through Black colleges whose central locations in Black communities facilitate their reaching a substantial audience.[7] The program is particularly complementary to those institutions which offer a degree in jazz studies.

Library Programs

Black academic libraries have broadened their prospectus from that of procuring published documents and manuscript miscellanea to the implementation of cultural programs which promote the sustentation of Black heritage. With a grant from NEH, Dr. Jessie Carney Smith, University Librarian for Fisk, developed and directed a project titled "Themes in the Black American Experience: A Learning Library Program." The project called for a series of lectures on various aspects of Black culture and the publication of corresponding brochures. Among the brochures relative to Black music are "Of Minnie the Moocher and Me" (viz, Cab Calloway), "Black Music: The Contemporary Scene," by Arnold Shaw, and "Black Song and Dance" by Dena Epstein.

The Fisk library and NEH also sponsored the university's Second Annual Black Folklife Festival, which was held on October 13, 1984. This ethnic jubilee traced

[7] "The Black College Jazz Network Tour: History of Jazz Involvement," Brochure by Alaina Moss, Tour Coordinator, Clark College.

"the development of Black folklife from its African roots through its development in America." Music naturally played an important part. At various scheduled points throughout the day were performances of jazz, blues, gospel, spirituals, and African music.

The Third Annual Black Folklife Festival, held on October 5, 1985, was sponsored by the Fisk library and funded by the Tennessee Arts Commission. A part of Fisk's state-wide program titled "'Making Do': Black Folk Arts in Tennessee," it too featured guest performers, choirs, and ensembles which rendered various types of Black music.

The Fisk library and NEH also sponsored "I've Been to the Mountain Top: A Civil Rights Legacy" which presented a series of lectures and exhibits between September 1985 and February 1987. The music of the civil rights era was discussed on October 6, 1985 by Dr. Bernice Reagon who, during the sixties, was a member of the Freedom Singers, an affiliate of the Student Nonviolent Coordinating Committee (SNCC).

Dr. Smith, through her procuring of these programs has contributed meritoriously to Black music preservation at Fisk, a school replete with musical history. She is perhaps the continuum in the legacy and fecundity of litterateur Arna Bontemps who, while university librarian at Fisk, edited W. C. Handy's autobiography, *Father of the Blues* (1941), and was instrumental in acquiring Carl Van Vechten's George Gershwin Memorial Collection and the Scott Joplin Collection for Fisk.[8]

Under the initiative of Dr. Lelia G. Rhodes, Dean of Libraries at Jackson State University (with the consultation of Dr. Jessie Carney Smith), the H. T. Sampson Library at Jackson also secured an NEH grant to fund a Library Learning Program for 1985–86. Their theme was "The Afro-American Heritage: Viewing the Past from Mississippi." The first of its programs, "The Evolution of Afro-American Music," occured on July 14, 1985 at the Jackson Municipal Auditorium, and included performances of spirituals, blues, gospel, jazz, and Black art music. On April 26, 1986 the program sponsored a lecture-demonstration on jazz piano styles given by James Williams, a pianist, composer, and arranger. And on April 28, 1986 it featured Dr. James Standifer in a program titled "Music and Music Traditions in the Southern Afro-American Cultures."

Institutional Publications

A number of Black colleges and universities hold strategic positions within the preservation matrix by means of their publishing interests. The books, journals, and newsletters dispersed by these schools provide historic and current information to both the campus community and the scholastic populace. Among the publications of Fisk University Press are *The Story of Music at Fisk* and John Wesley Work's *Folk Song of the American Negro* (1915). And among the publications of

[8] See these collections inventoried with the archival holdings of Fisk University (Chapter 2).

Hampton Institute Press are the 1874, 1891, 1909, and 1927 editions of *Religious Folk Songs of the Negroes*, and *Some Songs of the Hampton Institute Quartette* (1927).

Since 1974 Hampton University has been publishing *The Hampton Institute Journal of Ethnic Studies* (formerly *The Journal of African-American Studies*). Howard University has been publishing the *Journal of Negro Education* since 1932 and its Divinity School *The Journal of Religious Thought* since 1944. Atlanta University still publishes *Phylon*, the journal founded by W. E. B. DuBois in 1940, and its constituent seminary has been publishing *The Journal of the Interdenominational Theological Center* since 1973.

Although all of these scholarly journals are available sources for the publication of relevant research on Black music, only the *Black Music Research Journal*, founded in 1980 by its editor Samuel A. Floyd, Jr. of Fisk University, is devoted to the subject.[9] Its precursor was *The Negro Music Journal* a monthly publication founded in 1902 by its editor J. Hilary Taylor. This premier Black music journal came under the auspices of the Washington [D.C.] Conservatory of Music in 1903 when Taylor joined its distinguished Black faculty. The journal was not, however, published beyond that year.

Journals no longer published, but once available for pertinent Black music research, are Central State University's *Journal of Human Relations* (1952–1973), Wilberforce University's *Negro College Quarterly* (1943–1947), which was preceded by the *Wilberforce University Quarterly* (1939–1942), Dillard University's *Arts Quarterly* (1943–1947), and Hampton Institute's *Southern Workman* (1872–1939).

Of the journals not specializing in music, the *Southern Workman* has bequeathed an inestimable appanage to its documentation and sustentation. Such scholars as R. Nathaniel Dett (a contributing editor), Benjamin Brawley, Guy B. Johnson, Natalie Curtis-Burlin, Henry Hugh Proctor, Robert Russa Moten, Clarence Cameron White, and Edith Armstrong Talbot contributed scholarly articles on the subject.[10]

Music departments at Black schools have occasionally sponsored the publication of newsletters of interest to students and scholars of Black music. At the suggestion of his departmental chairman, Dr. Frederick D. Hall, Leonard R. Ballou (now the archivist at Elizabeth City State University) founded and edited *Tones and Overtones* (1953–1959) while a music professor at Alabama State University.[11] Orrin Suthern, now retired from Lincoln University (Pennsylvania), founded and

[9] The *Black Music Research Journal*, is now published by the Center for Black Music Research at Columbia College, Chicago, as is its corresponding newsletter. Dr. Floyd, its editor, is director of the Center.

[10] See the "Bibliography of Articles on Black Music in Non-Music Journals Published by Black Schools" at the close of this Introduction.

[11] Issues of *Tones and Overtones* can be found in the Maud Cuney-Hare Collection at Atlanta University (Chapter 1) and the Raymond I. Johnson Collection at Jackson State University (Chapter 5).

edited a similar newsletter, the *Music Department Bulletin* (1968–1972) while a music professor there.[12] Although both of these were duplicated typescripts, they were far more than departmental "bulletin boards," in that they included scholarly articles on Black music.

Distributed on a national level is the newsletter formerly of Fisk University, the *Black Music Research Newsletter*, founded in 1980 by its editor Dr. Samuel A. Floyd, and *Music Rap*, the newsletter of Morgan State University's music department, founded in 1984 by its editor Dominique-René de Lerma. These publications include short articles on Black music and musicians and pertinent news for their academic readership.

College yearbooks, bulletins, and newspapers can also be of historic value to Black music researchers. By following yearbook issues one can trace the development of choral and instrumental ensembles at Black institutions. Bulletins which keep track of successful graduates may also include information on distinguished music alumni.[13] And newspapers, amid general campus news, customarily chronicle and review current musical events. Many of these documents will be of future worth, just as some of the dated college yearbooks, bulletins, and newspapers are of historic value today.

In sum, it is at Black schools that spirituals are still arranged by choral directors and sung by their choirs, that traditional and contemporary styles of gospel are performed by gospel choruses, that Black faculty composers are creating Black music and recitalists rendering it, that ethnomusicologists are retrieving Black culture and documenting Black history, that campus chapels are maintaining Black religious music traditions and the homiletical folk song of the Black preacher, that curriculums are offering courses and degrees in jazz studies and sacred music, and that libraries are procuring documents on and by Blacks and sponsoring learning library programs. This is the cultural matrix of preservation in which campus printers assume their seminal part of publishing books, journals, newsletters, yearbooks, bulletins, and newspapers which disseminate historic and current information to the Black scholar, student, and public. It is the cultural duty of these printing media to document the historic song as the Black school sings.

---

[12] The newsletter was sometimes titled *Music Department News*. Issues of these can be found in the collection at Lincoln University (Chapter 6).

[13] For example, see "John Wesley Work," *Fisk News*, Spring, 1967; and "John Work Receives Alumni Award," *Fisk News*, June, 1948. These clippings can be found in the John Wesley Work III Collection at Fisk University (Chapter 2).

BIBLIOGRAPHY
Articles on Black Music in Non-Music Journals
Published by Black Schools

Adams, Eldridge L. "The Negro School Settlement," *Southern Workman*, 44 (March 1915), 161–65.

Alilunas, Leo J. "Negro Music in American Culture," *Journal of Human Relations*, 10, No. 4 (Summer 1962), 474–94.

Allen, Mary Emma. "A Comparative Study of Negro and White Children on Melodic and Harmonic Sensitivity," *Journal of Negro Education*, 11, No. 2 (April 1942), 158–64.

"American (Negro) Music," *Southern Workman*, 2 (May 1873), 2.

Armstrong, Robert G. "Talking Drums in the Benue-Cross River Region of Nigeria," *Phylon*, 15, No. 4 (1954), 355–63.

Arvey, Verna. "William Grant Still: Creative Aspects of His Work," *Arts Quarterly*, January–March, 1938.

Barrett, Harris. "Negro Folk Songs," *Southern Workman*, 41 (April 1912), 238–45.

Bartholomew, Marshall. "Your Own Music," *Southern Workman*, 57 (Sept. 1928), 398–401.

Beckham, Albert Sidney. "The Psychology of Negro Spirituals," *Southern Workman*, 60 (Sept. 1931), 391–94.

Benston, Kimberly W. "Tragic Aspects of the Blues," *Phylon*, 36, No. 2 (1975), 164–76.

Brawley, Benjamin. "A Composer of Fourteen Operas [H. Lawrence Freeman]," *Southern Workman*, 62 (July 1933), 311–15.

———. "The Singing of Spirituals," *Southern Workman*, 63 (July 1934), 209–13.

Brown, Sterling A. "The Blues," *Phylon*, 13, No. 4 (1952), 286–92.

———. "Negro Folk Expression: Spirituals, Seculars, Ballads and Work Songs," *Phylon*, 14, No. 1 (1953), 45–61.

Bruce, John E. "History of Negro Musicians," *Southern Workman*, 45 (Oct. 1916), 569–73.

Bryant-Jones, Mildred. "Association of Negro Musicians," *Southern Workman*, 54 (Sept. 1925), 388–89.

Cinquabre, Pierre. "African Dances," *Phylon*, 5, No. 4 (1944), 355–60.

Clark, Edgar Rogie. "Music Education in Negro Schools," *Journal of Negro Education*, 9, No. 4, 580–90.

Cooper, B. Lee. "Music: An Untapped Resource for Teaching Contemporary Black History," *Journal of Negro Education*, 48, No. 1 (Winter 1979), 20–36.

Cudjoe, S. D. "The Technique of Ewe Drumming and the Social Importance of Music in Africa," *Phylon*, 14, No. 3 (1953), 280–91.

Curtis–Burlin, Natalie. "Negro Music," *Southern Workman*, 47 (July 1918), 323–24.

Davis, Jane E. "Negro Music," *Southern Workman*, 49 (May 1920), 202.

———. "A Notable Negro Concert," *Southern Workman*, 43 (July 1914), 381–83.

———. "Popularity of the Spirituals," *Southern Workman*, 55 (April 1926), 149–50.

———. "Recognition of Negro Music," *Southern Workman*, 49 (Jan. 1920), 6–7.

Dett, R. Nathaniel. "As the Negro School Sings," *Southern Workman*, 56 (July 1927), 304–05.

———. "The Emancipation of Negro Music," *Southern Workman*, 47 (April 1918), 172–76.

———. "Glee Club Tour," *Southern Workman*, 57 (April 1928), 184.

———. "A Hampton Music Festival," *Southern Workman*, 45 (May 1916), 272.

———. "John W. Work (Obituary)," *Southern Workman*, 54 (Oct. 1925), 438–39.

———. "National Music Contest," *Southern Workman*, 50 (Feb. 1921), 58–59..

———. "Negro Music," *Southern Workman*, 47 (July 1918), 323–24.

———. "Negro Music of the Present," *Southern Workman*, 47 (May 1918), 243–47.

———. Rev. of *The Book of American Negro Spirituals*, eds. James Weldon Johnson and J. Rosamond Johnson, *Southern Workman*, 54 (Dec. 1925), 653–65.

———. Rev. of *Negro Workaday Songs*, by Howard W. Odum and Guy B. Johnson, *Southern Workman*, 56 (Jan. 1927), 45–46.

Fryer, Paul H. "'Brown-Eyed Handsome Man': Chuck Berry and the Blues Tradition." *Phylon*, 42, No. 1 (1981), 60–72.

Gillum, Ruth H. "The Negro Folksong in the American Culture," *Journal of Negro Education*, 12, No. 2 (Spring 1943), 173–80.

Graves, Neil. "Richard Wright's Unheard Melodies: The Songs of Uncle Tom's Children," *Phylon*, 40, No. 3 (1979), 278–90.

House, Grace B. "The Hymn in the Camps," *Southern Workman*, 47 (Oct. 1918), 476–78.

Howe, R. Wilson. "The Negro and His Songs," *Southern Workman*, 51 (Aug. 1922), 381–83.

Hughes, Langston. "Songs Called the Blues," *Phylon*, 2, No. 2 (1941), 143–45.

Johnson, Guy B. "The Negro and Musical Talent," *Southern Workman*, 56 (Oct. 1927), 439–44.

Kerlin, Robert T. "Canticles of Love and War," *Southern Workman*, 50 (Feb. 1921), 61–64.

Kirton, Stanley D. "Cultural Values in Music," *Journal of Human Relations*, 6, No. 3 (Spring 1958), 136–43.

Klotman, Phillis R. "Langston Hughes's Jess B. Semple and the Blues," *Phylon*, 36, No. 1 (1975), 68–77.

Lane, Leonora C. "A Journey into the Realm of Music: What Research in Music Education Reveals," *Journal of Human Relations*, 4, No. 4 (Summer 1956), 89–98.

Lovell, John, Jr. "The Social Implications of the Negro Spiritual," *Journal of Negro Education*, 8, No. 4 (Oct. 1939), 634–43.

McGinty, Doris E. "African Tribal Music: A Study of Tradition," *Journal of Human Relations*, 8, Nos. 3–4 (Spring–Summer, 1960), 739–48.

McLaughlin, Wayman B. "Symbolism and Mysticism in the Spirituals," *Phylon*, 24, No. 1 (1963), 69–77.

McMartin, Sean. "Music for One Hand Only," *Phylon*, 30, No. 2 (1969), 197–202.

Margetson, Edward. "Folk Music and Nationalism," *Southern Workman*, 56 (Nov. 1927), 487–92.

Mary, (Sister) Esther. "Spirituals in the Church," *Southern Workman*, 63 (Oct. 1934), 308–14.

Matthews, Miriam. "William Grant Still—Composer," *Phylon*, 12 (1951), 106–12.

Moton, Robert Russa. "Negro Folk Music," *Southern Workman*, 44 (June 1915), 329–30.

———. "Negro Music," *Southern Workman*, 42 (April 1913), 195–97.

———. "A Universal Language," *Southern Workman*, 56 (Aug. 1927), 349–51.

"[Negro Folk-Song]," *Southern Workman*, 24 (Feb. 1895), 30–32.

"Negro Musician: Blind Tom of Georgia," *Southern Workman*, 5 (May 1876), 34.

Nketia, J. H. Kwabena. "The Music of Africa," *Journal of Human Relations*, 8, Nos. 3–4 (Spring–Summer 1960), 730–38.

Peabody, Charles. "Notes on Negro Music," *Southern Workman*, 33 (May 1904), 305–09.

Phenix, George P. Rev. of *Religious Folk-Songs of the Negro*, ed. R. Nathaniel Dett, *Southern Workman*, 56 (April 1927), 151–52.

Proctor, (Rev.) Henry Hugh. "The Theology of the Songs of the Southern Slave." *Southern Workman*, 36 (Nov. and Dec. 1907), 584–92, 652–56.

Rathbun, F. G. "The Negro Music of the South," *Southern Workman*, 22 (Nov. 1892), 174.

"Religious Song of the Yoruba People," *Southern Workman*, 25 (Jan. 1896), 5.

"A Remarkable Evening of Music at Hampton Institute," *Southern Workman*, 7 (June 1878), 42.

Simms, David M. "The Negro Spiritual: Origins and Themes," *Journal of Negro Education*, 35, No. 1 (1966), 35–41.

"Songs of the Races," *Southern Workman*, 20 (March 1891), 160.

Stewart, James B. "Perspectives on Black Families from Contemporary Soul Music: The Case of Millie Jackson," *Phylon*, 41, No. 1 (1980), 57–71.

Szwed, John F. "Musical Style and Racial Conflict," *Phylon*, 27, No. 4 (1966), 358–66.

Talbot, Edith Armstrong. "True Religion in Negro Hymns," *Southern Workman*, 51 (May 1922), 260–64; (June 1922), 260–64; (July 1922), 334–39.

Terry, Anna M. "The Role of Music in Fostering Human Relations," *Journal of Human Relations*, 1, No. 3, 35–43.

Weldon, Abe. "The Street Corner Sound," *Hampton Institute Journal of Ethnic Studies*, 6, No. 2 (Nov. 1978), 1–11.

Whalum, Wendell P. "James Weldon Johnson's Theories and Performance Practices of Afro-American Folksong," *Phylon*, 32, No. 4 (1971), 383–95.

White, Clarence Cameron. "The Musical Genius of the American Negro," *Southern Workman*, 62 (March 1933), 108–18.

Wimberly, Anne S. "Spirituals as Symbolic Expression," *Journal of the Interdenominational Theological Center*, 5, No. 1 (Fall 1977), 383–95.

Wintersgill, H. G. "The Orchestras of Central Africa," *Southern Workman*, 34 (Dec. 1905), 657–62.

Wood, Mabel Travis. "Community Preservation of Negro Music," *Southern Workman*, 53 (Feb. 1924), 60–62.

Woode, Charles Henri. "The Negro Musician: His Contribution to Inter-Group Relations," *Negro College Quarterly*, 4, No. 1 (March 1946), 28–34.

Work, John Wesley, III. "Modern Music: Its Implications to the Listener," *Arts Quarterly*, June 1939.

PART I
ARCHIVAL COLLECTIONS

INTRODUCTION

What follows is an in-depth description of Black music manuscripts and miscellanea in archival collections at ten of the seventeen Black universities and colleges constituting this study. Included in this chapter by chapter inventory are discographies, bibliographies, catalogs of compositions, published articles, and manuscript writings, descriptions of journals, diaries, scrapbooks, correspondences, photographs, programs, broadsides, brochures, and so on.

The approximate time spans designated particular collections are not necessarily those specified by the librarian who processed the papers, for my research occasionally disclosed items which extended given dates. Undated collections are dated whenever the period can be determined with reasonable accuracy.

An individual colligation, and even an archive's entire corpus may sometimes seem to be misrepresented in terms of actual volume. Both the C. Eric Lincoln papers at Atlanta University and the entire archival division there appear to be relatively minute, for instance, when in fact they are quite voluminous. It must be re-emphasized that the inventories herein consist only of materials relative to Black music. This is the reason the archives at Savannah State, South Carolina State, and Xavier are not inventoried; they house no germane collections. By the same token Clark, Morehouse, Morris-Brown, and Spelman Colleges are constituent members of the Atlanta University Center, and share in its centralized Special Collections Division.

Biographical data is frequently provided on persons mentioned in an inventory, and excerpts are occasionally quoted from constituent correspondences and documents of interest. The purpose is to give this catalogue-raisonné the scholarly and literary ingredients of an encyclopedic history.

CHAPTER 1
ATLANTA UNIVERSITY

In the Special Collections and Archives Division of Atlanta University's Robert W. Woodruff Library are to be found a vertical file of selected clippings, items in the C. Eric Lincoln Collection, and the Maud Cuney-Hare Collection.

Vertical File Clippings

Music. Included are newspaper and magazine clippings, news releases, and programs. There are articles on James Brown, Alston Burleigh, Natalie Curtis-Burlin, Thomas Dorsey, Samuel A. Floyd, Stephen Foster, Andrew Frierson, Scott Joplin, Albert King, Harriet Gibbs Marshall, Thelonious Monk, William A. Rhodes, Nipsey Russell, Dione Warwicke, the Great Troubadours (Black Minstrels), the St. Louis Negro Symphony, as well as articles on Black folk music, spirituals, minstrel music, blues, rhythm and blues, and disco. There is one program each of music by composers Stephen Chambers and Howard Swanson, and one titled "Drums of Afro-Cuba by Claude Marchaut and Company." The news release is regarding *The Book of American Negro Spirituals* (1925) by James Weldon Johnson and J. Rosamond Johnson.

Also in this file are several issues of *The RCA Baton*, a publication which featured articles by and about Black musicians. Found herein are the January, October, and November 1955, and March–April and May–June 1956 issues. These have articles on such Black musicians as Marian Anderson, Harry Belafonte, Diahann Carroll, William Dawson, W. C. Handy, Natalie Hinderas, Lena Horne, James Weldon Johnson, Dorothy Maynor, Fats Waller, Ethel Waters, and the Modern Jazz Quartet.

Musicians. Included are newspaper and magazine clippings about local and national composers, performers, historians, and music educators: Muhal Richard Abrams, Marian Anderson, Louis Armstrong, Count Basie, Harry Belafonte, Allen Brown, Lawrence Brown, H. T. Burleigh, Gary Burton, Blanche Calloway, Cleota J. Collins, Maud Cuney-Hare, William Dawson, Dorothy Donegan, Duke Ellington, James Reese Europe, Stephen Foster, Lawrence Gellert, Azalia Hackley, Helen E. Hagan, Adelaide Hall, Lionel Hampton, Kemper Harreld, R. C. Jackson, Mildred Bryant Jones, Albert King, B. B. King, Albert McNeil Jubilee Singers, Lincolnia C. Morgan, Nellie Moore Mundy, Jessie Estelle Muse, Louise Parker, William Richardson, Paul Robeson, William R. Tatlen, Fats Waller, Aida Ward, Chick Webb, Joe Wright.

Programs. Besides a few clippings and news releases, this file consists primarily of programs of concert performances by Maud Cuney-Hare, Margaret

Bonds, the Jubilee Singers, the Booker T. Washington Choral Society (Albany, New York), the Carib Singers, and the Mwalimu Festival Chorus (African music ensemble). There is a program for a performance of Gershwin's *Porgy and Bess*, and programs for two concerts, one titled "Music of Negro Composers," and the other "Contest in Musical Composition for Composers of the Negro Race." On many of these programs are portraits of the artists.

C. Eric Lincoln Collection

Distinguished scholar, author, and professor of religion at Duke University, Dr. C. Eric Lincoln (b. 1924) is also an amateur musician. Included among his papers are five of his original compositions in manuscript: (1) "Atlanta Girl" for guitar, piano, and strings, with text by the composer. (2) "Candle in the Window" for guitar, piano, winds, and strings. (3) "Charlie, Cock Your Pistol," with text and melody only. (4) "Once On a Time of Love" for guitar, piano, and winds. (5) "Waiting," with melody and chord symbols only, and text by the composer.

Maud Cuney-Hare Collection, 1900–1936

This rich collection was compiled by Maud Cuney-Hare (1874–1936), concert pianist, historian, and author of *Negro Musicians and Their Music* (1936). It includes a large quantum of sheet music and song collections principally by Black composers:

Aaronson, Lazarus A. "I See Tho My Eyes are Closed."

Abbot, Francis H. and Alfred J. Swann, eds. *Eight Negro Songs*.

Adams, Wellington. "L'il Black Child" (Lullaby).

Alexander, Josef. *Negro Spirituals*.

"Amalgamation Waltz."

Andrews, Ismay. "Traditions." Arr. Hall Johnson.

Ball, Ernest R. "Who Knows." Text by Paul Laurence Dunbar.

Barbour, J. Berni. "Sphinx"(Egyptian Intermezzo).

Bares, Basile J. "La Sedvisante."

———. "Les Varietes du Carnaval."

———. "The Wedding."

Belliot, P. M. "Hymne a 'Toussaint Louverture.'"

Berger, Jean. "Four Songs."Texts by Langston Hughes.

Blake, Charles D. "Down Among de Sugar Cane."

Blake, Eubie. "Blue Thoughts.".

———. "Fantasy." MS.

———. "Scherzo No. 1." MS.

Bland, James. "Carry Me Back to Old Virginny."

———. "Carry Me Back to Old Virginny." Piano solo arr. by Leopold W. Rovenger.

———. "In the Evening by the Moonlight."

"Boatman's Song." Minstrel.

Bonds, Margaret. "The Ballad of the Brown King." Text by Langston Hughes.

———, arr. "Ezek'el Saw the Wheel."

———. "The Negro Speaks of Rivers." Text by Langston Hughes.

———. "Three Dream Portraits." Text by Langston Hughes.

———. "To a Brown Girl Dead."Text by Countee Cullen.

Bradford, Perry and James P.Johnson. *Dixieland Echoes* (A Collection of Five Descriptive Negro Songs).

Braham, David. "Hhist! The Bogie Man." Minstrel.

Bron, J. Harl, arr. "Don't Be Weary Traveller."

———, arr. "Hail the Crown."

———, arr. "Hear Me Pray."

———, arr. "I Wish I'se in Heav'n Set'in' Down."

Brooks, Shelton. "Swing Thing."

Brown, Lawrence, arr. *Spirituals* (Five Negro Songs).

Bryan, Lou. "We Share in His Dream" (In Memoriam: Dr. Martin Luther King). MS.

Burleigh, H. T., arr. "By and By."

———, arr. "De Blin' Man Stood on de Road an' Cried."

———, arr. "By the Pool at the Third Roses."

———, arr. "Deep River."

———, arr. "Don't Be Weary Traveler."

———, arr. "Don't You Weep When I'm Gone."

———. "Dream Land" (Cradle Song).

———. "Ethiopia Saluting the Colors."

———, arr. "Ev'ry Time I Feel de Spirit."

———. "Five Songs of Laurence Hope."

———. "Folk Song."

———. "Fragments."

———. "From the Southland."

———, arr. "Give Me Jesus."

———, arr. "Go Down in the Lonesome Valley."

———, arr. "Go Down Moses."

———, arr. "Go Tell It On the Mountains!"

———, arr. "De Gospel Train."

———. "The Grey Wolf."

———, arr. "Hard Trials."

———. "Have You Been to Lons."

———, arr. "Heav'n, Heav'n."

———. "Heigh-Ho!"

———, arr. "He's Jus' de Same To-Day."

———. "His Word is Love."

———, arr. "I Don't Feel No-Ways Tired."

———, arr. "I Know de Lord's Laid His Hands On Me."

———, arr. "I Stood on de Ribber ob Jerdon."

———, arr. "I Want to be Ready."

———, arr. "In Christ There Is No East or West."

———. "In the Wood of Finvara."

———. "Jean."

———, arr. "John's Gone Down on de Island."

———, arr. "Joshua Fit de Battle ob Jericho."

———. "Just Because."

———. "Just My Love and I."

———. "Just You."

———, arr. "Let Us Cheer the Weary Traveller."

———, arr. "Little Child of Mary."

———, arr. "Little David, Play On Your Harp."

———. "Little Mother of Mine."

———. "Lovely Dark and Lonely One." Text by Langston Hughes.

———. "Love's Dawning."

———. "Mammy's L'il Baby."

———, arr. "My Lord, What a Mornin'."

———, arr. "My Way's Cloudy."

———, arr. "Nobody Knows de Trouble I've Seen."

———. "O Love of a Day."

———. "O Perfect Love."

———, arr. "O Rocks, Don't Fall On Me."

———, arr. "Oh Peter Go Ring-a dem Bells."

———, arr. "Oh Wasn't dat a Wide Ribber?"

———. "Passionate" (Four Songs). Texts by James Weldon Johnson.

———. *Plantation Melodies:Old and New*.

———, arr. "Saracen Songs."

———. "Savior Divine."

———. "Since Molly Went Away."

———, arr. "Sinner, Please Doan Let dis Harves' Pass."

———. "Somewhere."

———, arr. "Stan' Still Jordan."

———, arr. "Steal Away."

———, arr. "Swing Low, Sweet Chariot."

———. "Tide."

———, arr. "'Tis Me, O Lord."

———. "The Trees Have Grown So."

———. "Two Poems."

———. "You Ask Me If I Love You."

———, arr. "You May Bury Me in de Eas'."

———. "The Young Warrior." Text by James Weldon Johnson.

———, arr. "Weepin' Mary."

———, arr. "Were You There?"

Carver, Wayman A. "Jolly Roger." Orchestral MS.

———. "Metropolis." Solo Clarinet MS.

Charlton, Melville. "Poeme Erotique."

Christy, E. P. "Old Folks at Home" (Ethiopian Melody).

Clapp, Augustus, arr. *Jim Crow Jubilee* (A Collection of Negro Melodies).

Coates, Frederick and Al Piantadosi. "My Prayer."

Cohen, Cecil. "As at Thy Portals Also Death." MS.

Coleridge-Taylor, Samuel. "African Dances."

———. "African Romances."

———. "Ballad in D Minor."

———. "Candle Lightin' Time." Text by Paul Laurence Dunbar.

———. "Danse Negre."

———. "Four Characteristic Waltzes."

———. "Gipsy Movements."

———. "Low Breathing Winds."

———. "Onaway, Awake, Beloved" (From *Hiawatha's Wedding Feast*).

———. "The Soul's Expression" (Four Sonnets).

———. "A Tale of Old Japan."

———. "Tell, O Tell Me."

———. "Two Choral Ballads." Texts by Longfellow.

———. "Valse-Caprice."

Cook, John H. "Evah Dahkey is a King." (Minstrel).

Cook, Will Marion. "Abyssinia."

———. "Cruel Papa!"

———. "An Explanation." Text by James Weldon Johnson.

———. "We're Marching On."

———. "Wid de Moon, Moon, Moon."

Corrister, W. D. "Dianah's Serenade" (Ethiopian Melody).

Cotter, Joseph S., Sr. "Going to Georgia 1863–1937." MS.

———. "I'm Wondering."

———. "I'm Wondering." MS.

Crabtree, Ray. "Christmas Greetings." MS.

———. "Easter Poem."

———. "I Know the Light Will Shine."

———. "Lullaby."

Cuney-Hare, Maud. "Aurore Pradere" (Creole Love Song).MS.

———. "Child's Funeral Song."MS.

———. "Dialogue d'Amour" (Creole Folk-Song). MS.

———. "Garde Piti Militat la." MS.

———. "My Heart to Thy Heart." Text by Paul Laurence Dunbar.

———. "Near the End of April." Text by William Stanley Braithwaite. MS.

———. "To le Paces Po Blanc (Tou-Cou-Tou)." MS.

———. "War Down a Monkland" (Jamaica Song). MS.

———. "Xosa Weddysent." MS.

"Dandy Jim from North Carolina" (A Popular Negro Melody).

Davis, Gussie L. "When Nelly was Raking the Hay." Minstrel.

Davis, John Walter. "Tired." Arr. by E. Clifford Davis.

Dawson, William. "We're On God's Side." Arr. by Clarence Gaskill and Clarence Williams.

"Dearest Mae" (Sung by Harmoneons). Minstrel.

Decker, Harold A., arr. "Bow Low, Elder."

Dett, R. Nathaniel, arr. "America the Beautiful."

———. "Enchantment" (Piano Suite).

———, arr. "Go Not Far from Me, O God."

———, arr. "I'm So Glad Trouble Don't Last Alway."

———. "Magic Moon of Molten Gold."

———. "Magnolia" (Piano Suite).

———, arr. "O Mary Don't You Weep."

———. "Poor Me."

———, arr. "There's a Meeting Here Tonight."

———. "A Thousand Years Ago."

Diton, Carl R., arr. "Deep River."

———, arr. "Ev'ry Time I Feel the Spirit."

———, arr. "Little David, Play On Your Harp."

———, arr. "Pilgrim's Song."

———. "Rhapsody in E." MS.

———, arr. "Swing Low, Sweet Chariot." Organ.

Dodge, May Hewes and John Wilson. "In Old Louisiana" (A Romance on the Old South). Musical Comedy in 3 Acts.

Dorsey, Thomas A. "If You See My Savior."

———. "My Desire."

———. "Our Father Who Art in Heaven."

Ehrlich, S. "Tompkins Blues Quick Step."

Elie, Justin. "Meringues Populaires Haitiennes."

Emilio, Manuel. "Little Eva: Uncle Tom's Guardian Angel."

"Emma Snow" (The Celebrated Ethiopian Song and Chorus as Sung by the Campbell Minstrels). Arr. for piano.

Emmett, Dan. "Dixie's Land." Arr. by W. L. Hobbs.

———. "Jordan is a Hard Road to Travel."

"Ethiopian Airs Composed with Variations for the Piano Forte."

Europe, James Reese. "Queen Louise."

Evanti, Lillian. "Himno Pan-Americano."

———. "The Mighty Rapture."

———. "My Little Prayer."

———. "Speak to Him Thou."

———. "Twenty-Third Psalm."

Freeman, H. Lawrence. "If Thou Didst Love."

Frey, Hugo, arr. "Heav'n, Heav'n."

———, arr. "It's a Me, O Lord."

———, arr. "Oh! Wasn't dat a Wide Ribber."

———, arr. "Swing Low, Sweet Chariot."

Gatty, Alfred Scott. *Six Plantation Songs*, vols. 1–3.

Gaul, Harvey, arr. "Dere's a Man Goin' Roun' Takin' Names."

Gordon, Taylor. "Don't Say You're No Longer Mine."

———. "Oh, Go On Ma."

Griffin, G. W. H. "Poor Old Slave." Minstrel.

Guion, David W., arr. "De Ol' Ark's a-Moverin'."

"Gumbo Chaff" (A Negro Song).

Hackley, E. Azalia. "Carola"(Spanish Serenade).

Hall, Purnell Fleetwood. "I Will Lift Up Mine Eyes." Psalm 121.

Handy, Elizabeth. "Stay" (A Torch Ballad).

Handy, Lucile Marie. "Deep River Blues" (A Meditation).

Handy, William Christopher. "Aframerican Hymn."

———. "Annie Love."

———. "Aunt Hagar's Blues."

———. "Beale Street Blues."

———. "Beale Street Blues." Arr. by J. Lawrence Cook.

———. "The Big Stick Blues March."

———. "Careless Love."

———. "East Saint Louis."

———. "Ever After On."

———. "Friendless Blues."

———, arr. "Give Me Jesus."

———. "Go and Get the Enemy Blues."

———. "Golden Brown Blues."

———. "Hail to the Spirit of Freedom" (March).

———. "Harlem Blues."

———. "Hesitating Blues."

———. "I Think of Thee."

———, arr. "I'll Never Turn Back No More."

———. "I'm Drinking from the Fountain."

———, arr. "I've Heard of a City Called Heaven."

———. "John Henry Blues."

———, arr. "Let Us Cheer the Weary Traveller."

———. "Loveless Love."

———. "Memphis Blues."

———. "Mozambique."

———. "Negrita." Text by W. C. Handy, Music by D. Arteaga.

———, arr. "Nobody Knows the Trouble I See."

———. "Ole Miss Blues."

———. "Opportunity."

———. "Pasadena."

———. "St. Louis Blues."

———, arr. "Shine Like a Mornin' Star."

———. "Shoeboot's-Serenade."

———. "Somebody's Wrong About dis Bible."

———. "Sounding Brass and Tinkling Cymbals."

———, arr. "Stand on the Rock a Little Longer."

———, arr. "Steal Away to Jesus."

———. "Sundown Blues."

———. "They that Sow in Tears (Shall Reap in Joy)". Psalm 126.

———. "Vesuvius" (There's a Real Glow in the Sky Above Vesuvius).

———. *W. C. Handy's Collection of Blues* (1925).

———. "Wall Street Blues."

———. "Way Down South Where the Blues Began."

———, arr. "We'll Go On and Serve the Lord."

———. "When the Black Man Has a Nation of His Own."

———. "Yellow Dog Blues."

——— and Clarence M. Jones. "Wool-Loo-Moo-Loo-Blues."

Harper, Emerson. "The Eagle." Text by Langston Hughes.

———. "Freedom Road."

Harper, Toy and LaVills Tullos. "This is My Land." Text by Langston Hughes.

Hawthehorne, Alice. "I Set My Heart Upon a Flower."

———. "What is Home Without a Mother."

———. "Yes, I Would the War Were Over."

Hebron, J. Harvey. "Good-Night." Text by Paul Laurence Dunbar.

Heiser, F. "Climbing Up the Golden Stairs." Minstrel.

Heyward, Sammy. "Ballad of Harry Moore." Text by Langston Hughes.

Hill, Alexander. "A Song" (How the First Song was Born).

Hill, Edwin. "Evening Zephyrs."

———, arr. "Jerusalem."

———. "Serenade: Rest Thee True Heart."

"I've Seen Her at de Window" (Performed by the Sable Harmonists).

Jackson, (Rev.) C. L., arr. "Death's Black Train is Coming." Arr. by L. Stevens.

Jackson, Zaricor, arr. "All God's Chillun."

———. "The Spanish Garden."

Jamieson, S. W. "Creole Dance."

Jeanty, O. "La Fusion" (Chant Patriotique).

Jessye, Eva. "Simon the Fisherman."

———. "Sol' Away to Georgia" (Negro Slave Song).

"Jim Crack Corn" (For the Virginia Minstrels).

Johnson, Georgia Douglas. "Come All Nations."

———. "I Want to Die While You Love Me." MS.

———. "Little Brown Bomber Lullaby."

Johnson, Hall, arr. "City Called Heaven."

———. "Singin' Roun' the World" (Hand-Clapping Song). MS.

Johnson, J. Rosamond. "The Awakening." Text by James Weldon Johnson.

———. *De Chain Gang* (Based on Work Songs of the Southland). A Musical Episode.

———, arr. "Did'nt My Lord Deliver Daniel."

———, arr. "Dry Bones."

———. "Excuse Me Mister Moon." Text by James Weldon Johnson.

———, arr. "Go Chain de Lion Down."

———, arr. "Go Down Moses."

———, arr. "I Ain't Goin' Study War No More."

———, arr. "Joshua Fit de Battle o' Jerico."

———. "Lift Every Voice and Sing" (National Negro Hymn). Text by James Weldon Johnson.

———. "Lift Ev'ry Voice and Sing." Arr. by Robert Cray for Band.

———. "De Little Pickaninny's Gone to Sleep." Text by James Weldon Johnson.

———. "Love Song." MS.

———. "Lovely Daughter of Allah." Text by James Weldon Johnson.

———, arr. "O, Wasn't That a Wide River."

———. "The Pathway of Love." Text by James Weldon Johnson.

———, arr. "Same Train."

———. "Since You Went Away." Text by James Weldon Johnson.

———. *Sixteen New Negro Spirituals* (1939).

———. "Song of the Heart." Text by Margaret Graham.

———, arr. "Steal Away to Jesus."

———, arr. "Walk Together, Children" (Negro March Song).

———, arr. "Who Built de Ark?"

————. "You Go Your Way and I'll Go Mine." Text by James Weldon Johnson.

Johnson, James P. "Aintcha Got Music?"

————. "Anima Anceps (Or Negro's Heart). Arr. by Steve Stevens.

————. "I Was So Weak (Love Was So Strong)."

————. "My Headache, There Goes My Headache."

————. "Stop That Dog."

————. "Yamekraw" (Negro Rhapsody).

————. "Yours All Yours."

Kemmer, George W., arr. "L'il David, Play On Yo' Harp."

King, Lovett. *Six Plantation Songs*.

Koenig, Martha E. and W. C. Handy. "Bright Star of Hope."

Krucer, Fr. "Lovetrick Polka."

Kurka, Robert. "From the Dark Tower." Text by Countee Cullen. MS.

Landeck, Beatrice, comp. *"Git On Board": Folk Songs for Group Singing* (1944).

Lawrence, Will. "The Freedom Song." Text by Countee Cullen.

Loomis, Harvey Worthington, arr. "Religion is a Fortune."

Lovelace, Henrietta and Lorenzo McLane. "A Fool Must Have His Day."

McCanns, Shirley Graham. "I Promise."

McCosh, D. S., arr. "Hear dem Bells."

McKay, Claude. *Songs from Jamaica* (1912).

MacGimsey, Robert. "Sweet Little Jesus Boy."

Mack, Cecil and Jimmy Johnson. "Charleston."

———— and Jimmy Johnson. "Ginger Brown."

———— and Jimmy Johnson. "Love Bug."

———— and Jimmy Johnson. "Old Fashioned Love."

———— and Jimmy Johnson. "Open Your Heart."

Mather, Henry. "Boys, the Old Flag Never Touched the Ground."

Meyerowitz, Jan. "On a Pallet of Straw." Text by Langston Hughes.

Miller, James E. "Prelude Novena."

Noir, A. Jack. "Lord, I Ain't Got Long to Stay" (From the Symphonic Poem *Etude en Noir*).

Oglesby, D. A. "Gone." MS.

"Oh! Carry Me Back." (Christy's Minstrels).

Onygjva, A. Nagerj. "Ethiopian Quadrilles." [Title page only].

Pace, Chas. H., arr. *Negro Spirituals* (1926).

Peyton, Thomas Roy. "West-View March."

Pinkard, Maceo. "Sugar (That Sugar Baby o' Mine)."

Pitcher, Gladys, arr. "Scandalize' My Name."

Porter, James W. "Ella Ree."(Christy Minstrels).

Razaf, Andy, Eubie Blake, and Chas. L. Cooke. "We Are Americans Too."

Rector, (Rev.) W. I. "All the Way."

Reddie, J. Milton. "Took Mah Babe Away" (A Negro Lamentation).

"Rosa Lee." (Christy's Minstrels).

Saracini, Joseph A. "There Will Be No Colored Line."

Sax, M. C. "Fight On, America."

Scherpt, John C. "Sugar Cane Green" (African Quadrille).

Scott, Tom. "The Creation." Text by James Weldon Johnson.

Sedgwick, A. "Keemo Kimo." Minstrel.

Sheffer, C. H. "New Coon Done Gone." Minstrel.

Siegmeister, Ellie. "A New Wind A-Blowin'." Text by Langston Hughes.

Simmons, Hiram. "Around the Great White Throne."

———. "Hear Us O Father When We Pray."

———. "Holy Jesus Love Divine."

———. "I Know that My Redeemer Liveth."

Sims, Dorothy Greer, ed. *Old Time Prayer Meeting Hymns* (1970).

"Sitting On a Rail" or "The Racoon Hunt" (A Celebrated Comic Extravaganza).

Smith, Chris and Billy Johnson. "Good-Bye, I'll See You Some More."

Smith, Lawrence. "The Spring that Did Not Become Summer." Text by Langston Hughes.

Smith, Russel. "Let Not Your Heart Be Troubled."

Smith, Ulysses. "Heart Break Avenue." MS.

Southall, Mitchell B. "Elf Dance."

———. "Impromptu in D Minor."

———. "Romance."

Stewart, Hilbert Earl. "Love Song."

Still, William Grant. "In Memoriam: The Colored Soldiers Who Died for Democracy."

———. *Twelve Negro Spirituals.*

Stor, Jean, arr. "I Want Jesus to Walk with Me."

Stout, Peter F. "Juliana, Phebiana, Constantiana, Brown." Minstrel.

Swanson, Howard. "And When I Think." Text by Countee Cullen.

———. "Joy." Text by Langston Hughes. MS.

———. "The Junk Man." Text by Carl Sandburg.

———. "The Negro Speaks of Rivers." Text by Langston Hughes.

Thomas, Millard. "America's Sweetheart, the Girl Behind the Guy Behind the Gun."

Tobin, Lew. "Bells of Freedom."

Treharne, Bryceson. "Crucifixion" (Based on a Plantation Spiritual).

Tyler, Gerald. "Afterglow."

Vandeveer, William J. "My Sweet Little Irish Girl."

Vodery, Will H. "O, Let Us Sing a New Song." Text by Noble Sissle.

Weaver, Paul J., arr. "I Got a Key to the Kingdom."

———, arr. "I Got My Sword in My Hand."

———, arr. "New Buryin' Ground."

———, arr. "Toll de Bell, Angel."

Webb, Chick and Ella Fitzgerald. "Spinning the Web."

Weill, Kurt. "Lost in the Stars."

———. "Street Scene." Text by Langston Hughes.

White, Clarence Cameron. "Cradle Song."

———. "Dance Caprice."

———. "Slave Song."

Willet, Chappie. "'Let My People Go'—Now!"

Williams, Warwick. "Come Back to Maryland." (Moore and Burgess Minstrels).

Wilson, Clarence Hayden, arr. "They Have Led My Lord Away."

Winston, Edward A. "My Heart is Calling You."

Work, John W. "For All the Saints."

CHAPTER 2
FISK UNIVERSITY

The Special Collections division of the Fisk University library holds the music and miscellanea of Scott Joplin, W. C. Handy, John Wesley Work III, the Fisk Jubilee Singers, Pauline Hopkins, Arthur Cunningham, and Bobby Hebb, as well as some of the scholarly papers of Eileen Southern and Dominique René de Lerma. Inventoried herewith are the George Gershwin Memorial Collection, the Black Oral History Collection, and the Langston Hughes Record Collection.

Scott Joplin Collection, 1899–1953

This material was compiled by Samuel Brunson Campbell (1884–1953), a white ragtime pianist known as the "Ragtime Kid," who studied under Scott Joplin (1868–1917). Herein are correspondences between "Brun" Campbell and Arna Bontemps (1902–1973), longtime head librarian at Fisk (1943–1966), regarding the former's effort to preserve Joplin's legacy and the latter's interest in procuring the collection for the university. In the letter of March 24, 1948, Bontemps informed Mrs. Joplin that Fisk had finally secured the Joplin collectanea from Campbell.

Included herewith are typescripts of articles written by Campbell: (1) "The Ragtime Kid," an autobiography, (2) "From Rags to Riches," a biography on Joplin, (3) "A Hop Heads Dream of Paradise," an article about the lavish Chicago and St. Louis clubs in which Joplin and others performed, and (4) a published copy of "Ragtime Begins: Early Days with Scott Joplin Recalled by S. Brunson Campbell." There are also programs for performances of Joplin's compositions, clippings of reviews, and photographs.

The outstanding feature is the assemblage of Joplin's piano rags: "Antionette" (1906), "The Chrysanthemum: An Afro-Intermezzo" (1904), "Country Club" (1909), "The Easy Winners" (1901), "Elite Syncopations" (1902), "The Entertainer" (1902), "Eugenia" (1906), "Euphonic Sounds: A Syncopated Novelty" (1909), "The Favorite" (1904), "Felicity Rag," with Scott Hayden (1911), "Fig Leaf Rag" (1908), "Kismet Rag," with Scott Hayden (1913), "Magnetic Rag" (1914), "Maple Leaf Rag" (1899), "March Majestic" (1902), "Nonpareil" (1907), "Palm Leaf Rag" (1903), "Paragon Rag" (1909), "Pine Apple Rag" (1908), "Pleasant Moments" (1909), "The Ragtime Dance" (1906), "Reflection Rag" (1917), "Rose Leaf Rag: Companion to Maple Leaf Rag" (1907), "Searchlight Rag" (1907), "Scott Joplin's New Rag" (1912), "Solace" (1909), "Sugar Cane" (1908), "Sunflower Slow Drag," with Scott Hayden (1901), "Swipsy Cake Walk," with Arthur Marshall (1900), "The Sycamore: A Concert Rag" (1904), "Wall

Street Rag" (1909), and "Weeping Willow" (1903). Adjoined are the original score of *Treemonisha* (Opera in Three Acts) published by Joplin in New York in 1911, and two volumes of ragtime pieces: *Scott Joplin's World Famous Jazz Classics for Piano* and *Original Rags* (picked by Scott Joplin and arranged by Charles N. Daniels).

William Christopher Handy Collection, 1916–1973

Among these papers are numerous correspondences (1945–1954) between W. C. Handy (1873–1958) and Arna Bontemps, University Librarian for Fisk, who edited the former's autobiography, *Father of the Blues* (1941). As illustrated in his letter of February 3, 1945, Handy often commented on issues pertinent to Black music: "[R. Nathaniel] Dett did not come up in the deep south as I did, and too, he had much of the education of a man who is trying to keep us in a certain category, as it relates to what we call Negro music." Herewith is a correspondence of May 13, 1946 from Handy's daughter, Lucile Handy, to Langston Hughes, and one of June 11, 1956 from Nat King Cole to Arna Bontemps.

Included is a resumé of Handy memorials dated 1931–1973, clippings, programs, and photographs of him from the time of his childhood, including one of 1938 with Cab Calloway. And, of course, there is a compilation of his published sheet music: "Aframerican Hymn" (1916), "Atlanta Blues" (1924), "Aunt Hagar's Children Blues" (1922), "Basement Blues" (1924), "Beale Street Blues" (1917), and "Black Patti" (1940). In addition, there is a large assortment of his blues compositions arranged by other writers.

George Gershwin Memorial Collection, 1931–1953

This assemblage amassed by Carl Van Vechten (1880–1964), philanthropist, collector, music critic, and author of the novel *Nigger Heaven* (1925), was named in honor of his personal friend, George Gershwin (1898–1937). Among the Black music-related materials are manuscripts of William Grant Still's ballet *La Guiablesse* (1953), and J. Rosamond Johnson's choral arrangement of Gershwin's *Rhapsody in Blue*, as well as a large colligation of compositions by W. C. Handy, and a pair of volumes entitled *Rag and Jazz Music*.

The highlight of the collection is the sizeable file of photographs taken of Black musicians between 1931 and 1941: Marian Anderson, Bricktop, H. T. Burleigh, Cab Calloway, William Dawson, Dean Dixon, Ruby Elzy, Ella Fitzgerald, Taylor Gordon, W. C. Handy, Nora Douglas Holt, Lena Horne, Elsie Houston, J. Rosamond Johnson, James Weldon Johnson, Dorothy Maynor, Etta Moten, Paul Robeson, Bessie Smith, Ethel Waters, and Frederick J. Work (the son of John Wesley Work III). Also included are miscellaneous programs and a selection of phonograph records.

John Wesley Work III Collection, 1915–1967

John Wesley Work III (1901–1967), author of *American Negro Songs* (1940), was a graduate of Fisk (1923) and a music educator there (1927–1966), during which time he served as director of the Jubilee Singers and as Chairman of the music department. It is fitting, then, that his papers would be bequeathed to the university.

Herein are biographical and autobiographical documents, photographs, correspondences, speeches, and papers related to his association with the American Society of Composers, Authors and Publishers (ASCAP). Relative to his 1956 European tour as director of the Jubilee Singers are correspondences, contracts, programs, news releases, clippings, a diary, and an itinerary.

Amid the miscellany are Work's unpublished writings on Black music: (1) "The Arts" (2) "The Composer is not Free" (3) "The Cultural Contributions of Negroes in Tennessee" (4) "Haitian Songs Make Good Hunting" (5) "The Story of the Jubilee Singers" (6) "The Significance of Jubilee Day" (7) "More On Calypso: Culture of Trinidad" (8) "The Music We Must Listen To Today" (9) "Negro Folk Music." Herewith are papers based on his research into Haitian and Brazilian music, including musical transcriptions.

Among these are his published writings extracted from periodicals: "Changing Patterns in Negro Folk Songs" from the *Journal of American Folklore* (April–June, 1949), "Musical Contributions of the Negro" from *Classnote* (January 1947), "The Plantation Meistersinger" from the *Musical Quarterly* (January 1941), "The Spiritual in Today's Church" from *The Missionary Seer* (November 1963), and "Sweet Chariot Goes to Church" from *The Epworth Highroad* (January 1938).

Several archival boxes apparently contain Work's complete published and unpublished compositions (thus precluding the need for a lengthy listing). His cantatas, anthems, chorales, hymns, songs, concerted spirituals, folksong arrangements, piano, organ, and orchestral works are enumerated on a master list adjoining the collection at Fisk. Also found therein is his compilation of compositions by other Black composers: James Bland, Edward Boatner, Margaret Bonds, H. T. Burleigh, James Cleveland, Samuel Coleridge-Taylor, William Dawson, R. Nathaniel Dett, Thomas Dorsey, Lillian Evanti, Werner A. Jaegerhuber (Haitian), William Laurence James, Hall Johnson, Ulysses Kay, Franck Lessegue (Haitian), Lamothe Ludevic (Haitian), Undine Smith Moore, Evelyn LaRue Pittman, Noah Ryder, William Grant Still, Clarence Cameron White.

Work also kept memorabilia on his father, John Wesley Work II (1873–1925), who was a Fisk graduate (1895), educator (1898–1923), and director of the Jubilee Singers. Enclosed in this one box are both the manuscript and published copy of his *Folk Song of the American Negro* (1915), his folk song arrangements, and some biographical writings.

Fisk Jubilee Singers Archives

General Collection, 1928–1947. Nine boxes contain biographical data, photographs, clippings on concert performances, programs, news releases, publicity broadsides, CBS and NBC radio broadcast scripts, fan mail, contract correspondences, tour itineraries, and accounting data.

Vault Inventory, 1867–1956. Four boxes contain autographs written for the original Jubilee Singers, programs, brochures, photographs, and scrapbooks. Included are a number of letters (1875–1878) from America Robinson, one of the original singers, letters (1873–1875) from Gustavus D. Pike, author of *The Jubilee Singers, And Their Campaign for Twenty Thousand Dollars* (1873) and *The Singing Campaign for 10,000 Pounds* (1875), and letters from George L. White, the first director of the Jubilee Singers and co-compiler (with T. F. Seward) of *Jubilee Songs: As Sung by the Jubilee Singers* (1875). With these items is a diary and clippings of the Jubilee Singers' 1956 European tour under the direction of John Wesley Work III.

Pauline Elizabeth Hopkins Collection, 1881–1899

This collection of Pauline E. Hopkins (1856–1930), playwright and soprano of Hopkins' Colored Troubadours, contains several manuscript drafts of a three-act musical comedy which was performed on September 29, 1881 at the Boston Musical Hall as *The Flight for Freedom; Or, The Underground Railroad.* Orchestrated parts for the musical are adjoined, along with Hopkins' scrapbook containing clippings and programs of the performance.

Arthur Cunningham Collection, 1966–1969

A graduate of Fisk (1951), composer Arthur Cunningham (b. 1934) donated a number of his compositional manuscripts to the university's Special Collections: (1) *Basis*, a double-bass quartet (2) *Concentrics* for orchestra (1968) (3) *Dim Du Mim* for orchestra (1969) (4) *Fragment* for orchestra (1968) (5) *The Garden of Phobus* for choir (1968) (6) *House by the Sea* (libretto only, 1966) (7) *Louey Louey*, a mini-opera in one act with text by the composer (8) *Octet* for percussion instruments (1968) (9) *Omnus* for string quintet (1968) (10) *Septet* for woodwinds (1968) (11) *Theatre Piece* for orchestra (1966) (12) *Trio* for violin, viola, and cello (1968).

Bobby Hebb Collection

This collection consists primarily of original compositions by Robert Hebb (b. 1938). "Good Evening, Eve" and "Judy" are piano pieces, and the remaining are jazz ballads with melody, text, and chord symbols given: "Eskimo," "Fat Cats and Chubby Meow-Meows," "Five Senses," "Funny Faces," and "Pretty as a Picture" have texts by Sandy Baron. "The Love Bird Has Flown" has its text by Anita Angliara. "I've Learned to Care," "My Love is Today," "She Gives a Damn," and "This Bird Will Be Free" have texts by the composer. And "I'll Remember Satch" has its text and music by Bobby Hebb and Hampton Reese.

Eileen Jackson Southern Papers, 1963–1974

The collection of Eileen Southern (b. 1920), Harvard University music professor since 1976, as well as co-founder, publisher, and editor of *The Black Perspective in Music* (f. 1973), contains biographical data, correspondences, miscellaneous programs, speeches, her books, *The Music of Black Americans* (1971) and *Readings in Black American Music* (1971), in addition to her published articles. Of the articles, three are on the subject of Black music: (1) "New Needs and New Directions: Needs for Research in Black-American Music" from the *College Music Symposium*, vol. 13 (Fall 1973), (2) "An Origin for the Negro Spiritual" from *The Black Scholar*, Vol. 3, No. 10 (Summer 1972), (3) "Some Guidelines: Music Research and the Black Aesthetic" from *Black World*, Vol. 23, No. 1 (November 1973).

Dominique René De Lerma Papers, 1973–1974

This collection of De Lerma, music professor at Morgan State University and the Peabody Conservatory of Music, contains three items: (1) "Discography of Music by Black Concert and Spiritual Composers in the Private Library of D. De Lerma" (2) A bibliography titled "Black Music Journals" (AAMOA Resource Papers, No. 4), and (3) "Humanistic Perspectives from Black Music," an extract from his book *Reflections on Afro-American Music* (1973).

Black Oral History Interviews

Herein are interviews with a variegation of Black musicians: (1) Gilbert Askey, composer and arranger (2) James Hubert [Eubie] Blake (1883–1983), songwriter and pianist (3) Robert J. Bradley (b. 1920), gospel performer (4) Veda Butcher (b. 1923), Howard University educator (5) Bennie Carter (b. 1907), jazz musician and arranger (6) Todd Duncan (b. 1903), opera singer, baritone (7) Ernest Dyson (b. 1930), jazz musician and historian (8) Robert Hebb (b. 1938), songwriter and singer (9) Ted Jarrett (b. 1925), songwriter (10) Dorothy Maynor (b. 1911), concert soprano (11) Undine Smith Moore (b. 1904), composer and educator (12) Daniel E. Owens (b. 1922), band musician (13) Joe Lewis Perkins (b. 1935) (14) Reuben Lawrence Phillips (1920–1974), director of the Appollo Theatre's house band (15) Don Q. Pullen (b. 1934), musician with the 6th U.S. Army Band (16) William O. Smith (b. 1917), performer with Bessie Smith's band, Marcus Garvey's UNIA Band, and the Nashville Symphony Orchestra (17) William Grant Still (1895–1978), composer (18) Clark Terry (b. 1920), jazz trumpeter (19) Benjamin Tucker, jazz musician.

Langston Hughes Record Collection

Although principally regarded as a poet, Langston Hughes (1902–1967) had a scholarly appreciation for Black music, as evidenced by his books, *Famous Negro*

Music Makers (1955) and *The First Book of Jazz* (1955), and his valuable colligation of 33 ⅓ RPM phonograph records:

The Art of Roland Hayes.

At the Embers (Dorothy Donegan).

Belefonte Returns to Carnegie Hall.

Big Bill Broonzy Sings Country Blues.

The Black Caribs of Honduras.

The Black Saint and the Sinner Lady (Charles Mingus).

Blues and Roots (Charles Mingus).

The Bridge (Sonny Rollins and Others).

Brother John Sellers Sings Baptist Shouts and Gospel Songs.

Chicago Jazz Album.

Claire Austin Sings "When Your Lover Has Gone" and Other Songs of Unrequited Love.

Count Basie in Kansas City.

Dancing Calypso Belly to Belly.

Deep River and Other Spirituals (Robert Shaw Chorale).

A Drum is a Woman (Duke Ellington).

Drums of the Yoruba of Nigeria.

Edmond Blair, "They Had a Thing Going On": A Highly Emotional Sermon.

Ellington Uptown.

Elsie Houston Sings Brazilian Songs.

Everybody Wants Freedom (Songs by Carolina Freedom Fighters).

Eye of the Storm (Fisk Choir and Jubilee Singers).

Father of the Blues (W. C. Handy).

Fun Life (Diahann Carroll).

Gentlemen, Be Seated!: A Complete Minstrel Show.

The Glory of Negro History.

Gospel Harmonettes.

The Gospel Truth: Sung by Sister Rosetta Tharpe.

A Hand is on the Gate: An All-Negro Revue.

Hoagy Carmichael Sings with the Pacific Jazzmen.

Howard Swanson: "Seven Songs."

I'm Going to Work till Day is Done: Alex Bradford (Spirituals).

Jamaican Cult Music.

Jazz.

Jazz Canto: An Anthology of California Music.

Jesus Keep Me Near the Cross: Alex Bradford (Hymns and Spirituals).

Jimmy Lunceford in Hi-Fi.

The Jo Jones Special (Jazz).

Langston Hughes' "Jericho-Jim Crow" (A Play with Incidental Music).

Let's Misbehave: Billy Dee Williams.

Little Niles: Randy Weston's Music.

The Louis Armstrong Story.

Man Here Plays Fine Piano (Don Ewell Quartet).

Mingus at the Bohemia.

Mingus at Montery.

Muddy Waters at Newport.

Muddy Waters Sings "Big Bill" (William Broonzy Songs).

Music and Extracts from the Sound Track of the Film "Satchmo the Great."

The Music of New Orleans: Recorded by Samuel B. Charters.

A Musical History of Jazz.

The Nashville Sit-In Story (Civil Rights Songs).

Nina Simone Sings the Blues.

One Step: Alex Bradford (Spirituals).

Randy Weston Live at the Fivespot.

Roots: An Anthology of Negro Music in America.

Satch Plays Fats.

Scott Joplin: Classic Solos Played by the King of Ragtime Writers and Others from Rare Piano Rolls.

Snooks Eaglin, New Orleans Street Singer.

Songs: Sam Cooke (Civil Rights Songs).

The Soul of Haiti: Songs of Magic, Love, and Voodoo Ritual.

Soul, Soul Searching: Sacred Songs Sung by Katie Bell Nubin with Dance Orchestra.

Sparrow (Calypsoes).

Staple Singers: "Uncloudy Day."

W. C. Handy's St. Louis Blues.

The Weary Blues and Other Poems (Langston Hughes poems read to incidental music).

CHAPTER 3
HAMPTON UNIVERSITY

Belonging to the Hampton University Archives in the Hollis P. Huntington Library are the collected papers of R. Nathaniel Dett, Natalie Curtis Burlin, Dorothy Maynor, Ruben T. Caluza, Orpheus M. McAdoo, Julian Bagley, William O. Tessman, Charles H. Flax, Roland M. Carter, and Jon Michael Spencer. In addition to these are the assembled papers of the Hampton Quartet, Camera Club, Musical Arts Society, Music Department, and Choir, the Hampton Songs and Folklore Collections, and miscellaneous recordings of historic value. Also inventoried herewith are the Hampton Scrapbook and Vertical File Collections, which are found in the Peabody Room adjacent the Archives.

Robert Nathaniel Dett Collection, 1911–1937

R. Nathaniel Dett (1882–1943), author, composer, performer, and choral director, was a music educator at Hampton Institute from 1913–1932. Among his papers are numerous programs of performances given throughout the country by the college choir he directed. Of particular interest are programs of concerts given at Carnegie Hall on April 16, 1928, at Symphony Hall (Boston) on March 10, 1929, at Queen's Hall in London on May 3, 1930, and at Constitution Hall on March 21, 1931. Each of these programs contain historic notes written by Dett on the subject of Negro folk song.

Herewith are programs of recitals sponsored by the Hampton Choral Union (later the Hampton Choral Society), and a miscellaneous one of May 25, 1929 titled "National Negro Music Festival," which contains program notes on Black composers. There are also a number of broadsides announcing various concerts of Negro music.

Dett accumulated a voluminous number of newspaper pieces concerning Negro music, himself, and his choir, especially articles regarding their tour of Europe in 1930. An itinerary, programs, and foreign newspaper reviews together paint an accurate picture of the tour. One review in the Austrian *Vienne Der Tag* perhaps summarized its success: "And now that the Negro singers from the renowned Hampton Institute proceed in triumph through European concert halls they are not looked upon as foreigners but as interpreters of human experience common to mankind."[1]

---

[1] Research indicates that the article in which this translation appears, "Hampton Choir Sings Here Monday Night," is extracted from a Chicago newspaper, March 1931.

A number of photographs are also to be found among the papers. Several are of Dett, including one of him (as department chairman) overlooking the work of a music instructor and student; another profiles the Hampton Institute (Male) Quartet.

There are a number of correspondences to and from Dett. Included are letters and annual reports addressed to James E. Gregg, principal of the institution (1918–1929), regarding the school's music program. In one typescript nearly 40 pages long, Dett reports to Gregg on the topics: "Why I Am At Hampton," "The Choir," "The Choral Union," "Religious Music," "The Glee Club," "The Orchestra," and "The Whittier School."

On April 21, 1930 came a critical correspondence from the college principal, George P. Phenix, regarding Dett's choral treatment of folk-song: "As sung by the choir a week ago, our spirituals were in a sense de-spiritualized. . ." Too, there is a letter from concert soprano and Negro folk song enthusiast E. Azalia Hackley (18? –1922) to "Mr. Dett and Miss Drew" labeled "suggestions." The suggestions were to prove beneficial to Dett as he sought to implement an efficient music program during his first year of employment at Hampton.

There are also four manuscript writings (1912–1914) by Mme. Hackley on "Voice Culture," as well as typescripts and journal reprints on the subject of Negro music (the latter from the *Southern Workman*). There is a reprint from the *Hampton Bulletin* titled "A Brief Biography of Dr. Robert Nathaniel Dett" (1945) by Marguerite Pope, and a reprint of Dett's article, "A Musical Invasion of Europe: The Hampton Choir Abroad," which was published in *The Crisis* (December 1930).

A few valuable books are amid his collectanea: (1) Thomas P. Fenner's *Cabin and Plantation Songs as Sung by the Hampton Students* (1889 and 1891) (2) *The Dett Collection of Negro Spirituals*, vols. 1–4 (1936) (3) An anonymous hand-written booklet with song texts, titled *Spiritual Songs of the People of St. Helena Is., South Carolina* (1862) (4) Dett's book of original poetry, *Album of a Heart* (1911) and (5) His unpublished volume of poetry, *The Song of Seven*.

A most interesting item is Dett's music theory notebook for his study at Eastman School of Music where he received the Master of Music degree in composition in 1931. Original motivic ideas, two-part inventions written for his counterpoint class, and a four-voice contrapuntal piece titled "Scene," dated October 24, 1931, comprise its contents.

This colligation of Dett's miscellaneous papers would not be complete without an assemblage of his original compositions and spiritual arrangements:

"America the Beautiful" (arr.)	"L'Envoi" (arr.), MS.
"Done Made My Vow to the Lord" (arr.)	"Go Not Far From Me, O God" (arr.)
"Don't Be Weary Traveler" (arr.)	"Hampton! My Home By the Sea"
"Enchantment" (A Romantic Suite for the Piano)	"I'll Never Turn Back No More" (arr.)

"I'm So Glad Trouble Don't Last Alway" (arr.)

"In the Bottoms" (Characteristic Suite for the Piano)

"Iorana," MS.

"Juba: Dance from the Suite 'In the Bottoms'."

"Let Us Cheer the Weary Traveler"

"Listen to the Lambs" (arr.), MS. (and published copy)

"Magic Moon of Molten Gold"

"Magnolia" (Suite for Piano)

"Music is Mine"

"O Holy Lord"

"O Lord, the Hard-Won Miles," MS. (Text by Paul Laurence Dunbar)

"The Ordering of Moses"

"The Palms," MS.

"Poor Me" (Arr. by Ruth Gillum)

"Ramah: Air Characteristic" (violin)

"Rise Up, Shepherd and Follow" (arr.)

"Sit Down, Servant, Sit Down: Negro Folk Scena," MS.

"Somebody's Knocking at Your Door"

"Son of Mary"

"There's a Man Goin' Roun' Takin' Names" (arr.), MS.

"There's a Meeting Here Tonight" (arr.)

"Way Up Yonder Children," MS.

Natalie Curtis Burlin Collection, 1918–1922

A number of writings by this white folklorist and author, Natalie Curtis Burlin (1875–1921), were the result of her ethnomusicological research at Hampton Institute. Of her two Hampton-related volumes, *Songs and Tales of the Dark Continent* (1920) consisting of pieces rendered by C. Kamba Simango while a student at the college (c. 1915), and her four volume work, *Hampton Series Negro Folk-Songs* (1918–1919), only the latter is contained herein.

Among her papers are two articles: "Folk-Lore from Elizabeth County, Virginia" by A. M. Bacon and E. C. Parsons, a reprint from the July-September 1922 issue of *The Journal of American Folklore*, and "The Significance of Hampton's Fifty Years: Special Correspondence" by Natalie Curtis, a brief essay from the July 4, 1919 issue of *The Outlook* (pp. 197–98).

With these items is a poem by Burlin titled "Hymn of Freedom," which she intended to be sung to the tune of the spiritual "O Ride On, Jesus". A printed program titled "The Choral Art Club of Brooklyn (Eighth Season, 1919–1920) Private Concert March 30, 1920," includes historic notes which accompanied the performance of Negro folk songs recorded by Burlin. And there are four letters to Hollis Burke Frissell, Hampton Institute Principal from 1893–1917.

Dorothy Maynor Collection, 1939–1976

Dorothy Maynor (b. 1910), a graduate of Hampton Institute (1933) where she studied with R. Nathaniel Dett, enjoyed a successful career as a concert soprano before devoting her energies to The Harlem School of the Arts (HSA), which she founded in 1965. Regarding HSA is a 1972 brochure and letter from Maynor, its Executive Director until 1980.

Among the assembled items are eleven photographs of the distinguished artist, and nearly a dozen programs of solo recitals and concert appearances with symphony orchestras throughout the country. An itinerary reveals her concert schedule for October and November of 1959.

Over 30 newspaper clippings review her performances. More intensive coverage is documented in articles collected from the December 1939 issue of *Life*, the January 1969 issue of *Stereo Review*, the October 1974 issue of *Opera News*, and the April 21, 1976 issue of *The Christian Century*. Additional biographical data is provided by a two-page type-written letter of February 18, 1947 from Marion C. Deane to L. C. White, and an anonymous three-page typescript. Finally, there is a two-page article by Maynor, "The St. James Program," whose publication source is unidentified.

Ruben Tholakele Caluza Collection, 1910–1937

This African ethnomusicologist and composer of the Zulu Tribe matriculated to Hampton Institute to study music under the departmental administration (1931–1935) of the renowned Clarence Cameron White (1880–1960). He graduated from the college in 1934 and went on to receive his masters degree in music from Columbia University. Among several clippings is one with the caption, "Zulu Makes Musical History: First African to Get Doctor's Degree."[2] There is no indication, however, as to where he might have received what must have been an honorary degree.

The clipped articles provide information on Caluza's musical background. It is documented that even before entering Hampton, he had made major ethnomusicological accomplishments. First, he went to London in 1930 with a choir of five men and five women to record over 150 folk songs for the Gramophone Record Company. Of this number fully half, 45 originals and 30 arrangements, were of his own composition. One of the enclosed clippings has a photograph of the group with percussion instruments which they apparently played while singing. He also published a collection of patriotic Zulu songs.

Neither the recordings nor the Zulu folk song collection are contained here. There is, however, an article titled "African Music" from the April 1931 issue of the *Southern Workman*, in which Caluza writes on Zulu music. And there is a bachelor's degree thesis in music by Zelda de Beer titled "Analysis of Choral Works by the Zulu Composer: Professor R. T. Caluza."

Belonging to the collection are several letters from Caluza to Hampton Institute President (1930–1940) Arthur Howe, and a letter of August 25, 1935, from him to music department chairman Clarence Cameron White.

---

[2] See this article reprinted in the *Hampton University Alumni Magazine*, Vol. 119, No. 3 (Spring 1986), p. 3.

Orpheus M. McAdoo Papers, 1886–1901

Orpheus McAdoo (1858–1900), a student at Hampton Institute from 1873–1876, became a member of the Hampton Quartet in 1886. Along with a photograph (c. 1886–1888) of the group (James H. Evans, William H. Daggs, R. H. Hamilton, and Orpheus McAdoo) are several clippings about him and his work with the ensemble.

Adjacent are correspondences from McAdoo to Hampton's founder (1868) and first principal (until 1893), Samuel Chapman Armstrong (1839–1893), of which only one is dated—May 6, 1889. Herewith is a letter of November 20, 1901 to Armstrong's successor, Hollis Burke Frissell.[3]

Julian Bagley Papers, 1919–1973

A graduate of Hampton Institute (1917) and a teacher at its Whittier School for children (1917–1922), Julian Bagley is principally remembered for his work at the San Francisco Opera House. The introduction to an oral history transcript reads: "Julian Bagley's position—concierge, tour conductor, welcomer—put him at the front door, as well as behind the scenes, for forty years of performances, visits, and meetings, at the San Francisco Opera House."[4] During the interview, references were made to Marian Anderson and other Black performers who passed through San Francisco.

The title of a newspaper feature, "Candle-Lighting Time for Julian Bagley," printed Sunday, January 23, 1972 in the Jacksonville *Times-Union and Journal*, alludes to his publication of 18 children's folk tales, *Candle-Lighting Time in Boddidalee* (1971). With these items are clippings of two other publications of his: "Moving Pictures in an Old Song Shop," whose source is unidentified, and "Unlettered Day," a story of the race problem printed in *The Outlook*, vol. 23, no. 2 (September 10, 1919), pp. 49–52.

William O. Tessman Papers, 1911–1919

Among these papers of William Tessman (1869–1940), director of the Hampton Institute college band from 1894–1938, are a number of handwritten correspondences regarding the work of the school band. Several (1911–1917) are addressed to Hampton Principal Hollis Burke Frissell, one (1918) to Vice Principal George P. Phenix, and another (1919) to Hampton Principal James E. Gregg. Herewith is a letter of January 17, 1913 from E. Azalia Hackley to Frissell.

---

[3] See the Hampton Quartet Collection later in this chapter.

[4] *Julian Bagley: Welcome to the San Francisco Opera House*. Interview by Suzanne Riess. Bancroft Library, Regional Oral History Office, University of California, Berkeley, 1973, p. ii.

Charles H. Flax Papers, 1963–1978

During his tenure at Hampton Institute, Charles Flax (1906–1980) served as Music Instructor, Assistant Chaplain, Acting Chaplain, Director of the Chapel Choir, and Director of the Choir Directors-Organists Guild of the Hampton Institute Ministers Conference. He is perhaps best remembered, however, as Director of the Crusaders Male Chorus. Organized on February 12, 1939, the group performed throughout Virginia's Tidewater Area and along the eastern seaboard. Documents among his papers indicate that they were known as "Hampton's Ambassadors of Good Will."

Among the printed programs is one of a concert given by the Crusaders on April 27, 1969 at Union Baptist Church in Baltimore. It is titled "Songs of Black America: The Negro Speaks Through the Spiritual," and includes historic notes on the spiritual and biographical notes on the choir.

A number of correspondences (1971–78) regarding the Crusaders are enclosed. In a letter of June 28, 1971 to W. R. Curry, for instance, Flax discussed the group's rendering of spirituals: "...you will find that many of the Negro Spirituals lend themselves to the forced syncopated beat as well as to the constant fundamental. Also the harmonies are so constructed that oft'times foreign notes are enjoined with a great deal of flourish." Some of the correspondences are relative to the Choir Directors-Organists Guild, of which he was director from 1956 to 1980. In addition, there are minutes of the 1963 meeting and programs of the guild's Sacred Concerts which always close the conference week.

Not only did Flax collect newspaper segments regarding the Crusaders and himself (as its director), but principally during the sixties he kept a clippings file on various subjects of interest to him—Hampton Institute, religion, and music. Most, if not all of these are from the daily newspaper to which he apparently subscribed, the Newport News, Virginia *Daily Press*. On the subject of worship, and more specifically music and worship, he accumulated a number of pamphlets, articles, and clippings.

Roland Marvin Carter Collection, 1963–1986

Since Roland Carter (b. 1942), a Hampton Institute graduate (1964), has been Hampton's Choir Director since 1965, was Assistant Director of the Choir Directors-Organists Guild from 1965 until he became its Director in 1980, has been Director of the Crusaders Male Chorus since 1980 and Music Department Chairman since 1986, it is fitting that the university archives house his agglomeration of school-related papers; for the crux of the collection has to do with the Hampton Institute Choir and him as its director.

There are innumerable correspondences, clippings, photographs, and programs, many of which are relative to the choir's tour of the Scandinavian countries July 28 through August 14, 1970. And there are programs of concerts given by the Peninsula Youth Orchestra which Carter directed from 1974–1980.

Miscellaneous photographs of Carter, soprano Marilyn Thompson (for whom he has been recital accompanist since 1982), R. Nathaniel Dett, James Weldon Johnson, and J. Rosamond Johnson are also included in the collection. Along with a family photo album is uncountable memorabilia.

Most of Carter's choral arrangements of spirituals and original choral compositions are located here. Many of these are published by his own company, Mar-Vel: "Behold the Days Come," "Done Made My Vow to the Lord," "First Thing Monday Morning" (from *Purlie*), "Five Choral Responses Based On Afro-American Spirituals," "Give Me Jesus," "Great Day," "I Want to Die Easy," "Lift Every Voice and Sing" (including an orchestral arrangement in pencil manuscript), "A Mighty Fortress," "Precious Lord, Take My Hand," "Ride On King Jesus," "Steal Away," "'Tis the Ol' Ship of Zion," and "You Must Have that True Religion."[5]

Along with these compositions are two manuscript musical arrangements of Noah Ryder, "Long John (Negro Convict Song)" and "This Ol' Hammer," one by Weldon J. Irvine, "Sometimes I Feel Like a Motherless Child," and Danmark's "The Moving Picture Rag."

Jon Michael Spencer Papers, 1978–1986

This collection of composer, music educator, and Hampton Institute alumnus (1978), Jon Michael Spencer (b. 1957), contains newspaper clippings and programs relative to performances of his original compositions. His compiled works include: (1) *Cantata: Six Jazz Poems* for tenor and baritone soloists, choir, and piano (1982) (2) *Concerto for Alto Saxophone and Orchestra* (1982) (3) *Confide in Sleep Eternal: A Dramatic Poem for Soprano and Piano* (1983) (4) *The Hampton Institute Sonata* for alto saxophone and piano (1978) (5) *Jubilis* (Opera in One Act) (1980) (6) *This Land Shall Overcome: Hymn for World Peace* (1983) (7) *Sonata for Alto Saxophone and Piano* (1981) (8) *Suite for Two Guitars* (1979) (9) *To Everything there is a Season and a Time,* anthem for choir (1982) (10) *Two Poems with Incidental Music* (1979) (11) *Wedding Cantata*, three duets for soprano and tenor with keyboard accompaniment, processional and recessional (1983).

Enclosed is his Ph.D. dissertation, *The Writings of Robert Nathaniel Dett and William Grant Still on Black Music* (Washington University, 1982), his published articles (principally on the subject of Black music), and papers and printed programs of presentations given for such organizations as the Society for Ethnomusicology, the American Musicological Society, the Mississippi Folklore Society, and the Music Library Association.

Hampton Quartet Collection, 1889–1938

In this collection are broadsides and programs of concerts given nationwide by the Hampton Quartet, as well as clippings announcing and reviewing their 1930

---

[5] See the complete collection of choral works by Carter in the Black Music Archive at North Carolina Central University (Chapter 8).

tour of Europe. Concert programs and an itinerary indicate that they performed in Bristol, Oxford, London, Windsor, Canterbury, York, Manchester, and Liverpool. In the latter city the concert was held on July 2 in the Liverpool Cathedral.

Pertaining to this tour is an eleven-page typescript by Hampton Institute faculty member (1921–1941) George Franklin Ketchan (1895–1965), dated October 29, 1929, entitled "Possibilities for Hampton Choir: Europe 1930." Ketchan concludes the paper with a most philanthropic comment: "It would be one thing if the Hampton Choir and the small group were to go abroad as ordinary concert attractions, but it is quite another thing to have them go as living demonstrations of the potentialities of the Negro race."

Several anonymous articles about the group are enclosed. Three of them are one page typescripts, the first titled "Negro Quartet," the second "Hampton Institute and the Hampton Negro Quartet," and the third being a brief biographical sketch on the members of the 1916 ensemble—F. W. Crawley, Samuel E. Phillips, C. H. Tynes, and J. H. Wainwright. With reference to the Hampton Quartet is a two-page article by historian John Tasker Howard, Jr. entitled "Capturing the Spirit of the Real Negro Music."

There are three glass slide plates of the quartet, and four photographs, one of which is dated 1889, and another 1898. Of interest is a pamphlet of song texts published by the college in 1927, "Some Songs of the Hampton Institute Quartet."

Camera Club Collection, 1886–1900

Belonging to this collection of photographs are several pertinent to Black folk music on the Hampton campus. A few are worthy of description: (1) Three elderly Black men, one with a guitar, reclining on a cabin porch. (2) Boys at the Butler School in 1886, one in a marching uniform with a drum. (3) Four photographs of Miss. Alice M. Bacon (1858–1918), Hampton Institute faculty member. (4) The Hampton Choir in 1888. (5) A photograph of the school band in the 1890's. (6) Boys of the Mandolin Club in 1900, four with mandolins, four with guitars, two with banjoes, and one with a cello. (7) A posed photograph of a young man courting a lady with a banjo, titled "When Malindy Sings," used as an illustration in Paul Laurence Dunbar's book of the same title (1906).

Hampton Songs Collection, 1893–1930

This collection consists principally of class songs, alma maters, and dedicatory pieces written for special Hampton occasions. All are either in manuscript or are printed clippings from the *Southern Workman* or *Hampton Script*:

Bacon, Alice M. "Memorial Hymn to General Armstrong." Text by Ernest Trow Carter (1893). MS.

————. "Song of the Class of '97." Text by W. A. Drake. MS.

Blackwell, M. H. "Greeting Song." (Class of 1897). Text by W. A. Drake. MS.

————. "Tree Song" (Class of '97). Text by W. A. Drake.

————. "Use What You Have." Text by W. A. Drake.

Cleveland, Bessie. "Armstrong." Text by Alice M. Bacon.

Curtis-Burlin, Natalie. "Hymn of Freedom" (Text only). Tune: "O Ride On, Jesus!" (1918).

Dett, R. Nathaniel. "Hampton! My Home By the Sea." MS. (and published copy from the *Southern Workman* (February 1914).

Fields, C. W. "Exercises in Honor of the Aged: Consisting of Original Recitations, Songs, Responses, etc."

Fletcher, Joseph G. "Hampton Flight Song." From *Hampton Script* (October 25, 1930).

"Freedom, God, and Right" (Trade School Song). (Text only).

Gilder, Richard Watson. "Hymn" (Written for the Service held on April 26, 1903 in memory of Dr. J. L. M. Curry (Text only). Tune: "Duke Street."

"Grace Before Meat at Hampton."

Hamilton, R. H. "Dedication Hymn" (Written for and Sung at the Dedication of the New Armstrong Hall. Normal School, Hampton, Virginia). Text by (Mrs.) F. E. W. Harper.

Hill, D. R. "Class Song." Text by Maggie Fisher.

Ludlow, Helen. "For Dedication" (Text only). Tune: "Air," Russian Hymn.

————. "For Dedication of the Collis P. Huntington Library, Hampton Institute" (Text only). Tune by Joseph Haydn.

————. "Song of the Armstrong League" (Based on Hawaiian Hymn).

Northern, Chauncey. "Hampton: A Song of Service, Love and Loyalty." Text by Sarah Collins Fernandis. Published in the *Southern Workman* (December 1928). Early version of the Alma Mater.

"Slave Songs of the South, by the Virginia Choirsters."

Stevens, Marie F. "Memories of Hampton" (Text only, 1899).Tune: "America."

Folklore Collection, 1895–1938

Contained herein are these items: (1) A letter of March 6, 1895 from an ill Mrs. Fanny D. Bergen of North Cambridge, Massachusetts to the director of the Hampton Singers, requesting that the choir come to her home to sing, for a fee, during their forth-coming visit to Boston. (2) Natalie Curtis-Burlin's *Hampton Series Negro Folk Songs*, Books 1–4 (1918–1919). (3) A printed program of April 22, 1915 titled "Folklore Concert," which includes historic notes on Negro folk song and early Black composers. (4) A 33⅓ RPM record titled *Virginia Traditions: Non-Blues Secular Black Music*. (5) Clippings (1935–38) on the Hampton Folk Singers, a group organized in 1935 at the request of college president Arthur Howe.

Musical Arts Society Papers, 1919–1986

The Musical Arts Society, founded at Hampton Institute in 1919 by R. Nathaniel Dett, brought to the campus such renowned musicians as Marian Anderson, H.

T. Burleigh, Duke Ellington, Roland Hayes, Dorothy Maynor, William Warfield, and Camilla Williams. More recently it has sponsored the appearances of Grace Bumbry, Miles Davis, Roberta Flack, Natalie Hinderas, Billy Taylor, and Andre Watts.

The collection consists principally of pertinent programs and newspaper clippings. One program of May 20, 1933, conducted by Clarence Cameron White, was titled "Musical Arts Society Presents the Hampton Institute Choral Society and the Hampton Players in S. Coleridge-Taylor's 'Hiawatha's Wedding Feast'."

Music Department Papers, 1918–1983

In addition to programs and clippings relative to visiting artists of the Musical Arts Society, are those of faculty recitals. Herewith is a typescript titled "Music at Hampton Institute," and two pamphlets, the first titled "Mr. Harry Burleigh, Baritone: Concert—Song Recital, Private Musicales,"and the second "The Hampton Institute Glee Club with R. Nathaniel Dett."

Hampton Institute Choir Papers

This small collection duplicates some of the larger ones, in that it contains clippings and photographs of the Hampton Institute Choir and the Hampton Folk Singers. Included are several typescripts on the history of the former.

Recordings, 1880–

Two recordings in the Hampton Institute Archives are of inestimable value. First, there is a wax cylinder recording of spirituals being sung at Hampton in the 1880's. Believed to be the oldest music recording in the country, a cassette taped reproduction is made available to researchers. Second, there is a 78 RPM three-set record titled *Negro Spirituals: Dorothy Maynor, Soprano, With Unaccompanied Male Choir* (RCA Victor).

Hampton Scrapbook Collection, 1894–1922

Available in the Peabody Room adjacent the Archives are music scrapbooks, each consisting of a compilation of clippings centered around a specific subject heading: (1) "Harry T. Burleigh: A Man of Rare Musical Gifts and Modest" (2) "Daniel Emmett: The Composer of 'Dixie'" (3) "James Reese Europe: 'The Jazz King'" (4) "Madame Azalia E. Hackley: The Race's Leading Prima Dona" (5) "Roland Hayes: From Slave Cabins to the Hall of Fame" (6) "S. Coleridge-Taylor: A Genius in Music" (7) "Music and Negro Music: 1894–1913" (8) "Negro Music: 1914–16" (9) "Negro Music: 1917–18" (10) "Negro Music: 1919–22" (11) "Negro Musicians" (12) "Cole Z. Johnson: Negro Music and Musicians."

Peabody Room Vertical Clippings File

Music—Classical. Included are clippings on Grace Bumbry, Carl Diton, Duke Ellington, Dorothy Maynor, Sheila Maye (present vocal instructor and soprano recitalist at Hampton), Leontyne Price, William Grant Still, William Warfield, Camilla Williams, as well as on the Negro Symphony Orchestra (Los Angeles) and a performance of *Porgy and Bess*.

Black Musicians—1984. Herein are clippings on such contemporary Black musicians as Count Basie, Marvin Gaye, Lena Horne, the Jackson Five, Michael Jackson, B. B. King, Wynton Marsalis, Prince, and Stevie Wonder.

Music—Popular. Assembled here are clippings on such popular artists as the Bar-Kays, Harry Belafonte, Earth, Wind and Fire, B. B. King, Hubert Laws, Lou Rawls, and Muddy Waters.

Music. Enclosed are clippings on Louis Armstrong, R. Nathaniel Dett, Duke Ellington, Paul Freeman, Roland Hayes, Dorothy Maynor, Billy Taylor, and Andre Watts. There are also clippings on African drumming, the Fisk Jubilee Singers, and *The Book of American Negro Spirituals* (1925) by James Weldon Johnson and J. Rosamond Johnson. Therewith are clippings of articles written by Dett and Clarence Cameron White.

Music—Spirituals. The clippings here are relative to spirituals, gospel music, and the Fisk Jubilee Singers. The colligation consists primarily of spirituals clipped from the *Southern Workman*.

Photograph Collection. Belonging to this file are glossy prints, posters, and photographs clipped from magazines and newspapers: Marian Anderson, H. T. Burleigh, Samuel Coleridge-Taylor, Sammy Davis, Jr., Carl Diton, Zelma Watson George, Azalia Hackley, W. C. Handy, Roland Hayes, Lena Horne, Alain Locke, Philippa Duke Schuyler, and the 368 Regiment [Black] Band (World War I).

CHAPTER 4
HOWARD UNIVERSITY

The foundation of Howard University's Moorland-Spingarn Research Center is built on the extensive personal libraries of bibliophiles Jesse E. Moorland (1863–1940) and Arthur B. Spingarn (1878–1971) which were acquired in 1914 and 1946 respectively. To these were added the Manuscript Division, the four departments of which are inventoried in the succeeding pages: Music Department, Manuscript Department, Oral History Department, and Prints and Photographs Department. Also inventoried is the clippings file belonging to the Library Division.

Music Department[1]

Arthur B. Spingarn Collection

Over 2,200 compositions were acquired with the Spingarn collectanea in 1946. It appears that all of the major historic Black composers are represented: Thomas Bethune, Eubie Blake, James Bland, H. T. Burleigh, Cab Calloway, Bob Cole, Samuel Coleridge-Taylor, Thomas Dorsey, Duke Ellington, James Reese Europe, Lillian Evanti, Ella Fitzgerald, H. Lawrence Freeman. Scott Joplin, Ulysses Kay, Noble Sissle, William Grant Still, and Howard Swanson, to name just a few. Rare among the pieces are works by Afro-Cuban composer Amadeo Roldan and Afro-Brazilian composer A. Carlos Gomes.

Jesse E. Moorland Collection

Bearing Moorland's name as a memorium only, this collection consists of compositions donated to the research center by musicians and music enthusiasts. Approximately 433 LP recordings and over 800 compositions by 180 different composers represent every form of Black American music. In addition to the classics of the historic Black composers, are pieces by such contemporary gospel writers as James Cleveland, Robert Fryson, and Kenneth Morris, and such contemporary classical writers as Aldolphus Hailstork. The latter, a graduate of

[1] For further detail see "The Guide to the Music Department Collections at the Moorland Spingarn Research Center" compiled by Deborra A. Richardson. This guide remains at present unpublished but is available to visiting researchers.

Howard University (1963), has donated over 50 of his original compositions to the collection.

Alain L. Locke Collection

This collection was compiled by the noted social philosopher Alain Locke (1886–1954), Howard University professor (1912–1954) and author of such well known books as *The New Negro* (1925) and *The Negro and His Music* (1936). In addition to being a social commentator and bibliophile, Locke had a deep appreciation for Black music, which lead him to accumulate approximately 53 pieces. The majority of the works are spirituals, both arrangements by such composers as H. T. Burleigh and John Wesley Work, and volumes like Nicholas Ballanta-Taylor's *Saint Helena Island Spirituals* (1925) and Natalie Curtis-Burlin's *Hampton Series Negro Folk Songs* (1918).

Washington Conservatory of Music Collection

This Black-owned and operated conservatory (1903–1960) was founded by Harriet Gibbs Marshall (1869–1941), author of *The Story of Haiti* (1930). Under Marshall the conservatory amassed over 350 music compositions by approximately 121 Black composers. Represented among the number of historic figures are: Wellington A. Adams, Eubie Blake, Edward Boatner, H. T. Burleigh, Arthur W. Calhoun, Melville Charlton, Samuel Coleridge-Taylor, Will Marion Cook, William Dawson, R. Nathaniel Dett, Carl Diton, Duke Ellington, Ray Forrest, H. Lawrence Freeman, W. C. Handy, Maud Cuney Hare, James P. Johnson, J. Rosamond Johnson, Florence Price, Noah Francis Ryder, Philippa Duke Schuyler, Noble Sissle, Jean Stor, Lillian Evanti, Clarence Cameron White, as well as Haitian composers Franck Lassegue and Lamothe Ludevic, and Afro-Cuban composer Jose Manuel Jimenez.

Manuscript Department[2]

Marian Anderson Collection, 1939–1943

The central theme of this colligation is the racial controversy surrounding Marian Anderson (b. 1902) and the Daughters of the American Revolution (D.A.R.) who, in January 1939, refused to allow the renowned Black contralto to sing in Constitution Hall. Among the newspaper clippings is a broadside which summarizes the entire event: "The D.A.R. would not let her sing in Constitution

---

[2] For a more general description of these collections see *Guide to Processed Collections in the Manuscript Division of the Moorland-Spingarn Research Center*, comp. Greta S. Wilson, and published by the center in 1983.

Hall. The Board of Education made it impossible for her to sing in Central High School. But Under the Auspices of Howard University Marian Anderson Sings Free in the Open Air to the people of Washington on Easter Sunday, April 9 At Five o'clock in the afternoon at the Lincoln Memorial." A printed program indicates that Anderson opened the Easter concert with "America" and closed it with the spiritual "My Soul is Anchored in the Lord."

Another printed program is for the commemorative occasion held in Washington's Interior Department Auditorium on January 6, 1948: "Presentation of the Marian Anderson Mural Commemorating the Easter Sunday Concert of 1939." Lastly, there is a promotional pamphlet by S. Hurok which includes an essay, "Marian Anderson to Me," by Irving Kolodin, music editor for the *Saturday Review*.

Owen Vincent Dodson Papers, 1930–1968

Owen Dodson (b. 1914), poet, playwright, novelist, and author of such volumes as *The Confession Stone: Song Cycles* (1970), taught at Atlanta University, Spelman College, and Hampton Institute, before settling at Howard University's drama department in 1947. Among his papers is a typescript of the aforementioned anthology, musical settings of his poems in the manuscript of Morris Mamorsky, and a musical score written in 1943 by Edgar Rogie Clark for his play, "Everybody Join Hands."

Dodson collected an assortment of photographs of Lillian Evanti (1891–1967), concert soprano and opera star, and a Howard University graduate (1917). Included with the pictures is a typescript of Evanti's song cycle, "Naturama: A Cycle of Songs of the Seasons."

Gregoria Fraser Goins Papers, 1843–1962

The enclosed biographical data on Mrs. Goins (1883–1964) indicates that she taught piano and voice in her Gregorian Music Studio in Washington, D.C., and started a women's string orchestra. She was also a member of the city's Treble Clef Club and The National Association of Negro Music and accumulated organizational data.

Andrew Franklin Hilyer Papers, 1893–1913

Born a slave in Georgia, Andrew Hilyer (1859–1925) received law degrees from Howard in 1885 and 1886, and later served the university as a trustee from 1913–1935. Hilyer, along with his wife Mamie Nichols Hilyer (1863–1916) who started the Treble Clef Club in 1897, were instrumental in founding the Samuel Coleridge-Taylor Society in 1901 which sponsored the visit of the Black English composer (1875–1912) to the United States in 1904 and 1906. Since Hilyer was its treasurer, his papers contain pertinent correspondences, including some with the composer. There is also a miscellaneous correspondence with E. Azalia Hackley.

Louia Vaughn Jones Collection, 1912–1960

Louia Vaughn Jones (1895–1965), a graduate of the New England Conservatory (1918) taught music at Howard University for 30 years (1930–1960) while also enjoying a successful career as a concert violinist. Four scrapbooks (1912–1960) contain pertinent programs, broadsides, correspondences, and newspaper reviews. In addition to being called "a fiddler for royalty" in Europe, Jones received high acclaim among the Black academic community after rendering masterful performances at such schools as Howard and Xavier. At the latter, he gave a joint recital with pianist Camille Nickerson on April 12, 1935.

Progams enclosed indicate that he preferred the classics of the Romanticists. The works of Brahms, Schubert, Chopin, Franck, and Debussy were standard in his repertoire. He also performed such works as S. Coleridge Taylor's *Deep River*, R. Nathaniel Dett's *Ramah* and Ulysses Kay's *Sonatina in C Minor*.

Alfonce Mizell and Freddie Perren Collection, 1969–1971

This collection consists of 17 musical scores arranged by Mizell and Perren for records produced by the Jackson Five. The songs are "All I Can Give to You," "Bridge Over Troubled Water," "Can You Remember," "I Found That Girl," "I Want You Back," "I'm So Happy," "It's Great to Be Here," "The Love I Saw in You Was Just a Mirage," "The Love You Save," "Mamas Pearl," "Maybe Tomorrow," "Merry Little XMas," "My Little Baby," "Nobody," "She's Good," "Sugar Daddy," and "To the Top: Up On the House Top."

Andy Razaf Papers, 1913–1973

Songwriter Andy Razaf (1895–1973), the prolific lyricist who collaborated with such greats as Louis Armstrong, W. C. Handy, Eubie Blake, and James P. Johnson, was most noted for his teamwork with Fats Waller. The two produced such songs as "Ain't Misbehavin'" and "Honeysuckle Rose," as well as the Broadway musical, *Keep Shufflin'* (1928). But that was only one of the half-dozen Broadway musicals Razaf wrote in collaboration with other musicians.

His papers consist principally of two bound volumes of his songs dated 1913–1962. Herewith is a scrapbook containing programs, newspaper clippings, and letters relative to his career.

Isabele Taliaferro Spiller Papers, 1906–1954

Included herein is biographical data relative to the careers of Isabele Spiller (1888–1974) and her husband William N. Spiller (1876–1944), who were members of The Musical Spillers, a vaudeville act founded in Chicago by the latter in 1906. Newspaper articles, broadsides, and photographs (1906–1940) reveal the group's success throughout the United States, Canada, Europe, Africa, and South America. Additionally, there is information regarding The Musical Spillers' School, which was organized in New York by William Spiller in 1926. With his wife as co-director of the music school, they often contracted the most talented students to perform with their vaudeville act. Biographical data is given on several of these group members.

LeRoy Tibbs Collection, 1921–1949

Herein are two scrapbooks (1927–1947) containing clippings, programs, and correspondences relative to the New York nightclub career of jazz pianist, arranger, and bandleader Roy Tibbs.[3] Tibbs' successful career led him to perform at such establishments as The Cotton Club and Cafe Society Uptown. Among the newspaper articles regarding his career are a number on Black music and musicians in general. He kept, for instance, a piece from the August 25, 1945 *Amsterdam News* which had the caption "Cab Calloway Slugged Me, Claude Hopkins Charges." The third scrapbook enclosed is relative to the career of Tibbs' wife, Marie Young Tibbs, a New York actress.

Charles Pickard Ware Papers,

Charles Ware (1840–1921) is co-author with William Francis Allen and Lucy McKim Garrison of the first published collection of spirituals, *Slave Songs of the United States* (1867). The papers assembled here concern his administration of a group of plantations in the South Carolina Sea Islands, a position asigned him by the government after that Confederate territory was brought under Union control. The Allen, Ware, and Garrison book probably draws on some of his observations while on the islands.

Washington Conservatory of Music Records, 1887–1966

Founded "with the ideal of encouraging and developing the Negro's own racial self-expression in music," Marshall's 1937 addition of the National Negro Music Center to the conservatory was intended to aid in the research and preservation of Black musical heritage through the maintenance of a library, the presentation of concerts, and the like. This effort was furthered by the publication of *The Negro Music Journal*. Founded in 1902 by its editor, J. Hilary Taylor, this monthly journal came under the conservatory's auspices in 1903 when Taylor joined the

---

[3] LeRoy Tibbs the nightclub pianist is not to be confused with LeRoy Wilford Tibbs (1888–1944), the pianist and organist who taught music at Howard University from 1914–1944, and who married Lillian Evans Tibbs, the opera star known on stage as Madame Evanti.

faculty; which consisted of such distinguished musicians as E. Azalia Hackley and Clarence Cameron White. Only a copy of the November 1903 (vol. 2, no. 15) issue is enclosed. It opens with an article, "Music as a Profession," by Harriet Gibbs (Marshall).

Among the records of the conservatory and its adjunct research center are clippings, publicity, programs, and photographs pertaining to performances it sponsored between 1913 and 1933, as well as articles, programs, and biographical data pertaining to its faculty (1903–1937). Herewith is biographical data on nearly two dozen Black musicians and composers: Amanda Ira Aldridge, Nellie Constance Allen, H. T. Burleigh, Melville Charlton, S. Coleridge-Taylor, Will Marion Cook, R. Nathaniel Dett, James Reese Europe, Edwin Francis Hill, J. Rosamond Johnson, Walter Loving, Eugene Mars Martin, Bernard Lee Mason, Ruth Norma, Magda Pfeiffer, Florence B. Price, Vivian Scott, Marie Selika, Oliver Sims, and Clarence Cameron White.

Glenn Carrington Collection,[4] 1844–1974

A graduate of Howard University (1925), where he came under the lasting influence of Professor Alain Locke, Glenn Carrington (1904–1975) amassed a large quantity of books, broadsides, programs, recordings, and sheet music, all of which was bequeathed to the university upon his death. Of the 41 pieces of music dating from 1844–1959 are works by such composers as Eubie Blake, James Bland, H. T. Burleigh, Will Marion Cook, R. Nathaniel Dett, W. C. Handy, J. Rosamond Johnson, and Noble Sissle.

Highlighted among his collection of 500 LP recordings are those of Duke Ellington (130), George Lewis (28), Fats Waller (18), Ella Fitzgerald (16), Louis Armstrong (14), Odetta (14), Bobby Short (11), Mable Mercer (10), Johnny Hodges (9), Jelly Roll Morton (9), and Art Tatum (7). Also represented with several albums are such artists as Ma Rainey, Billie Holiday, Leadbelly, Blind Lemon Jefferson, Mahalia Jackson, Paul Robeson, and Dorothy Maynor.

Oral History Department[5]

Ralph J. Bunch Oral History Collection, 1967–1974

This collection consists of transcripts of nearly 700 interviews with persons who were involved in the civil rights movement, especially in leadership positions.

---

[4] For a listing of the sheet music and recordings, see *The Glenn Carrington Collection*, compiled by Karen L. Jefferson and Bridgette M. Rouson, and published by the center in 1977, pp. 96–119.

[5] For a complete listing of the Ralph J. Bunch Oral History Collection with annotations, see *Bibliography of Holdings of the Civil Rights Documentation Project*, edited by Vincent J. Browne and Norma O. Leonard, and published by the center in 1974.

A number of the interviewees refer to the singing of protest songs, which were typically adaptations of extant spirituals and gospels. The following interviews were conducted in 1967.

Marion Barry (b. 1936), the first Chairman of the Student Nonviolent Coordinating Committee (SNCC), referred to Harry Belafonte's financial support of the protest movement. He also spoke briefly of the Freedom Singers of SNCC who he said performed on college campuses throughout the country.

Dion T. Diamond (b. 1941), a former SNCC field representative, recalled his 49 days in Mississippi's Parchman Prison, and how nightly they would have song fests. He said the other prisoners often encouraged their singing: "Everybody would join in and the guys on the other side I do believe they were behind us."

John Lewis (b. 1940), chairman of SNCC from 1963–1965, spoke of the Nashville movement and the part played by Guy Carawan (of Guy Carawan and the Freedom Singers), whom he believed first introduced "We Shall Overcome" to the movement.

Wyatt T. Walker (b. 1929), Executive Director of the Southern Christian Leadership Conference (SCLC) from 1960–1965, made reference to the involvement of Harry Belafonte, Mahalia Jackson, Nat King Cole, Eartha Kitt, Lena Horne, and Sammy Davis, Jr., all of whom either gave money to the movement or sponsored benefits to raise it. The two names which stand out among them, says Walker, are Belafonte and Davis, with the former being the principal supporter: "I would say that Belafonte, by far, has done more than any other person in the entertainment world, to my knowledge."

Television Transcripts Collection, 1959–1971

Among the nearly 100 television transcripts of programs produced on the ABC, CBS, NBC, and NET television networks are two with segments on Black music. The first was a CBS News Special titled "Body and Soul" aired on July 30, 1968. Of the two parts, "Body" and "Soul," the latter was essayed by rhythm and blues singer Ray Charles. Although Charles talked principally about blues from its conception up to the Billie Holiday era, he did mension other musical genre and such performers as Mahalia Jackson, Duke Ellington, Count Basie, and Aretha Franklin.

The second program, Black Journal #11, was aired on the National Educational Television Network (NET) in New York on April 28, 1969. A portion of the show was a tribute to Paul Robeson on his 71st birthday.

Prints and Photographs Department

The Mary O'H. Williamson Collection of Colored Celebrities Here and There, 1947–1957

Photographs, post-cards, posters, magazine and newspaper articles convey images of a variety of Black musicians: Ira Aldridge, Gilbert Allen, Marian Anderson, Louis Armstrong, Clyde Barrie, Count Basie, James Bland, Carol Brice, Shelton Brooks, Anne Wiggins Brown, Ivan Harold Browning, H. T. Burleigh, Cab Calloway, Melville Charlton, Chevalier de St. George, Will Marion Cook, William Dawson, R. Nathaniel Dett, Dean Dixon, Randolph Dunbar, Todd Duncan, Duke Ellington, Ruby Elgy, Lillian Evanti, Ella Fitzgerald, Eugene Gasch, Shirley Graham, Elizabeth T. Greenfield, E. Azalia Hackley, The Hampton Institute Choir, Lionel Hampton, W. C. Handy, Maud Cuney Hare, Josephine Harreld, Hazel Harrison, Erskin Hawkins, Roland Hayes, Lena Horne, Billy Horner, Caterina Jarboro, Hall Johnson, J. Rosamond Johnson, Louia Vaughn Jones, Thomas Kerr, Andy Kirk, Virginia Lewis, Walter A. Loving, June McMechan, Dorothy Maynor, Mills Brothers, Abbie Mitchell, Etta Moten, Camille Nickerson, Chauncey Northern, Sylvia Olden, Aubrey C. Pankey, Robert Parrish, Muriel Rahn, Leon René, C. L. Roberts, Philippa Schuyler, Southern Airs, Kenneth Spencer, William Grant Still, S. Coleridge-Taylor, Roy Tibbs, Charlotte Wallace, Fats Waller, Chick Webb, Lawrence Whisonant, Clarence Cameron White, Camilla Williams.

The Rose McClendon Memorial Collection of Photographs of Celebrated Negroes by Carl Van Vechten, 1932–1965

This collection of photographs was given to Howard by Van Vechten as a memorium to the distinguished actress Rosalie Scott McClendon (1884–1936). A significant number of these black and white prints are pictures of Black musicians: Marian Anderson, Pearl Bailey, Reginald Beane, Gladys Bentley, H. T. Burleigh, Dan Burley, Cab Calloway, John Carter, Sammy Davis, Jr., Leonard de Paur, Dean Dixon, Todd Duncan, Ella Fitzgerald, Dizzy Gillespie, W. C. Handy, Billie Holiday, Lena Horne, Mahalia Jackson, Raymond Jackson, Hall Johnson, James Weldon Johnson, Ulysses Kay, Mabel Mercer, Evelyn LaRue Pittman, Paul Robeson, Philippa Duke Schuyler, George Shirley, Bobby Short, William Grant Still, Billy Strayhorn, Howard Swanson, Ethel Waters, William Warfield, Clarence Cameron White, Josh White, Camilla Williams, and John Wesley Work.

The Griffith Davis Collection of Photographs of Liberia, 1948–1952

This extensive collection of photographs taken by Griffith Davis consists of contact prints of a panorama of Liberian scenes and social occasions. There are, for instance, pictures of tribal dancing and singing accompanied by drumming and clapping. Another photograph is of an African man playing a guitar in his village. Many similar musical scenes are to be found therein.

The Howardiana Collection, 1867–1986

The photographs relative to Howard University's department of music are dated 1950–1953. Among them are pictures of concert violinist Louia Vaughn Jones, the String Ensemble he directed, the university orchestra, choir, and band, and a group-shot of the music faculty.

Library Division

Clippings File, 1800–1986

Programs, broadsides, and articles from newspapers, magazines, and journals cover all forms of Black American music, as well as the music of Africa, Brazil, and the West Indies, more specifically, Trinidad (calypso) and Jamaica (reggae). Musical artists, ensembles, and organizations represented herein are Carl Diton, Charles Ezzard, Paul Robeson, Ester Mae Scott (Mother Scott), Rosetta Tharpe, Muddy Waters, and James Lesesne Wells; Bradford Harmonizers, De Paul's Infantry Chorus, Fifth Dimension, Fultz Quartet, Golden Gate Quartet, Hall Johnson Negro Choir, Jackson Five, Nickerson's Ladies Orchestra, Temptations, and Wings Over Jordan Choir; African Music Society, Metropolitan Music Society, Negro Folk Music Festival, New York Musicians Jazz Festival, and Washington Blues Festival.

The first of two printed programs herein is titled "Contest in Musical Composition for Composers of the Negro Race." The other is sequential, "Second Contest for Composers of the Negro Race for One Thousand Dollars in Prizes Offered by Rodman Wanamaker."

CHAPTER 5

JACKSON STATE UNIVERSITY

Located in the Special Collections at Jackson State University are archival files on Opera/South, William Grant Still, Frederick Douglass Hall, William Walton Davis, Aurelia Norris Young, and Raymond I. Johnson. Located therewith is a small gathering of sheet music.

Opera/South Collection, 1969–1984

Opera/South is a Black-operated opera company founded by Sister Mary Elise, a white Catholic nun who once served as music director at Xavier University. Still managed by Jackson State University, Tougaloo College and Utica Junior College, the organization opened with the 1969–70 season. The archive contains pamphlets about the company, business correspondences, news releases, newspaper reviews, and its newsletter, *Rapnotes*.

A complete file of programs reveals its repertoire of standard European operas as well as the operas of Black American composers. Too, they document the list of distinctive Black performers, such as Benjamin Matthews and Jackson alumnus (1959) William Albert Brown (b. 1938), who have performed under the baton of such Black maestros as Leonard de Paur (b. 1915), Paul Freeman (b. 1935), and James DePreist (b. 1936).

Among the programs and clippings are those pertaining to the two operas of Ulysses Kay (b. 1917). The first, *The Juggler of Our Lady* (1958), was performed by Opera/South in 1972. The second, *Jubilee* (1974/76), was commissioned by the company. Its text, by Opera/South stage director Donald Dorr, is based on the novel of the same title by Margaret Walker (b. 1915), a Mississippian who taught at Jackson State from 1949–1979. Opera/South rendered its world premier under the baton of DePreist in the Jackson Auditorium on November 20, 1976. Program notes provide a scenario along with information on the composer, librettist, novelist, conductor, and performers.

William Grant Still, the first Black American composer to have an opera performed by a major company,[1] had his *Highway #1, U.S.A.* (1963) performed by Opera/South in 1972; and his *A Bayou Legend* (1940) received its debut 34 years after its completion. That historic performance took place under the conductorship of maestro De Paur in the Municipal Auditorium in Jackson, Missis-

[1] That opera, *Troubled Island* (1941), was premiered by the New York City Opera Company on March 31, 1949.

sippi on November 15, 1974. The printed program contains notes on Still, the librettist (who happens to be his wife Verna Arvey), and a scenario. Among the miscellany are photographs of the composer and scenes from the opera. In addition, a guide for Mississippi Public Television (June 14–20, 1981) gives notes on the opera which was aired on June 15, 1981.

William Grant Still Collection, 1931–1971

As the "Dean of Afro-American Composers," William Grant Still (1895–1971) not only composed concert works in every conceivable musical genre, but early in his career arranged music for the bands of such notables as W. C. Handy, Sophie Tucker, Paul Whiteman, and Artie Shaw. Dean Still's collection seems to be an outgrowth of materials accumulated relative to Opera/South's premier of *A Bayou Legend* in 1974.

Among the printed programs is one documenting a Lyceum Recital at Southern University with William Grant Still conducting the New Orleans Symphony Orchestra on February 25, 1955. Listing this occasion as one of his historic "firsts," Still claims to have been the first Black to conduct a major symphony orchestra in the deep south. Adjacent are published scores of his *Afro-American Symphony* (1931) and *Seven Traceries* (1940).

Assembled here are several of Still's 36 published articles on various aspects of Black music and American music in general: "Fifty Years of Progress in Music," "Music: A Vital Factor in America's Racial Problem," and "My Arkansas Boyhood." Herewith are several pieces about him: "An Outstanding Arkansas Composer—William Grant Still" by Mary D. Hudgins, and "Afroamerican Music Memo" and "Still Opera Points the Way" by Verna Arvey. Adjoined is a bibliography of articles by and about him.[2]

Along with a printed program of November 8, 1970, "Oberlin College Conservatory of Music Presents a 75th Birthday Celebration in Honor of William Grant Still," is an article taken from the January 1971 issue of Oberlin Alumni Magazine, "Oberlin Marks William Grant Still's 75½ Birthday." This recognition is given him as one who not only studied at Oberlin, in 1917 and 1919, but who was awarded the honory Doctor of Music Degree by the college in 1947.

Frederick Douglass Hall Collection, 1921–1975

Having received his undergraduate training at Morehouse College (1921), Frederick D. Hall (b. 1898) gave back to Black education the excellent training he had received: first to Jackson State (1921–27) as music director, then to Dillard

---

[2] For a compilation of 34 published articles by Still and an analysis of their content see the doctoral dissertation of Jon Michael Spencer, "The Writings of Robert Nathaniel Dett and William Grant Still on Black Music" (Washington University, 1982), located in the Spencer collection at Hampton University.

(1936–41), Alabama State (1941–55), Southern (1955–59), and once again to Dillard (1960–74). Jackson State University acknowledged the contributions of this Black educator par excellence by naming its music building after him. An enclosed program indicates that Hall was present for the dedicatory event. Alongside it is a photograph of him as a young man on the university's faculty.

There are clippings and some correspondences, but the item of real historic value is Hall's curriculum vitae which lists his educational training, fellowships, honors, memberships, research interests, service to the community, compositions and arrangements, books in preparation, consultations, and lectures. The list of lectures probably consists of topics Hall covered as he spoke throughout the country: "The Romance of the Spiritual," "The Structure of the Negro Voice," "Music in the Church-Related Negro College," "History of the Afro-American Concert Artist," "Trends in Afro-American Music, 1925–1975," and "Music in Christian Worship."

William Walton Davis Collection, 1916–1981

Formerly a musician with Cab Calloway's band, an enclosed newspaper clipping indicates that William Davis (1922–1981) was Jackson State's first band director (1948–1981). With printed programs of band concerts is a tribute to his 27 years of service to the school in the October 29, 1982 issue of the university's newsletter, *Scope*.

Davis also composed and arranged music for the band. Among his few original compositions is "Symphonic Portrait of Jackson Fair," Davis's band arrangement of the alma mater, "Jackson Fair," written by Thomas D. Pawley in 1916 and arranged by Frederick D. Hall in 1921. All three versions are enclosed.

Aurelia Norris Young Collection, 1972–1983

Mrs. Young served on Jackson State University's music faculty from 1963–1979. Along with a photograph of her and newspaper clippings regarding her career, are three items of her composition: (1) An article, "Black Folk Music," taken from the *Mississippi Folklore Register* (the journal of the Mississippi Folklore Society), vol. 6, no. 1 (Spring 1972) (2) A speech, "Taking the High Road," delivered on Honors Night, April 28, 1983, at Jackson State, and (3) A composition, "Centennial Hymn," written for the university's centennial celebration in 1977.

Sheet Music Collection

Aside from "Sunflower Slow Drag" by Scott Joplin and Scott Hayden, the other pieces of this collection are not by Black composers, but instances of the derogatory minstrel ditty which satirizes Blacks: (1) "Happy Hours in Coon Town" by

Charles B. Brown (2) "My Honey Lou (A Darkey Love-Song)" by Thurland Chattaway, and (3) "My Bamboo Queen" by Harry Von Tilzer.

Raymond I. Johnson Collection, 1930–1980

Raymond I. Johnson served Jackson State University as choir director and choral coordinator of Opera/South for many years. Upon his death the music department received his extensive collectanea.[3]

Outstanding in the agglomeration are approximately 280 choral compositions by Black writers, most of which are arrangements of spirituals. Included are over 40 published pieces and 20 unpublished manuscripts of Hall Johnson, in addition to works by Edward Boatner, Margaret Bonds, H. T. Burleigh, Noble Cain, John Carter, Edgar Rogie Clark, S. Coleridge-Taylor, William Dawson, Leonard de Paur, R. Nathaniel Dett, Carl Diton, Ruth Gillum, Jester Hairston, Frederick Hall, Willis Laurence James, Ulysses Kay, Undine Smith Moore, Camille Nickerson, Julia Perry, Evelyn LaRue Pittman, Clarence J. Rivers, Robert Shaw, John Wesley Work, and many others.

Among the unpublished manuscripts are Kenneth Billups' "Kappa Alpha Psi Hymn," Florence Cole-Talbert's "Delta Sigma Theta Hymn," and John Duncan's *The Resurrection: A Chamber Cantata*, *An Easter Cantata*, *Journey of the Holy Family*, *Remember Now Thy Creator*, *Six Bible Choruses*, and *God Don't Like It*. Herewith are two of Raymond Johnson's own works dated 1950: *Suite* (3 parts for clarinet and piano) and *Quartet for Woodwinds*.

Comprising the miscellaneous items are a letter from John Duncan to Raymond Johnson, a promotional pamphlet from Black bass-baritone Benjamin Matthews, the vol. 3, no. 2 (Winter 1956) issue of *Tones and Overtones*, and printed programs of various musical events.

---

[3] When inventoried, this collection had just been received by the music department and was unprocessed. Aside from the portion given to the Special Collections, most of it remains unprocessed in the music building.

CHAPTER 6
LINCOLN UNIVERSITY

Located in the Special Collections division of the Langston Hughes Memorial Library at Lincoln University (Pennsylvania) are the papers of Langston Hughes, a complete collection of the school's *Music Department Bulletin*, and files of photographs and recital programs.

Langston Hughes Papers, 1925–1967

What makes the archival collection at Lincoln University so special are the personal papers of litterateur Langston Hughes (1902–1967), poet, short story writer, playwright, novelist, librettist, lyricist, and scholar. Rewarded the Honorary Literary Doctorate by Lincoln in 1943, only fourteen years after taking his bachelor's degree there in 1929, the "Dean of Black Letters" bequeathed a portion of his amassment to the institution.

Hughes' ardent passion for Black music is not only evident in his jazz and blues poetry and the pertinent books he published, but also in the articles and programs he accumulated. The clippings specifically evince a preoccupation with music of the West Indies: a magazine piece, "Road to Haiti" by Arthur R. Pastore, Jr., and a number of newspaper extracts, "Calypso," "Calypso Composers Now Sing of Trinidad Independence," "Jamaica Has Special Charm in Folk Music," "'Traump' Time in the Virgin Islands," and a picture of Virgin Islanders marching with musical instruments.

Three printed programs in Hughes' collection further implicate this interest: (1) A program for the West Indies Festival of the Arts, which took place in Trinidad in April of 1958. Inside are notes on a musical drama, *Drums and Colours*, its author Derek Walcott, and two pertinent essays, "Music in the West Indies" by Rev. T. Corcoran, and "Sounds of Our Time—The Steel Band" by Pat Castagne. (2) A program for the performance of *Drums and Colours*, which took place during April and May of 1958 at Royal Botanical Gardens, Port-of-Spain, Trinidad. Included is a synopsis of the musical. (3) Record-jacket notes for an album titled *Jamaica Cult Music* (Ethnic Folkway Library, No. P461).

There are also programs for the performance of an opera and three music dramas based on texts by Hughes: (1) *Port Town*, a one act opera (music by Jan Meyerowitz) performed on August 4, 1960 by the Boston Symphony Orchestra in Lenox, Massachusetts. (2) *Simply Heavenly* (music by David Martin), a folk comedy presented on May 5, 1959 by the Karamu Theatre, in Cleveland, Ohio. (3) *Black Nativity*, a gospel song-play performed December 23–30, 1962 at Philharmonic Hall in the Lincoln Center. (4) *The Gospel Glow*, a Christmas gospel song-play presented in October of 1962 by the Eastern Christian Leadership Conference at Washington Temple Church of God in Christ, in Brooklyn, New York. In the program notes, Hughes wrote: "The Gospel Glow—The first Negro passion play, depicting the Life of Christ from cradle to cross, is projected in terms of the Negro spirituals."

Two additional printed programs document performances based on Hughes materials: (1) *Voice of His People*, a musical narrative by George Bass based on the life of Hughes, produced on March 26, 1961 by the Jamaica Branch of the NAACP, in St. Albans, New York. (2) "Delores Martin Singing Songs by Langston Hughes at Brooklyn Museum," a birthday celebration for the poet/lyricist sponsored by the National Association of Negro Musicians on February 19, 1964.

Among miscellaneous items is a postcard titled "Dudley Smith's Steel Orchestra," the curriculum vitae of Hughes, and a bibliography of his poetry, plays, lyrics, and librettos. One of the principal pieces listed in the bibliography is William Grant Still's opera *Troubled Island* (1941), for which Hughes wrote the libretto. H. T. Burleigh (1866–1949), Howard Swanson (1909–1978), and Margaret Bonds (1913–1972) are also among the many composers who have set his poetry.

Music Department Bulletin Collection, 1968–1972

The *Music Department Bulletin* was founded in 1968 by its editor, Orrin Clayton Suthern II (b. 1912), organist and choir director who served Lincoln University for over three decades (1950–1983). This departmental journal was a letter-size typescript which included original articles and reprints on the subject of Black music. Sometimes titled *Music Department News*, it also informed music students and faculty of upcoming concerts and pertinent television programs, and gave critical reviews of musical events on the campus. Examples are "The Gospel According to Jazz" by Phil Wilson (November 9, 1968 issue), "[Lionel] Hampton Asks New Jazz" by Otto Dekom (January 18–25, 1969 issue), and "Blues for the Negro College" by Thomas C. Dent, (July 8, 1969 issue).

Photograph Collection

In the picture file are photographs of Marian Anderson, Louis Armstrong, Mercer Cook, Danse de Negres, Billy Eckstine, Duke Ellington (with Billy Strayhorne and Louis Armstrong), Ella Fitzgerald, Dizzy Gillespie, Earl Hines and His Orchestra, Lena Horne, Mahalia Jackson, Eartha Kitt, Dorothy Maynor, Leontyne Price, Fats Waller, and the Charles Wilson Trio.

An additional source of pictures are the college yearbooks also housed in the Special Collections division. Together these provide a photographic history of musical activities on the Lincoln campus. In the 1923 issue, for instance, a picture of the 12-piece university orchestra displays a makeshift mixture of clarinet, saxophone, trumpet, violin, and several banjos. The 1939 issue portrays "Bonner's

Swinging Collegians," a six-piece jazz group consisting of flute, trumpet, alto and tenor saxophones, drums, and vocalist. In addition to these is a detached solitary glossy print of the school orchestra in 1904.

Recitals File

The printed programs gathered here are of concerts and faculty recitals. A few examples are: (1) The Pearl Williams Jones Trio on February 12, 1981, rendering classical pieces, gospel, and spirituals. Included are program notes on pianist and singer Pearl Jones (b. 1931), who received her musical training at Howard University (1953,1957). (2) A recital given by baritone Malcolm Poindexter on February 5, 1939, which also includes selections of Black spirituals. (3) A faculty recital given by baritone (composer and choir director) James E. Dorsey (b. 1905) on March 11, 1937. And (4) a faculty recital given by organist Orrin Suthern II on April 6, 1975.

CHAPTER 7
NORTH CAROLINA CENTRAL UNIVERSITY

The Black Music Archive at North Carolina Central University was founded in 1984 by Jon Michael Spencer with a grant from the Mary Duke Biddle Foundation. Located in the school's Fine Arts Library, its aim has been to assemble the published and unpublished music of Black composers for the academic and scholastic use of faculty, students, and visiting researchers.

The archive now holds approximately 500 pieces representing all forms of Black music by composers both historic and contemporary. Also included are hymnals of the historically Black denominational churches and other religious songbooks containing spirituals, gospels, and hymns by Black writers.

A prized possession of the music archive is the acquisition of manuscript compositions by Paul H. Jeffries (b. 1933), the jazz saxophonist, composer, recording artist, and Duke University professor since 1983 who has performed with such notables as Thelonious Monk, Charles Mingus, Clark Terry, Lionel Hampton, and Count Basie. Following the Jeffries collectanea in volume are the complete choral works (33 pieces) of Roland M. Carter (b. 1942), a music professor at Hampton University since 1965, the complete works (23 pieces) of Jon Michael Spencer (b. 1957), the present Black music curator who served on North Carolina Central University's music faculty from 1982–1986, seventeen works by Adolphus Hailstork III (b. 1941), a music professor at Norfolk State University since 1976, and fifteen works by John E. Price (b. 1935), a music professor at Tuskegee Institute since 1982.[1]

Also found here are the choral arrangements of three North Carolina Central University music educators: Ruth Gillum (from 1944–1971), Barbara Cooke (since 1964), a 1941 product of Fisk University where she studied under John Wesley Work III, and Charles H. Gilchrist (since 1968), a 1961 graduate of the school he now serves as music department chairman.

The Black Music Archive

Allen, Richard, comp. *A Collection of Hymns and Spiritual Songs*. Philadelphia: T. L. Plowman, 1801. (Photocopy).

AME [African Methodist Episcopal] Hymnal. Philadelphia: AME Book Concern, 1946.

---

[1] See the compositions of Roland M. Carter and Jon Michael Spencer in their respective collections in the archives at Hampton University (Chapter 3), and the works of Adolphus Hailstork in the Moorland Collection at Howard University (Chapter 4).

The AMEC [African Methodist Episcopal Church] Hymn and Tune Book. Philadelphia: AME Book Concern, 1946 [1897 hymnal].

AMEC Hymnal. Nashville: AMEC Publishing House, 1954.

American Folk Songs as Sung by Williams' Jubilee Singers. Chicago: Press of Rosenow, n.d.

Anderson, Thomas Jefferson. "Five Portraits of Two People." MS. Piano-Four Hands.

Banks, Estelle V. McKinley. "Shepherd, Where Are My Sheep?" Hymn.

Berger, Jean. "Hope for Tomorrow" (Text by Martin Luther King, Jr.). Anthem. SATB with Tenor Solo and Piano.

The Bicentennial Musical Celebration (A Gift from J. C. Penny). Music for chorus.

Black, Johnny S. "The Dardanella Blues." Voice and Piano.

Boatner, Edward, arr. "Oh, What a Beautiful City!" Spiritual. Voice and Piano.

Brewster, (Rev.) W. Herbert. "Surely God is Able" (Arr. by Virginia Davis). Gospel.

Bright, Houston. "I Hear a Voice A-Prayin'."

Brown, Uzee, Jr., arr. "I'm Buildin' Me a Home." Xerox MS. TTBB with Baritone Solo.

Bryan, Charles F., arr. "Amazing Grace." SATB with Alto Solo.

Burleigh, H. T., arr. *Album of Negro Spirituals*. Rockville Centre, New York: Belwin, 1969.

———, arr. "Behold that Star." Spiritual. SSA and Organ.

———. "Dear Old N.C.C." (North Carolina Central University Alma Mater). Voice and Keyboard.

———, arr. "Go Tell It On the Mountain!" Spiritual. SATB and Organ.

———, arr. "I Stood on de Ribber ob Jerdon." (Arr. by R. Vené). Spiritual. SATB and Piano.

———, arr. "My Lord, What a Mornin'." Spiritual. SATB.

———. "The Young Warrior" (Text by James Weldon Johnson). Voice and Piano.

Burton, Christina. "Oh Lord" (Arr. by Jeanette Tall). Gospel.

Cable, George W. *The Dance in Place Congo & Creole Slave Songs*. Np: Faruk von Turk, 1974.

Cain, Noble, arr. "Ain't Gonna Study War No More." Spiritual. SATB.

———, arr. "By and By." Spiritual. SATB.

———, arr. "Gonna Ride Up in de Chariot." Spiritual. SATB.

———, arr. "De Gospel Train." Spiritual. SATB.

———, arr. "It's Me, O Lord." Spiritual. SATB.

———, arr. "Joshua Fit de Battle ob Jericho." Spiritual. SATB.

———, arr. "Ole Ark's a-Moverin'." Spiritual. SATB.

Campbell, Lucie E. "Jesus Gave Me Water." Gospel.

Carter, Nathan, arr. "Precious Lord" (By Thomas Dorsey). Gospel Hymn. SATB.

Carter, Roland M. "Behold the Days Come." Xerox MS. Cantata. SATB and Piano.

———, arr. "Choral Responses Based On Old Hymn Tunes and Afro-American Spirituals." Xerox MS. SATB.

———, arr. "Come Here Jesus If You Please" (Prayer Response). Xerox MS. SATB.

———, arr. "Done Made My Vow to the Lord." Xerox MS. Spiritual. SATB with Soprano Solo.

———, arr. "Five Choral Responses Based On Afro-American Spirituals." SATB.

———, arr. "Go Tell It On the Mountain." Xerox MS. Spiritual. SATB with Tenor or Soprano Solo.

———. "A Hampton Portrait." Xerox MS. Anthem. SATB.

———, arr. "His Truth is Marching On." Xerox MS. SATB.

———, arr. "I Heard the Preaching of de Elders." Xerox MS. Spiritual. SATB.

———, arr. "I Remember Laura: Colorado Trail." Xerox MS. SATB with Soprano Solo.

———, arr. "I Want to Die Easy." Spiritual. SATB with Soprano Solo.

———, arr. "If You Love God Serve Him." Xerox MS. SATB with Soprano Solo.

———, arr. "I'm Troubled" (Prayer Response). Xerox MS. SATB.

———, arr. "In Bright Mansions Above." Spiritual. SATB and Keyboard.

———, arr. "Lift Every Voice and Sing" (By James Weldon Johnson and J. Rosamond Johnson). Anthem. SATB and Keyboard.

———, arr. "Lord, I Don't Feel No Ways Tired." Xerox MS. Spiritual. SATB.

———, arr. "A Mighty Fortress" (By Martin Luther). Xerox MS. SATB.

———. "No Room in the Inn" (From "Behold the Days Come").Xerox MS. SATB.

———. "[Oh Hampton On the Waters]." Xerox MS. Anthem. SATB with Tenor Solo.

———, arr. "Plenty Good Room." Xerox MS. Spiritual. TTBB.

———, arr. "Precious Lord" (By Thomas Dorsey). Gospel Hymn. SATB with Mezzo-Soprano or Baritone Solo.

———. "The Prophecy" (From "Behold the Days Come"). Xerox MS. SATB.

———, arr. "Ride On, Jesus." Spiritual. SATB.

———, arr. "Rise, Shine, For the Light Is a-Comin'." Xerox MS. Spiritual. SATB.

———, arr. "Same Train." Xerox MS. Spiritual. SATB with II Alto or I Tenor Solo.

———, arr. "Steal Away." Spiritual. SATB with Mezzo-Soprano or Baritone Solo.

———, arr. "Sweet Lil' Jesus Boy." Xerox MS. Spiritual. SATB with Soprano Solo.

———, arr. "Sweetest Sound I Ever Heard." Xerox MS. Solo Voice and Piano.

————, arr. "'Tis the Ol' Ship of Zion." Xerox MS. Spiritual. SATB.

————, arr. "Wayfaring Stranger." Xerox MS. TTBB with Bass Solo.

————. "Where Will He Be Born." Xerox MS. SATB.

————. "Wondrous Night" (From "Behold the Days Come"). Xerox MS. SATB.

————, arr. "You Must Have That True Religion." Xerox MS (And Published Copy). Spiritual. SATB.

Clark, Edgar Rogie, arr. "Six Afro-American Carols for Easter." Spirituals. SATB.

Clarke, Grant, et al. "Anything Nice If It Comes from Dixieland." Voice and Piano.

Clary, Salone, arr. "I Want to Live with God." Xerox Copy. Spiritual. SATB.

Coleridge-Taylor, Samuel. "Hiawatha's Wedding Feast." Cantata. Orchestral Score.

Cook, Will Marion. "Bon Bon Buddy." Voice and Piano.

Cooke, Barbara, arr. "Dere's No Hiding Place Down Here." Xerox MS. Spiritual. Solo Voice and Piano.

————, arr. "I Want Jesus to Walk with Me." Xerox MS. Spiritual. Flute and Piano.

————, arr. "I've Been 'Buked." Xerox MS. Spiritual. Violin and Piano.

————, arr. "My God Is So High." Xerox MS. Spiritual. Voice and Piano.

————, arr. "This Little Light of Mine." Xerox MS. Spiritual. Voice and Piano.

————, arr. "Wade in Water." Xerox MS. Spiritual. Solo Voice and Piano.

Cooke, Charles L., arr. "Go Tell It On the Mountain." Spiritual. SATB with Soprano Solo and Piano.

Crouch, Andrae. "I Don't Know Why (Jesus Loved Me)." Xerox Copy. Gospel. Voice and Piano.

————. "I'm Gonna Keep on Singin'." Gospel. SATB with Solo Voice and Piano.

————. "My Tribute." Gospel. SATB with Solo Voice and Piano.

Cunningham, Arthur. "Harlem Is My Home" (From "Harlem Suite"). SATB with Soprano Solo and Piano.

————. "Two Prayers." SATB.

Curtis, Marvin. "Praising Song." SATB.

Davenport, John and Eddie Cooley. "Fever." Voice and Piano.

Davis, Frank M. "Savoir, Lead Me, Lest I Stray." Gospel Hymn.

Dawson, William L., arr. "Ain'-a That Good News." Spiritual. SATB.

————. "Before the Sun Goes Down." SATB with SATB Solos.

————. "Behold the Star." SATB with Soprano and Tenor Solos.

————, arr. "Ev'ry Time I Feel the Spirit." Spiritual. SATB with Baritone Soli.

————, arr. "Ezekiel Saw de Wheel." Spiritual. SATB with Tenor Solo.

————. "Hail Mary!" SATB with Alto Solo.

————. "I Wan' to Be Ready." Spiritual. SATB with Alto and Baritone Solos and Piano.

————. "In His Care-O." SATB.

————, arr. "Jesus Walked this Lonesome Valley." Spiritual. SATB with Soprano Solo and Piano; and TTBB with Baritone Solo and Piano.

————, arr. "King Jesus Is a-Listening." Spiritual. SATB with Piano.

————. "L'il' Boy-Chile." SATB with Soprano and Baritone Solos.

————. "Out in the Fields." Xerox Copy. SATB.

————, arr. "Pilgrim's Chorus" (From Tannhauser by Richard Wagner). SATB with Soprano Solo.

————, arr. "Soon Ah Will Be Done." Spiritual. SATB.

————, arr. "Swing Low, Sweet Chariot." Spiritual. SATB with Solo Voice.

————. "Talk About a Child That Do Love Jesus." SATB with Soprano Solo and Piano.

————, arr. "There is a Balm in Gilead." Spiritual. SATB with Soprano Solo.

————, arr. "You Got to Reap Just What You Sow." Spiritual. SATB with Piano; and TTBB.

————. "Zion's Walls." SATB with Soprano Soli.

Dean, Emmett S., et al., eds. *New Victory Song Book for Christian Work and Worship.* Nashville: National Baptist Publishing Board, 1918.

Deas, E. C. "Thy Way, O Lord." Gospel.

De Cormier, Robert, arr. "Let Me Fly." Spiritual. SATB with Baritone Solo.

————, arr. "Obey the Spirit of the Lord." Spiritual. SATB with Solo Voice and Piano.

————. arr. "The Virgin Mary Had a Baby Boy." West Indian Spiritual. SATB with Bell or Finger Cymbals.

———— and Donald McKayle. "They Called Her Moses." Cantata. SATB, Soloists, Narrator, with Piano.

Dedrick, Chris, arr. "Kum Ba Yah." Spiritual. SATB with Piano.

De Paur, Leonard, arr. "Ye Ke Omo Mi" (Nigerian Lullabye). Xerox Copy. SATB with Soprano Solo.

Dett, R. Nathaniel. "Ave Maria." Anthem. SATB with Baritone Solo.

————. *The Dett Collection of Negro Spirituals*, Fourth Group. Minneapolis: Schmitt, Hall & McCreary, 1936.

————. "Don't Be Weary Traveler." Motet. SATB with Soprano, Tenor, and Baritone Solos.

————. "Gently, Lord, O Gently Lead Us." Anthem. SATB with Soprano Solo.

————. "I'll Never Turn Back No More." Anthem. SATB with Solo Voice.

————. "Listen to the Lambs." Anthem. SATB with Soprano Solo.

————. "O Holy Lord." Anthem. SATB.

[Dorrard?], R. "Blue Bossa." Xerox MS. Piano and Voice.

Dorsey, James E., arr. "Tone de Bells." Spiritual. SATB with Soprano Solo.

Dorsey, Thomas A., arr. "All Alone" (By G. T. Byrd). Gospel Hymn.

————. "Count Your Blessings from the Lord Each Day." Gospel Hymn.

————. "He is Risen for He's Living in My Soul." Gospel Hymn.

————, arr. "I Am On the Battle-Field for My Lord" (By Sylvava Bell and E. V. Banks). Gospel Hymn.

————. "I Just Can't Keep from Crying Some Time." Gospel Hymn.

————. "I Know Jesus." Gospel Hymn.

————. "It is Thy Servant's Prayer A-men." Gospel Hymn.

————. "My Desire." Gospel Hymn.

————. "Take My Hand, Precious Lord." Gospel Hymn.

————. "Watching and Waiting." Gospel Hymn.

Duncan, John. "Burial of Moses." MS. Cantata. SATB, Contralto and Baritone Solos, and Wind Symphony.

————. "An Easter Canticle." MS. SATB, Soloists, and 15 Wind Instruments.

Ellington, Duke. "Do Nothin' Till You Hear from Me." Voice and Piano.

————. *Duke Ellington's Song Folio*. New York: Mills Music, n.d.

————. Portrait of Duke Ellington. Arr. by John Cacavas for SATB and Piano. Melville, New York: Belwin Mills, 1974.

Exner, Max. "I Have a Dream" (Text by Martin Luther King, Jr.). Anthem. SATB.

Fax, Mark. "Whatsoever a Man Soweth." Xerox Copy. Anthem based on Galatians 6:7–9. SATB and Organ.

Fisher, Fred. "Savannah" (The Georgianna Blues). Voice and Piano.

Follet, Charles, arr. "Ain't it a Shame?" Spiritual. SATB with Piano.

Foster, Stephen. *A Treasury of Stephen Foster*. Ed. Deems Taylor, et al. New York: Random House, 1946.

Fryson, Robert J. "God Is." Gospel. SAT with Vocal Solo and Piano.

Furman, James. "Hehlehlooyuh." SATB with Soprano Solo.

Geld, Gary. "Walk Him Up the Stairs" (From "Purlie"). Arr. by "Bugs" Bower for SATB with Vocal Solos.

Gershwin, George. "Summertime." Solo Voice and Piano.

Gilchrist, Charles H., arr. "[Amazing Grace]." MS. SATB with Solo Voice and Piano.

————, arr. "American Medley." Xerox MS. SATB and Piano.

————, arr. "Give Me a Clean Heart." Xerox MS. SATB.

————. "God Bless the Fallout." Solo Voice and Piano.

————, arr. "He'll Understand and Say 'Well Done'." Xerox MS. SATB with Solo Voice and Piano.

————, arr. "In Memoriam to Dr. Martin Luther King, Jr."Xerox MS. SATB with Solo Voice and Piano.

————. "Psalm 127" (In Memory of My Father). Xerox MS. SATB with Solo Voice and Piano.

————, arr. "Rock-a-Mah Soul." Spiritual. SATB and Piano.

————, arr. "Show Me Thy Way." Spiritual. SATB with Solo Voice and Piano.

————, arr. "What a Friend We Have in Jesus." Xerox MS. SATB with Solo Voice and Piano.

Gillum, Ruth H., arr. "Choric Dance." SATB.

———, arr. "Roll Jordan Roll." Spiritual. SATB with Mezzo-Soprano Solo.

———, arr. "There's No Hiding Place." Spiritual. SATB with Piano.

Golden Gems: A Song Book for Spiritual and Religious Worship. Nashville: National Baptist Publishing Board, n.d.

Griffith, John E. and Ernest Kelley. "Detroit Renaissance." Piano.

Hailstork, Adolphus C. "Arise My Beloved." SATB.

———. "Bellevue" (Prelude for Orchestra).

———. "A Carol for All Children." SATB.

———. "Celebration!" Orchestra.

———. "The Clothes of Heaven" (Text by W. B. Yeats). Anthem. SATB.

———. "Crucifixion." Anthem. SATB.

———. "Easter Music." Cello and Piano.

———. "Ignis Fatuus." Piano.

———. "In Memorium: Langston Hughes" (Text by Edwin Markham). SATB.

———. "Let a New Earth Arise" (Texts by Margaret Walker, Mari Evans, Kahlil Gibran, Adolphus Hailstork). Anthem. SATB with Soprano Solo— Orchestral Reduction.

———. "Look to This Day." SATB and Orchestra; and Orchestral Reduction for Organ.

———. "Mourn Not the Dead" (Text by Ralph Chaplin). SATB.

———. "Piano Fantasy."

———. "Piano Rhapsody."

———. "The Pied Piper of Harlem." Solo Flute.

———. "Set Me as a Seal Upon Thine Heart." Anthem based on "The Song of Songs." SATB.

———. "Seven Songs of the Rubaiyat" (Text by Omar Khayyam). SATB with Baritone Solo.

———. "Sing of Your Life." SATB.

Hairston, Jester, arr. "Crucifixion." Spiritual. SATB.

———, arr. "Elijah Rock." Spiritual. SATB with Soprano Solo.

———, arr. "Give Me Jesus." Spiritual. SATB with Soprano Solo.

———, arr. "God's Gonna Buil' Up Zion's Wall." Spiritual. SATB and Piano.

———. "Great God A'mighty." SATB with Bass Solo.

———, arr. "In dat Great Gittin' Up Mornin'." Xerox Copy. Spiritual. SATB with Tenor Solo.

Handy, William Christopher. "Beale Street Blues." Voice and Piano.

———. "St. Louis Blues." Voice and Piano.

Hawkins, Edwin. *The Edwin Hawkins Choral Collection.* Arr. by Frank Metis. Westbury, New York: Kamma Rippa Music and Edwin Hawkins Music Companies, 1970.

———, arr. "Oh Happy Day." Gospel. Voice and Piano.

Hawkins, Walter. "Lord Give Us Time." Gospel. SATB with Piano and Guitar.

Hayes, Isaac and Betty Krutcher. "John Shaft." Arr. by Richard Averre for SATB with Rhythm Section.

Hayes, Mark, arr. "Go Down Moses." Spiritual. SATB with Piano.

Hicks, Charles E., and Jimmie James, Jr. "Praising God with Instruments" (A Complete Church Service Using Wind and Percussion Instruments).

Hill, J. H., arr. "It May Be the Best for Me" (By L. Edison). Gospel.

Howard, John Tasker. "O Did You Hear the Meadow Lark?" Voice and Piano.

————. "The Primrose." Voice and Piano.

Howorth, Wayne, arr. "There is a Balm in Gilead." Spiritual. SATB with Solo Voice.

"I Couldn't Hear Nobody Pray." Spiritual. Voice and Piano.

Isaac, E. W. D., et al. *Inspirational Melodies: A Choice Collection of Gospel Songs*. Nashville: National Baptist Training Union Board, National Baptist Convention, U.S.A., Inc., n.d.

Jackson, Myrtle. "But This I Pray, Oh Lord Remember Me." Gospel.

James, Willis Laurence. "Dark Water." SATB.

————. "Negro Bell Carol." SATB with Soprano or Tenor Solo.

————, arr. "Roun' de Glory Manger." Spiritual. SATB with Soprano Solo.

Jeffries, Paul H. "Acirema." MS. Jazz Combo—Piano Reduction.

————. "Acousia." MS. Jazz Combo.

————. "African Sunrise." Xerox MS. Jazz Ensemble.

————. "Bianca." MS. Jazz Combo—Piano Reduction.

————. "Big Bad Jam." MS. Jazz Combo.

————. "Brand X." MS. Jazz Combo.

————. "Cycles." MS. Jazz Combo.

————. "Druid." MS. Jazz Combo.

————, arr. "Eighty One" (By Ron Carter). MS. Jazz Ensemble.

————. "Four Nigerian Dances." MS. Jazz Combo.

————. "Grant." MS. Jazz Combo.

————, arr. "Hallucinations" (By Bud Powell). MS. Jazz Combo.

————. "Hiatus." MS. Jazz Combo.

————. "Jacoba's Song." MS. Jazz Combo—Piano Reduction.

————. "Kim." MS. Jazz Combo—Piano Reduction.

————. "Moon Madness." MS. Jazz Combo.

————. "Nicole and Nile." MS. Jazz Ensemble.

————, arr. "Oh Yeah" (By Sadik Hakim). MS. Jazz Ensemble.

————, arr. "Reincarnation of a Love Bird" (By Charles Mingus). MS. Jazz Combo.

————, arr. "Skippy" (By Thelonious Monk). MS. Jazz Combo.

————, arr. "So Sorry Please" (By Bud Powell). MS. Jazz Combo.

————, arr. "Stockholm Shortening" (By Quincy Jones). MS. Jazz Combo.

————. "Suite Newport." MS. Jazz Combo.

————. "Voices of Jazz." Xerox MS. Cantata. Boys Chorus with Solo Voices and Jazz Ensemble—Piano Reduction and Vocal Parts.

————. "Waltz Little." MS. Jazz Combo.

Jessye, Eva A., arr. "I Been 'Buked an' I Been Scorned." Spiritual. Voice and Piano.

Johnson, Hall. "Ain't Got Time to Die." SATB with Tenor Solo.

————, arr. "Cert'n'y Lord." Spiritual. SATB with Tenor and Bass Solos.

————, arr. "City Called Heaven." Spiritual. SATB.

————. "Doxology" Xerox MS (Transcribed by Roland Carter). SATB.

————, arr. "Elijah, Rock!" Spiritual. SATB.

————, arr. "His Name So Sweet." Spiritual. SATB.

————, arr. "Honor! Honor!" Spiritual. SATB with Tenor Solo.

————, arr. "I Cannot Stay Here By Myself." Xerox Copy. Spiritual. SATB with Alto Solo.

————, arr. "I've Been 'Buked." Spiritual. SATB.

————, arr. "Jesus, Lay Your Head in de Winder." Spiritual. SATB with Tenor Solo.

————, arr. "Oh, Freedom!" Spiritual. SATB.

————, arr. "Oh Lord, Have Mercy On Me." Spiritual. SATB with Soprano Solo.

————, arr. "Ride On, Jesus!" Spiritual. SATB with Soprano Solo.

————, arr. "Scandalize My Name." Spiritual. SATB with Tenor Solo.

————. "Take My Mother Home." Anthem based on St. John 19:26–27. SATB with Baritone Solo.

————, arr. *Thirty Negro Spirituals*. New York: G. Schirmer, 1949.

————, arr. "Trampin'." Spiritual. SATB with Contralto Solo.

Johnson, James Weldon. *God's Trombones*. Arr. by Roy Ringwald. Delaware Water Gap, Pennsylvania: Shawnee Press, 1955.

———— and J. Rosamond Johnson. "Lift Ev'ry Voice and Sing."Xerox Copy. SATB.

Jones, Charles P. "I'm Happy with Jesus Alone." Gospel Hymn.

Jones, Isaiah. "Aren't You Glad." Gospel. SATB with Tenor Solo and Piano.

Jones, Quincy, et al. "Selections from Quincy Jones' Roots." Arr. by Dick Averre for SATB with Piano and Percussion.

Judson, Alfred. "He Rose." Anthem. SATB with Piano.

Kay, Ulysses. "A Wreath for Waits." SATB.

Kerr, Thomas N., Jr. "Prayer for the Soul of Martin Luther King, Jr." Xerox MS. SATB.

Klickmann, F. Henri. "I've Got the Sweet Hawaiian Moonlight Blues." Voice and Piano.

Kubik, Gail. "Soon One Mornin' Death Comes Creepin'" (American Folk Song Sketch). SATB with Baritone Solo.

Leoni, Franco. "The Birth of Morn (Dawn)" (Text by Paul Laurence Dunbar). Voice and Piano.

Luboff, Norman. "African Mass." SATB, Solo Voices, and Tuned Drums.

————, arr. "Roll Jordan, Roll." Spiritual. SATB with Rhythm Section.

————, arr. "Steal Away." Spiritual. SATB with Rhythm Section.

McIntyre, Phillip, arr. "Hear the Lambs a-Crying." Spiritual. SATB with Soprano Solo.

————, arr. "O Lord, Let Me Ride." Spiritual. SATB.

McKinney, (Rev.) G. P. "Emancipation Hymn" (Music by Josephine Straughn). Xerox MS. SATB.

McLin, Lena J. "All the Earth Sing Unto the Lord." Anthem based on Psalm 96. SATB.

————, arr. "Amazing Grace" (By John Newton). SATB with Solo Voice and Piano.

————, arr. "Cert'nly Lord, Cert'nly Lord." Spiritual. SATB with Soprano or Tenor Solo.

————. "Free At Last!: A Portrait of Martin Luther King, Jr." SATB with Soprano, and Baritone or Mezzo-Soprano Solos, and Piano.

————, arr. "Give Me that Old Time Religion." Xerox Copy. Spiritual. SATB.

————, arr. "Glory, Glory, Hallelujah." Spiritual. SATB with Solo and Piano.

————. "If They Ask You Why He Came." SATB.

————. "Let the People Sing Praise Unto the Lord." SATB with Piano or Organ, and Trumpet.

————. "New Born King." SATB.

————. "Winter, Spring, Summer, Autumn." Cantata. SATB.

————, arr. "Writ'en Down My Name." Xerox Copy. Spiritual. SATB with Baritone Solo.

Martin, Roberta, arr. "At the End" (By Alex Bradford). Gospel. SATB.

————, arr. "Down On My Knees" (By H. J. Ford). Gospel. SATB.

————. "God Is Still On the Throne." Gospel. SATB.

————, arr. "He Laid His Hands On Me" (By Dorothy Norwood). Gospel. SATB.

————, arr. "He's Already Done (What He Said He Would Do)" (By Robert Sims). Gospel. SATB.

————, arr. "Since I Met Jesus" (By Alex Bradford). Gospel. SATB.

————, arr. **"Walk On By Faith" (By James Cleveland). Gospel. SATB.**

Martin, Sally and Kenneth Morris, eds. *Martin and Morris Gospelodiums*, No. 8. Chicago: Martin and Morris Music Studio, n.d.

Miller, Mayme White. "I Love the Name Jesus." Gospel.

Montague, J. Harold, arr. "Joshua Fit de Battle ob Jerico." Spiritual. SATB with Baritone or Contralto Solo.

Moore, Donald Lee. "Blues in Three-Quarter Time." Piano.

Moore, Undine Smith, arr. "Daniel, Daniel, Servant of the Lord." Spiritual. SATB.

————. "Lord, We Give Thanks to Thee." Xerox Copy. Anthem based on Leviticus 25:9. SATB.

Morris, Kenneth, arr. "Am I Living in Vain?" (By E. Twinkle Clark). Gospel.

————, arr. "Because I Love Him" (By S. C. Foster). Gospel.

————, arr. "Blessed and Brought Up By the Lord." Spiritual as Gospel. Voice and Piano.

————, arr. "Blessed Quietness" (By M. P. Ferguson.) Gospel.

————, arr. "Come Over Here" (By C. Johnson). Gospel.

————, arr. "Coming Up On the Rough Side of the Mountain" (By Rev. F. C. Barnes). Gospel. Piano and Voice.

————, arr. "Everybody Ought to Praise His Name" (By Curtis Wilson). Gospel.

————, arr. "Everything Will Be Alright." Gospel.

————, arr. "A Follower of Christ" (By J. W. Harris). Gospel. Piano and Voice.

————, arr. "God Cares" (By Evangelist Rosie Wallace). Gospel.

————, arr. "God Is Our Creator" (By John K. McNeil). Gospel.

————, arr. "God So Loved the World" (By J. Stainer). Gospel.

————, arr. "God's Goodness (You Don't Know How Good God is to Me)" (By Dorothy Love). Gospel.

————, arr. "Hallelujah" (By John K. McNeil). Gospel.

————, arr. "Happy in Jesus" (By George Jordan). Gospel.

————, arr. "He Will Take Care of You" (By G. D. Martin and W. S. Martin). Gospel.

————, arr. "The Healer" (By Dorothy Love Coates). Gospel.

————, arr. "Hush! Somebody's Calling My Name." Spiritual as Gospel.

————. "I Can Put My Trust in Jesus." Gospel.

————. "I Feel the Spirit." Gospel.

————, arr. "I Get a Blessing Every Day" (By James Cleveland). Gospel.

————, arr. "I Got to Serve the Lord" (By J. McNeil). Gospel.

————, arr. "I Serve a Living God" (By Richard Jackson). Gospel.

————, arr. "I Wont Be Back No More" (By James Herndon). Gospel.

————, arr. "If Everybody Was Like Jesus" (By Rev. C. Robinson). Gospel.

————, arr. "If I Can Help Somebody" (By A. Bazel Androzzo). Gospel.

————, arr. "If We Never Pass this Way Again" (By James Cleveland). Gospel.

————, arr. "I'll Be Resting in Beulah Land" (By Rev. Oris Mays). Gospel.

————, arr. "I'll Do His Will" (By James Cleveland). Gospel.

————, arr. "I'm Going Through" (By C. A. Tindley). Gospel.

————, arr. "I'm Willing to Run All the Way" (By Rev. I. C. Rector). Gospel.

————, arr. "I've Got to Make It" (By Lonnie Mack). Gospel.

————, arr. "Jesus Be a Fence Around Me" (By Sam Cooke). Gospel.

————, arr. "Jesus Can Work it Out" (By George Jordan). Gospel.

————. "Jesus, I Love You." Gospel.

————, arr. "Jesus In Me" (By C. George and James Herndon). Gospel.

————, arr. "Jesus Knows" (By J. Alexander). Gospel.

————, arr. "Jesus Lover of My Soul" (By Charles Wesley). Hymn as Gospel.

————. "Jesus Prayed for You and I." Gospel.

————, arr. "Lift Him Up" (By Kevin Yancy and Jerome Metcalfe). Gospel.

————, arr. "Meet Over There." Gospel.

————, arr. "Mother Bowed and Prayed for Me." Spiritual as Gospel.

————, arr. "My Soul Says 'Thank You, Lord'" (By B. Mays). Gospel.

————, arr. "Oh, To Be Kept By Jesus" (By Thurston Frazier).Gospel.

————, arr. "One More Time" (By James Cleveland). Gospel.

————, arr. "Over My Head." Spiritual as Gospel.

————. "Power of the Holy Ghost (Send it on Down)." Gospel.

————, arr. "Pressing On" (By the Spiritualaires). Gospel.

————, arr. "Shake My Mother's Hand" (By K. Turner). Gospel.

————, arr. "Somewhere List'ning for My Name." Spiritual as Gospel.

————, arr. "(Spirit of the Living God) Fall Fresh on Me" (By B. B. Mc-Kinney). Gospel.

————, arr. "Thank You for One More Day" (By Hattie Foster). Gospel.

————, arr. "Thank You, Lord, for One More Day." Spiritual as Gospel.

————, arr. "There's Peace in the Midst of the Storm" (By Stephen R. Adams). Gospel.

————, arr. "Trust in Him" (By Rev. Isaac Douglas). Gospel.

————, arr. "Victory Shall Be Mine" (By J. Hanson). Gospel.

————, arr. "Wait I Say On the Lord" (By James Cleveland). Gospel.

————, arr. "Walk Around Heaven All Day" (By Cassietta George). Gospel.

————, arr. "We Shall Be Changed" (By Clara Ward). Gospel.

————, arr. "Who Art Thou?" (By Dorothy Love). Gospel.

————, arr. "You Ought to Tell It" (By Charles Fold). Gospel.

Morris, Robert Leigh, arr. "I'll Never Turn Back No More." Spiritual. SATB with Solo Voice.

Mull, (Rev.) J. Bazzell, ed. *Gospel Quartet Music*, No. 1. Powell, Missouri: Albert E. Brumley and Sons, n.d.

National Baptist Jubilee Melodies.

New Songs of Pentecost. Philadelphia: Hall-Mack Company, 1916.

O'Kelly, C. Grant. "N. C. C. Loyalty." Piano and Voice.

Perkins, N. E. "Steal Away to Jesus." SATB with Piano.

Phillips, T. D. "South Carolina State Alma Mater" (Text by Robert S. Wilkinson). Xerox Copy. Voice and Keyboard.

Pittman, Evelyn LaRue, arr. "Any How." Spiritual. SATB.

Price, Florence, arr. "My Soul's Been Anchored in de Lord." Spiritual. Voice and Piano.

Price, John E. "Aptah Hymn." Xerox MS. Voice and Piano.

————. "Barely Time to Study Jesus." Xerox MS. Percussion.

————. "For Brass Quartet." Xerox MS.

————. "Identity." Xerox MS. Voice and Piano.

————. "Impulse for Cello." Xerox MS. Unaccompanied Cello.

————. "Invention for Piano." Xerox MS.

————. "Meditation and Change of Thought." Xerox MS. Brass Quartet.

————. "Psalm 117." Xerox MS. SATB.

————. "Quartet." Xerox MS. Violin, Viola, F Horn, Bassoon.

————. "Scherzo '1' for Clarinet and Orchestra." Xerox MS.

————. "Set I: A Hymn to God the Father." Xerox MS. Voice and Piano.

————. "Sonatine-1st." Xerox MS. Piano.

————. "Song on a Poem by Blake." Xerox MS. Voice and Piano.

————. "[Thirty-Three] 33 Hymns" (Nos. 1 & 33). Xerox MS.

————. "Two Typed Lines." Xerox MS. Voice and Piano.

Ray, Robert. "Gospel Mass." SATB with Vocal Solos and Rhythm Section.

Reece, Cortez D., arr. "Mary Had a Baby." Spiritual. SATB with Soprano Solo.

Roberts, Howard A., arr. "I Want Jesus to Walk with Me." Spiritual. SATB with Optional Percussion.

————, arr. "Let My People Go." Spiritual. SATB with Optional Percussion.

————, arr. "Motherless Child." Spiritual. SATB with Optional Percussion.

————, arr. "Sinner Man." Spiritual. SATB with Soprano and Tenor Solos, and Optional Percussion.

————, arr. "Soon I Will Be Done." Spiritual. SATB with Solo Voice.

————, arr. "Steal Away." Spiritual. SATB with Optional Percussion.

————, arr. "Talk About a Child." Spiritual. SATB.

————, arr. "Tumbando Cana." Cuban Folk Song. SATB with Drums.

Rosborough, William, et al. *National Anthem Series*. Nashville: National Baptist Publishing Board, 1906.

————. "Princes Awake" (Text by E. W. D. Isaac). Anthem. SATB with Soprano or Tenor Solo, and Baritone Solo, with Piano.

Rosenthal, Harry. "Georgia Rose." Voice and Piano.

Ryder, Noah Francis, arr. "He Aint Coming Here to Die No More." Spiritual. SATB with Contralto Solo.

Sawyer, Pamela and Marilyn McLeod. "Love Hangover." Voice and Piano.

Shackley, Frederick N. "A Message of Easter." Anthem. SATB with Soprano or Tenor Solo and Organ.

Shaw, Robert, arr. "All Creatures of Our God and King." SATB with Organ.

————, arr. "If I Got My Ticket, Can I Ride?" Spiritual. SATB with Tenor Solo.

———— and Alice Parker, arr. "John Saw duh Numbuh." Spiritual. SATB.

———— and Alice Parker, arr. "My God is a Rock." Spiritual. SATB with Baritone Solo.

———— and Alice Parker, arr. "Sometimes I Feel." Spiritual. SATB with Contralto Solo.

Shearing, George. "Lullaby of Birdland." Voice and Piano.

Siegmeister, Elie, arr. "American Street Cries." SATB.

Sleeth, Natalie. "Jazz Gloria." Xerox MS. SATB with Trumpets, Bass, and Bongos.

Smalls, Charlie. "Ease On Down the Road" (From "The Wiz"). Arr. by Stan Beard. Xerox Copy. SATB with Piano.

Smith, Nathaniel Clark. "The Tuskegee Song" (Tuskegee Institute Alma Mater, Text by Paul Laurence Dunbar). Voice and Keyboard.

Smith, Raymond Allyn, arr. "Ride On, King Jesus." Spiritual. SATB with Soprano, Alto, Baritone, and Bass Solos.

Smith, William Henry, arr. "Ride the Chariot." Spiritual. SATB with Soprano Solo.

Sowande, Fela, arr. "Wheel, Oh Wheel." Xerox Copy. Spiritual. SATB.

Spencer, Jon Michael. "Cantata: Six Jazz Poems." Text by the Composer. Xerox MSS. SATB with Tenor and Baritone Solos, Piano and Bass; Also Arr. for Jazz Combo.

———. "Classical Blues." MS. Jazz Combo.

———. "Classical Blues Part II." MS. Jazz Combo.

———. "Concerto for Alto Saxophone and Orchestra." Xerox MS.

———. "Confide in Sleep Eternal: A Dramatic Poem for Soprano and Piano." Text by the Composer. Xerox MS.

———. "Flowered Candies" (Contrapuntal Instrumental Pieces, and Pieces for Two Guitars). Xerox MS.

———. "The Hampton Institute Sonata." MS. Alto Saxophone and Piano.

———. "Halloween." MS. Violin Duet.

———. "I Am Lonely." Text by the Composer. MS. Soprano and Tenor with Two Guitars.

———. "Jazz is the Fountain of Youth." MSS. Jazz Ensemble Score and Instrumental Parts.

———. "Jubilis" (Opera in One Act). Libretto by the Composer. Xerox MS.

———. "Nightbird Song." MS. Two Flutes and Piano.

———. "River Sticks" (A Musical Drama). Text by the Composer. Xerox MS.

———. "Rondo." MS. Two Pianos, Two Flutes, and Viola.

———. "Sonata for Alto Saxophone and Piano." Xerox MS.

———. "String Quartet." MS.

———. "Suite for Two Guitars." Xerox MS.

———. "This Land Shall Overcome" (Hymn for World Peace). Text by the Composer. MS.

———. "To Everything There is a Season and a Time." Xerox MS. Anthem based on Ecclesiasties 3:1–8. SATB with Tenor Solo, Piano, and Organ.

———. "Two Poems with Incidental Music." Xerox MS.

———. "Variations for Saxophone Quartet." MS.

———. "Wedding Cantata." Three Duets for Soprano and Tenor with Piano Accompaniment. Xerox MS.

Stanton, Royal, arr. "Ev'ry Time." Spiritual. SATB.

Stevens, Vernon T., et al. "Plantation Lullaby." Voice and Piano.

Still, William Grant. "All That I Am." Xerox MSS. SATB with Tenor and Soprano Solos, and Organ; and Arranged for Orchestra by Ray Anthony Delia).

————. "And They Lynched Him on a Tree." Xerox MSS. Double Mixed Chorus, Contralto Solo, Narrator, and Orchestra; and Piano-Vocal Score.

————. "A Bayou Legend" (Opera in Three Acts). Xerox MSS. Orchestral Score; and Piano-Vocal Score.

————. "Blues" (From "Lenox Avenue"). Xerox MSS. Piano Reduction; and Piano-Conductor Score.

————. "Ennanga." Xerox MSS. Harp and String Orchestra; and Harp-Piano Reduction.

————. "Here's One." Xerox MSS. Violin; Also arr. for Violin and Piano by Louis Kaufman.

————. "Kaintuck" (Poem for Piano and Orchestra). Xerox MSS. Also Two-Piano Version.

————, arr. "Lift Every Voice and Sing." Xerox MSS. Piano-Conductor Score; and Parts for String Quintet and Flute.

————. "Quit dat Fool'nish." For Saxophone and Orchestra. Xerox MSS. Piano-Conductor Score; and Orchestra Parts.

————. "Romance." For Saxophone and Orchestra. Xerox MSS. Piano-Conductor Score; Orchestral Parts; Piano-Saxophone Version.

————. "Suite for Violin and Piano." Xerox MSS. Orchestral Score; and Piano-Violin Reduction.

————. "Summerland" (Arr. for Organ by Edouard Nies-Berger).

————. "Three Visions." Xerox MS. Piano.

Sweatman, Wilber C. "Boogie Rag." Piano.

Swift, Frederic Fay. "Fearin' of the Judgement Day." SATB.

Thomas, C. Edward, arr. "Mary and Martha." Spiritual. SAB.

Thomasson, Reginald. "Evening Song" (South Carolina State University). Xerox Copy and Xerox MS.

————. "[Was It Just a Dream]." Xerox MS. Voice and Piano.

Tindley, (Rev.) Charles Albert. "Some Day" (Arr. by F. A. Clark). Gospel Hymn.

Tobias, Thomas W. J. *National Anthem Series*. Nashville: National Baptist Publishing Board, 1908.

Ward, Clara. *Special Songs of Clara Ward and the Famous Ward Singers*, Vol. 3. Philadelphia: Ward's House of Music, n.d.

Weaver, Powell, arr. "Wash My Sins Away, Lord." Spiritual. SATB with Vocal Solos and Piano.

Whalum, Wendell, arr. "Give Me Jesus." Spiritual. SATB with Soprano Solo.

————, arr. "The Lily of the Valley." Spiritual. SATB.

White, Clarence Cameron, arr. "Bear de Burden" (Arr. by G. Ackley Brower). Xerox Copy. Spiritual. TTBB.

White, Vincent, arr. "I Wan' Jesus to Walk with Me." Spiritual. SATB.

Wilson, Harry Robert, arr. "Little David, Play on Yo' Harp." Spiritual. SATB.

Withers, Bill. "Lean On Me" (Arr. by William Sanford). Gospel. SATB with Soprano Solo and Rhythm Section.

Woods, Kenneth, arr. "Come Unto Me." Gospel.

Work, John Wesley, arr. "Done Made My Vow to the Lord." Spiritual. SATB
with Tenor or Soprano Solo.

————, arr. "Go Tell It On the Mountain." Spiritual. SATB with Soprano and
Tenor Solos.

————. "Grigi, Grigi" (Based on Haitian Folk Text). SATB with Soprano
Solo.

————, arr. "I Got a House in Baltimore." SATB with Solos.

————. "Into the Woods My Master Went." Anthem. SATB with Alto Solo
and Piano or Organ.

————. "I've Known Rivers" (Text by Langston Hughes). SATB with Narrator.

————, arr. "Lord, I'm Out Here On Your Word." Spiritual. SATB with Tenor
Solo.

————, arr. "Rock My Soul in the Bosom of Abraham." Spiritual. SATB with
Soprano Solo.

————, arr. "Rockin' Jerusalem." Spiritual. SATB with Soprano or Tenor Solo.

————. "Sing, O Heavens." Anthem Based on Isaiah 49:13,18; 52:9. SATB
with Alto Solo and Organ.

————, arr. "Sinner, Please Don't Let this Harvest Pass." Spiritual. SATB
with Soprano Solo.

————, arr. "'Way Over in Egypt Land." Spiritual. SATB.

Wright, N. Louise. "A Spiritual." Piano.

CHAPTER 8
SOUTHERN UNIVERSITY

The Archives of the John B. Cade Library at Southern University hold the papers of Leon T. René, a collection of antique recordings, and an assortment of religious songbooks and hymnals. Additionally, the adjacent Black Heritage Room maintains a vertical file which contains clippings and other printed matter relative to Black music.

Leon T. René Papers, 1920–1979

Leon René (b. 1902), a Wilberforce University graduate (1921) who studied for a period at Southern and Xavier Universities, went on to become a successful composer, music publisher, and recording executive. Enclosed newspaper clippings and papers containing biographical data indicate that his many hit songs (e.g., "Sleepy Time Down South" and "Rockin' Robin") were first recorded and published by his own Los Angeles companies, Exclusive Records and Leon René Publishers. These companies were co-founded by his older brother, Otis J. René (1898–1970), who was also a collaborator on some of the songs.

In 1979 Leon René received the Honorary Citizen's Awards and Keys to the Cities of Baton Rouge and New Orleans, places which have been immortalized in his songs "Sleepy Time Down South," and "A Place I Know Called New Orleans." According to René, the nostalgia of overlooking the Mississippi River as a student at Southern University was the inspiration behind "Sleepy Time." Made famous by Louis Armstrong, the song is now in the New Orleans Jazz Museum and ASCAP's Hall of Fame.

Among the René compositions in the collection are both of the above-mentioned in manuscript, and published copies of "All that Oil in Texas (And Not One Drop's Mine)," "Convicted," "Gloria," "God's Green Earth," "If Money Grew On Trees," "When the Swallows Come Back to Capistrano," and "When It's Sleepy Time Down South" (as recorded by Dean Martin). Herewith is a melodic theme catalogue of songs published by Leon René Publishers (his own songs included).

Several photographs of René are among the papers. The earliest of him is in 1920 in a group called Buddy Petit's Jazz Band. This is followed by a 1930 picture of a 9-piece jazz combo named Leon René's Southern Syncopators and another from 1932 of a 14-piece ensemble, Leon René's Orchestra, performing in a Hollywood musical drama titled "Lucky Day." Two photos from 1948 are of René with Herb Jeffries and Duke Ellington, and with Louis Armstrong, and one of 1950 with Count Basie. Also included is a scene from the 20th Century Fox

Production of "Stormy Weather" (with Lena Horne), for which René was a composer. Finally, there is a portrait of the successful songwriter and business executive posing alone at the piano in 1979.

Comprising miscellaneous items are some correspondences from René and a 45 RPM recording of his two songs, "The Sign of the Cross" and "When the Swallows Come Back to Capistrano."

Record Collection

Several large boxes contain antique 78, 45, and 33⅓ RPM recordings of historic value. Most of them are scratched, a few are even chipped, and the collection presently remains uncatalogued; however the titles alone comprise an instructive discography. The following is a select list:

Louis Armstrong and Ella Fitzgerald: "Would You Like to Take a Walk," "The Frim Fram Sauce," "You Won't Be Satisfied," and "Dream a Little Dream of Me" (45).

The Caravans: "Walk Around Heaven All Day" (33⅓).

The Quiet Side of the New Christy Minstrels (33⅓).

Nat King Cole: "My Dream Sonata" and "That's All there is to That" (45).

Lawrence Cook: Piano Roll Party on Hi-Fi [Rags and Spirituals] (33⅓).

Democratic National Committee Kennedy Civil Rights Spots (Series 3) [Songs performed by Harry Belafonte, Lena Horne, Nat King Cole, Ella Fitzgerald, Cab Calloway] (33⅓).

Fisk University Jubilee Quartette: "There is a Balm in Gilead" and "The Greatest Campmeeting" (78).

Fisk University Male Quartet: "Steal Away to Jesus" (78).

Lionel Hampton and His Orchestra: "On the Sunny Side of the Street," "Don't Be that Way," "Shoe Shiners Drag," and "Dream a Little Dream of Me."

W. C. Handy: "St. Louis Blues" (78).

Woody Herman and Billy Eckstine: "Here Come the Blues" and "I Left My Hat in Haiti" (45).

Noble Sissle and His Orchestra: "Rhythm of the Broadway Moon" and "I Take to You" (78).

Sarah Vaughn: "Make Yourself Comfortable" and "Idle Gossip" (45).

Fats Waller: "I'm Crazy 'Bout My Baby" and "Until the [Readning?] Comes Along" (78).

The Ward Singers: "Prince of Peace" and "I Heard the Voice of Jesus" (78).

Cootie Williams and His Orchestra: "Wrong Neighborhood" and "Let's Do the Whole Thing or Nothing at All" (78).

Religious Songbook and Hymnal Collection, 1900–1963

Assembled here are an assortment of religious songbooks and hymnals containing Black spirituals and gospel songs composed, compiled, and in most cases published by Black companies. The following bibliography also contains a miscellaneous program and musical composition:

Bowles Favorite Herald (No. 31). Chicago: Bowles Music House, 1953. [Contains spirituals and gospels by Kenneth Morris and other writers].

Chinn, (Rev.) W. Scott, comp. "Gospel Songs and Spirituals." [Program with song texts enclosed].

Deas, E. C., arr. *Songs and Spirituals of Negro Composition for Revivals and Congregational Singing*. Chicago: The Overton-Hygienic Co., 1921.

Franklin, (Mme.) Johnnie Howard, comp. *Songs of Love and Worship*. Chicago: Martin and Morris Music, 1960.

Frederick, Conrad, arr. and William Stickles, ed. *The Golden Gate Quartet* [Spirituals for male quartet]. New York: Leeds Music Corp., 1946.

Frye, Theodore R., comp. *Frye's Echoes*. Chicago: Anderson and Frye, 1959.

Gospel Pearls. Nashville: Sunday School Publishing Board, National Baptist Convention, U. S. A., 1921.

Hall, Frederick D. *Deliverance* (An Oratorio). Winona Lake, Indiana: The Rodeheaver Hall-Mack Co., 1963.

Hamilton, (Rev.) F. M. and (Bishop) L. H. Holsey, eds. *Songs of Love and Mercy*. Jackson, Tennessee: Publishing House of the C. M. E. Church, 1904. [Most of the hymns herein are by Rev. Hamilton].

Jackson, (Elder) H. C., comp. *The Jackson Bible Universal Selected Gospel Songs*. New Albany, Mississippi: Elder H. C. Jackson, n.d. [Texts only].

Johnson, J. Rosamond, arr. *Album of Negro Spirituals*. New York: Edward B. Marks Music Corp., 1940.

Martin, Roberta. *Songs of the Roberta Martin Singers* (Nos. 1 and 4). Chicago: The Roberta Martin Studio of Music, 1951, 1957.

Martin, Sallie, and Kenneth Morris, comps. *Caravan Specials*. Chicago: Martin and Morris Music Studio, 1958.

————, comps. *The Famous Davis Sisters* (Special Folio No. 26). Chicago: Martin and Morris Music Studio, 1957.

————, comps. *Martin and Morris' Gospel Songbook of the Singing "Caravans."* Chicago: Martin and Morris Music Studio, 1955.

————, comps. *Sallie Martin's Gospelodiums* (Nos. 1 and 25). Chicago: Martin and Morris Music Studio, n.d., 1956.

————, comps. *Special Songs of the Pilgrim Travelers* (No. 16). Chicago: Martin and Morris Music Studio, 1949.

The National Harp of Zion and B.Y.P.U. Hymnal. Nashville: National Baptist Publishing Board, 1900.

National Jubilee Melodies. Np: National Negro Doll and Company, 1916.

Vertical File Collection

In the Black Heritage Room adjacent the Archives are vertical files containing an array of printed matter pertinent to Black music. Included are concert programs, journal articles, and newspaper and magazine clippings regarding such figures as James Brown, Thomas Dorsey, E. Azalia Hackley, Scott Joplin, Muddy Waters, Little Richard, Dorothy Maynor, Lou Rawls, Dionne Warwick, and Stevie Wonder. Issues of *The RCA Baton*, *Tones and Overtones*, *Gospel Advocate*, *The BMI Journal*, and *The Black Perspective in Music* are also included, as are Alma Norman's *Ballads of Jamaica* (London: Longmans, 1967) and Al Bernard's *Complete Minstrel Folio* (New York: Amsco Music Publishing Co., 1935).

CHAPTER 9
TUSKEGEE INSTITUTE

In the Archives of the Hollis Burke Frissell Library at historic Tuskegee Institute are William L. Dawson and William Grant Still collections, an assortment of sheet music and songbooks, phonograph recordings of Black music, and an extensive vertical clippings file.

William L. Dawson Collection, 1920–1980

This gathering of miscellaneous materials pertains to composer and conductor William Dawson (b. 1899). A 1921 graduate of Tuskegee Institute, Dawson returned to the school to develop and direct its music department from 1930–1955. Although well-known for his celebrated "Negro Folk Symphony" (1931), Dawson is principally an arranger of Black spirituals. His choral directing and composing brought the Tuskegee Institute Choir to the height of national acclaim during the thirties and forties. Consequently, the corpus of the collectanea—clippings, concert programs, and photographs—pertains primarily to Dawson's accomplishments as director of the Tuskegee choir.

Also belonging to the collection are Dawson's curriculum vitaes, biographical articles, programs documenting his compositional performances and commemorative occasions given in his honor. His extensive choral output is meagerly represented with a manuscript of "Break, Break, Break" (for chorus and piano), and a published song titled "Forever Thine."

William Grant Still Collection, 1930–1978

This collection consists of clippings regarding William Grant Still (1895–1978), photographs of him, programs and reviews documenting his compositional performances, and a select few of his many essays on music. The item of especial interest is a typescript of a 1967 oral history interview with Still titled "Negro Serious Music."[1] Adjacent is a modest representation of his extensive compositional output: "Bells," "Here's One," "Three Visions," and *Six of the Twelve Negro Spirituals* (1937).

---

[1] "Negro Serious Music." Interviewed by R. Donald Brown. California Black Oral History Project, California State University, Fullerton, November 13 and December 4, 1967.

Sheet Music Collection

Rare in this assemblage of sheet music are pieces pertaining exclusively to Tuskegee Institute. First and foremost is the alma mater, "The Tuskegee Song." The lyric was written by Paul Laurence Dunbar (1872–1906) who was invited to the Tuskegee campus by Booker T. Washington (1856–1915) for that specific purpose. The music was composed by the school's bandmaster, Nathaniel Clark Smith (1877–1933) who served on Tuskegee's military faculty from 1907–1913.

After having organized the first Black Symphony Orchestra in Chicago (and perhaps in the nation) in 1903, N. Clark Smith established a band, orchestra, glee clubs, and instrumental ensembles at Tuskegee. His most famous piece, "Negro Folk Suite," was performed by the St. Louis Symphony Orchestra in January 1930, well before Dawson and Still had completed their respective pieces, "Negro Folk Symphony" and "Afro–American Symphony," in 1931. Smith's suite is not within the sheet music collection, but three other compositions of his are: "Frederick Douglass" (Funeral March), "The Inlisted Soldier," and "Rose" (A Plantation Love Song).

A manuscript copy of "The Tuskegee Song" as arranged by Carl P. Harrington is included, as is a piece by Alberta Lillian Simms (1888–1970) titled "Tuskegee's Washington." Simms, a music instructor and the college organist for Tuskegee from 1923–1960, dedicated the song to Booker T. Washington, the illustrious founder of Tuskegee Institute (f. 1881). Another piece entrenched in Tuskegee history, "Moton's Inaugural March," was composed by the Bandmaster who succeeded Smith, Frank L. Drye (1889–1957). Drye, who came to Tuskegee in 1915 at Washington's summons (to remain for 32 years of committed service), wrote the piece for the May 25, 1916 inauguration of Washington's successor, Robert Russa Moton (1867–1940). Moton, like Washington, was a Hampton Institute graduate (1890), and upon leaving for Alabama in 1915 he could count 25 years of devoted service to the Virginia college. He held the Tuskegee presidency until 1935.

Another piece treasured by Tuskegee is the "General 'Chappie' James Suite," by Roger Hogan. The manuscript, along with a phonograph recording of it, are kept in a room named as a memorium to Daniel "Chappie" James (1920–1978), the venerated Tuskegee graduate (1942) who became the first Black four-star General (United States Airforce).

Of no particular relationship to Tuskegee are three songbooks: *American Folk Songs as Sung by Williams' Jubilee Singers* (Chicago: Press of Rosenow, n.d.), Alexander Seymour's *Gospel Gems* (New York: Crest, 1936), and *Jubilee Songs as Sung by the Jubilee Singers of Fisk University* (New York: Biglow & Main, n.d.). What remains is an assortment of published sheet music:

Allen, Thos. S. "Goodbye Mister Green-back."

Ball, Ernest R. "Till the Sands of the Desert Grow Cold."

——. "Who Knows" (Text by Paul Laurence Dunbar).

Bland, James A. "Carry Me Back to Old Virginny."

Boatner, Edward, arr. "You Got to Reap."

Burleigh, H. T., arr. "By and By."

——, arr. "Deep River."

——. "Her Eyes Twin Pools" (Text by James Weldon Johnson).

——. "Just You."

——. "Mammy's Li'l' Baby."

——. "One Year, 1914–1915."

——. "Perhaps."

——, arr. "Sometimes I Feel Like a Motherless Child."

——. "The Young Warrior" (Text by James Weldon Johnson).

Burlin, Natalie Curtis. "Hymn of Freedom."

Coleridge-Taylor, Samuel. "The Lee Shore."

Cook, Will Marion. "Rain Song."

Delmore, Harry. "Peter Drop Your Net and Follow Me."

Dett, R. Nathaniel. "Enchantment." [Cover Only].

——. "Niagara Falls."

Foster, Stephen. "My Old Kentucky Home."

——. "Old Folks at Home."

Gershwin, George. "My Man's Gone Now" (from Porgy and Bess).

Heyward, Sammy. "Checkin' On the Freedom Train" (Text by Langston Hughes).

Johnson, J. Rosamond. "As Long as the World Goes Round."

——. "Lazy Moon" (Text by Bob Cole).

——. "A Little Bit of Love (Goes a Long Way)."

——. "De Little Pickaninny's Gone to Sleep" (Text by Bob Cole).

——. "The Pretty Little Squaw, From Utah" (Text by Bob Cole).

——. "The Same Old Silv'ry Moon is Shining" (Text by Bob Cole).

——. "Two Love-Songs" (Texts by James Weldon Johnson).

——. "You're All Right Teddy" (Republican Campaign Song) (Text by Bob Cole).

Jordan, Joe. "Lovie Joe" (Text by Will Marion Cook).

Levi, Maurice. "An Ethiopian Mardi Gras" (Two Step and Cake Walk).

Taylor, Jeanetta. "Onward" (Dedicated to Hampton Institute).

White, Clarence Cameron, arr. "Bear de Burden."

——, arr. "Down by de River Side."

Supplementing this sheet music collection is an amassment of some 500 phonograph recordings representing jazz, blues, gospel, and spirituals. These are being transferred to cassette tapes for preservation purposes and easy access.

Vertical Clippings File, 1911–1966

Having subscribed to approximately 145 newspapers between 1911 and 1966, Tuskegee Institute established what continues to be the most extensive clippings file on Black culture in the United States. The newspaper segments and the microfilm copies of them are delineated according to subject. Looking under the main heading of "music," under a specific musician's name, or such a topic as "church choirs," will lead to sizable drawers of newspaper pieces on Black music.

Akin to this is a complete program file of concerts given by the Tuskegee choir, band, and visiting artists as far back as R. R. Moton's administration. Moton, an ardent enthusiast of Black folk song, established an arts society of sorts which brought to the Tuskegee campus such renowned musicians as Roland Hayes, Marian Anderson, Dorothy Maynor, Duke Ellington, W. C. Handy, and Noble Sissle.

Also located in the vertical files are a selection of printed items which have been maintained intact: (1) The April 1917 (vol. 1, no. 8) issue of the Chicago publication, *The Champion Magazine* (A Monthly Survey of Negro Achievement), containing the John Wesley Work essay, "Negro Folk Music as a Basis of an American Music" (pp. 389–93). (2) The January 1929 issue of *The Negro Musician*, another Chicago magazine (founded in the twenties) which contains articles by and about Black musicians. (3) An article reprint from the October 1940 issue of the *Journal of Negro Education*, "Music Education in Negro School's and Colleges," by Edgar Rogie Clark. (4) Minutes of the Fourth Annual Meeting of the National Association of Negro Musicians, which met in Columbus, Ohio, July 25–27, 1922. (5) Rev. Henry Hugh Proctor's recondite volume on Black spirituals, *Sermons in Melodies* (Atlanta: Union Publishing Company, 1917).

The Negro Yearbook Collection, 1912–1952

A complete collection of *The Negro Yearbook: An Annual Encyclopedia of the Negro* is accessible. Published by the Tuskegee Institute Department of Records and Research from 1912–1952, the volume was founded, compiled, and edited by Monroe Nathan Work (1866–1945), bibliographer, sociologist, and director of the above-mentioned department. Having served Tuskegee Institute from 1904–1940, Work was the statistician with whom Booker T. Washington maintained close correspondence for socio-statistical data relative to southern Blacks.

The Negro Yearbook was and remains a valuable source of encyclopedic data on Black music and musicians, in that it covered both the historic and contemporary. The 1937–38 volume, for instance, contains a section titled "The Negro in Music." Therein are facts on a considerable number of Black musicians, some of whom have fallen into as much obscurity as this historic encyclopedia. There is plenty of data on such acclaimed artists as Marion Anderson, Elizabeth Taylor Greenfield ("The Black Swan"), Mme. Marie Selika, H. T. Burleigh, Roland Hayes, Chevalier de Saint Georges, George Bridgetower, Thomas Greene Bethune ("Blind Tom"), Samuel Coleridge-Taylor, Will Marion Cook, R. Nathaniel Dett, W. C. Handy, Maud Cuney Hare, J. Rosamond Johnson, Capt. Walter Loving, and many others. Also discussed are such topics as African and Black American folk music, ragtime, and jazz.

CHAPTER 10
VIRGINIA STATE UNIVERSITY

In the Special Collections of the Johnston Memorial Library are the papers of Luther Porter Jackson, Altona Trent-Johns, Anna Laura Lindsay, J. Harold Montague, E. Azalia Hackley, and William Henry Johnson. Also therein are the records of the music department, a vertical clippings file, audio tapes of concerts and lectures sponsored by The Black Man in American Music program, and a collection of rare phonograph records.

Luther Porter Jackson, Sr. Papers, 1920–1950

Though a history professor at Virginia State University (1922–1950) with expertise in the free antebellum Blacks of Virginia, Luther P. Jackson (1892–1950) was also a musician. He served the school and larger community, respectively, as director of the Mens Glee Club and the 100-voice Petersburg Community Choir. Pertaining to the latter are correspondences, records, and a brief history.

Jackson's wife, Johnnella Frazier Jackson (1897–?), was a graduate of Fisk University where she was piano accompanist for the Jubilee Singers. While at Virginia State as a piano teacher (1920–1965), she assisted her husband as accompanist for the Petersburg Community Choir. She is perhaps best remembered as the composer of the college's alma mater (1923), which is based on a text by Felicia Dorothea Anderson (d. 1969), former drama teacher in the Department of English.

Of singular interest are 15 hand-written letters (1940–1950) from opera and concert soprano Camilla Williams (b. 1922) to Mrs. Jackson, with whom she studied at Virginia State prior to graduating in 1941. In her letter of October 24, 1975, for instance, Mme. Williams tells Mrs. Jackson about an especial occasion: "...I visited Marian Anderson at her home. She was such a lovely person....We had an interesting conversation concerning my work at Virginia State College."

Herewith are two letters of 1943 and 1944 from John Wesley Work III, and one of 1923 from Mrs. Agnes Work, John Work's wife, addressed to Professor and Mrs. Luther P. Jackson. In the letter of September 3, 1943, Work discloses an intimate observation regarding the music program at Fisk: "There have been three professors of music at Fisk, but they have all been white. There has never been a Negro professor of music. This of course makes me feel bad at times."

Comprising the miscellaneous items are programs of concerts given in Petersburg and throughout the country. One is of a violin recital given by Clarence Cameron White on March 26, 1923 in the Virginia Union College Chapel.

Altona Trent-Johns Papers, 1938–1968

Altona Trent-Johns (1904–1977) taught music at Virginia State from 1952–1972, during which time she and Undine Smith Moore founded the Black Man in American Music program. Her step-daughter, Cleota Collins (1893–1976), a noted concert singer, was a student and protégé of E. Azalia Hackley. As head of the voice department at Virginia State University from 1940–1952, Collins passed along her excellent vocal training to Camilla Williams. Among the papers are photographs of Cleota Collins and several letters dated 1968 to her stepmother.

The remaining items are compositions and song collections: (1) "Five Spirituals" arranged by Margaret Bonds (2) "Hail Virginia State" (Evening Song) by Alston Waters Burleigh, who directed the school's Choral Society (3) "Two Spirituals" arranged by William L. Dawson (4) "W. C. Handy's Collection of Negro Spirituals" (5) "My Songs: Aframerican Religious Folk Songs Arranged and Interpreted" by Roland Hayes (6) "Daniel, Daniel, Servant of the Lord" and "Fare You Well" arranged by Undine Smith Moore, and (7) "A Song to Teachers College" by R. A. Laslett Smith (music) and Clara H. Perry (text).

Anna Laura Lindsay Papers, 1898–1937

Anna Laura Lindsay (1876–1961) not only founded the music department at Virginia State University, she taught there for nearly a half-century (1899–1947). In the collection are numerous correspondences. One, dated May 25, 1898, is from James A. Robinson, Principal of the Music Department at Fisk University.

Two unsigned items may have been authored by Lindsay: (1) a handwritten paper titled "The Three P's of Musicians" and (2) a manuscript composition, "[When Life is Dark and I Am Weary]." Herewith is a pamphlet on the life of Madame E. Azalia Hackley, a friend of Lindsay.

Also belonging to the collection are two religious songbooks, *National Jubilee Melodies*, 10th ed. (n.d.) and *Songs and Spirituals of Negro Composition for Revivals and Congregational Singing* (1921). Additionally, there are two miscellaneous compositions: (1) a manuscript copy of "A Song," a setting of Paul Laurence Dunbar's poem by David N. Baker, and (2) "Two Homeward Songs: 'My Journey Home' and 'Our Long Home'," a composition by Gordon Blaine Hancock arranged in 1965 by Pearl Wood. Hancock (1884–1970), the Baptist minister and noted sociologist who enjoyed a lengthy tenure at Virginia Union University, was also an enthusiast of Black spirituals.

J. Harold Montague Collection, 1930–1942

J. Harold Montague (1907–1950) served Virginia State as director of the music department ca. 1933–1947. A pianist and choir director, he conducted the college's Harry T. Burleigh Singers, an a cappella choir he organized in 1933.[1]

---

[1] For further information on the development of the school's music program, see J. Harold Montague,

Montague amassed a significant file of photographs relative to musical organizations and activities on the Virginia campus. There are pictures of Anna Laura Lindsay and her Lindsay Treble Clef Club, his own Harry T. Burleigh Singers, and the Mens Glee Club with its director, Luther P. Jackson. A picture of the Choral Society (1931–32) directed by Alston Burleigh also includes Undine Smith (Moore) as accompanist. Additionally, there are photographs of Johnnella Jackson, Camilla Williams, and Cleota Collins, as well as of Montague. Of real interest is a photograph of "the first state music clinic held for Negro music teachers" at Virginia State College, June 18–25, 1942. Photographed are the clinic participants, Montague, its director, and R. Nathaniel Dett, the guest consultant.

E. Azalia Hackley Papers, 1906

In this collection are some exclusive snapshots of Mme. Hackley in France, and with members of her family in Philadelphia. In a lengthy letter of September 2, 1906 to her father, Mr. Edwin H. Hackley of Philadelphia, she tells of her daily experiences in France. One most interesting statement in the form of a pun actually reveals little about her domestic life there but a lot about her sense of humor: "I will use my little stove, and do a little 'Bach-ing'," she says.

William Henry Johnson Papers, 1884–1935

Major William Henry Johnson (1884–1935), an 1878 graduate of Hampton Institute, commanded one of two battalions of the Black Virginia National Guard. In addition, he was a school teacher and a singer in a church quartet. Along with his many speeches and a scrapbook of photographs is a small picture of the Black Militia band and portraits of himself.

Records of the Music Department, 1920–1967

The records of the music department include photographs of the college band, choir, and Little Symphony Orchestra dating from 1947–1967. Also included are: (1) programs of student, faculty, and guest recitals, (2) programs of concerts given by the Mens Glee Club, Little Symphony Orchestra, choir, symphonic band, the college's Matoaca Laboratory School Band, and the All-State Band and Choir, (3) programs documenting opera and piano workshops, summer institutes, and clinics, (4) programs given by such organizations as the High School Music Festival, the Intercollegiate Music Association, the Lindsay Treble Clef Club, and the Black Man in American Music, and (5) the newsletter of the Music Conference of the Virginia Teachers Colleges (1955–57 issues).

"Music at Virginia State College," *Virginia State College Gazette*, 9, Nos. 3–4 (Dec. 1934), pp. 31–33. (Located in Special Collections).

Vertical File

The vertical file contains newspaper clippings on the Virginia State University band, choir and faculty. Among former music faculty covered are Johnnella Jackson, Anna Laura Lindsay, Undine Smith Moore, and D. Antoinette Handy. Current music faculty covered are Johnnella L. Edmonds, a voice teacher, and Buckner Gamby, a concert pianist.

A notable figure, about whom are numerous newspaper pieces, is F. Nathaniel Gatlin, a concert clarinetist who replaced J. Harold Montague as music department head in 1947. A symphonist at heart, Gatlin directed the school's Little Symphony and upon retirement in 1978 organized the Petersburg Symphony Orchestra which he still conducts today. He is also founder of the Intercollegiate Music Association (IMA), which comprises schools in the CIAA.[2]

Audio Tape Collection, 1967–1972

Assembled here are tapes of concerts and lectures sponsored by the Black Man in American Music program established at Virginia State University in 1967 by Undine Smith Moore and Altona Trent-Johns.

The tapes are of performances given by Marian Anderson, Ralph R. Simpson (organist), Rev. Gary D. "Blind" Davis, Brownie McGhee and Sonny Terry, Donald Bryd and the Howard University Jazz Band, the St. Simons Georgia Sea Island Singers, and Michael Babatunde Olatunji with his troupe of African dancers and drummers.

Lectures covered virtually every type of Black music, from African and Latin American to gospel and jazz. There are, for example, tapes of Halin El Dabh (of Howard University) lecturing on music of Northern Africa, Willia Daughtry (of Hampton Institute) on Sisseretta Jones, Frederick Hall (of Dillard University) on teaching African children's songs to elementary school children, and Margaret Butcher (of Howard University) moderating a composers forum.

Additionally, performances were given of Samuel Coleridge-Taylor's "Christmas Overture," Ulysses Kay's "Concerto for Orchestra," David Baker's "Black American Violin Concerto," and Ollie Wilson's "In Memoriam of Martin Luther King, Jr."

Phonograph Record Collection

The library has two record collections which presently remain unprocessed. The first is an assemblage of Duke Ellington records donated to the school by F. Nathaniel Gatlin.

The second grouping consists of 360 radio platters (33⅓ RPM), produced by the Allied Record Manufacturing Company in Hollywood for the United States

---

[2] The Special Collections at Virginia State University is the official repository for the records of IMA.

State Department. These recordings were aired on the worldwide radio broadcast, Voice of America, a division of the United States International Communication Agency established in 1942. The platters contain a wide selection of Black music, including performances by such artists as The Calloway Sisters, the Folk Singers, Dorothy Maynor, and Art Tatum.

The following select list not only comprises a rare discography, it also indicates the type of Black music which received an international audience through Voice of America:

Altanta-Morehouse-Spelman Choir. [Spirituals]. Kemper Harreld, Director.

Anderson, Marian. [Classics and Spirituals with Orchestra]. Donald Voorhees, Conductor.

Basie, Count. "One O'Clock Jump." Johnny Guarnieri Quintet.

Bethune-Cookman Negro College Choir. [Spirituals]. Alzeda C. Hacker, Director.

Camp Meeting Choir. [Spirituals]. J. Garfield Wilson, Conductor.

Chadwick, George. "Jubilee Overture." Orchestra Conducted by Edwin MacArthur.

Chariot Wheels Choir. [Spirituals]. Lawrence Mann, Director.

Coleridge-Taylor, Samuel. "The Bamboola." U. S. Army Band. Lt. Herbert Hoyer, Conductor.

————. "The Departure" (From "Hiawatha Suite"). CBS Concert Orchestra, Bernard Herrmann, Conductor.

————. "Sonnet d'Amour." The Symphonette, Mishel Piastro, Conductor.

Duncan, Todd (Baritone). [Creole Songs arr. Camille Nickerson, Haitian Songs arr. Jaegerhuber, and Spirituals arr. Hall Johnson].

Ellington, Duke. "All Day Long," "Sophisticated Lady," "The Hawk Talks," "Midriff," "Just a-Sittin' and a-Rockin'," "Caravan." Guy Lombardo Orchestra.

————. "Caravan." Cesar Petrillo Orchestra.

————. "In a Sentimental Mood." Bob Trendler and Orchestra.

————. "Mood Indigo," "Warm Valley," "The Eighth Veil," "Ting-a-Ling," "Happy-Go-Lucky Local," "Tea for Two." Duke Ellington Orchestra.

————. "Take the 'A' Train." Charlie Spivak Orchestra.

Fisk University Choir. [Spirituals]. John F. Ohl, Director.

Gould, Morton. "Minstrel Show." Minneapolis Symphony Orchestra, Dimitri Mitropoulos, Conductor.

————, arr. "Swing Low, Sweet Chariot." Alfredo Antonini Orchestra.

Hall Johnson Choir. [Spirituals]. Hall Johnson, Director.

Hampton Institute Choir. [Spirituals]. Henry F. Switten, Director.

Juan, P. San. "Initiation" (Afro-Cuban Suite, "Liturgia Negra"). NBC Orchestra. Henri Nosco, Conductor.

Kay, Ulysses. "Sinfonia in E." Eastman-Rochester Symphony Orchestra. Howard Hanson, Conductor.

Lincoln University Glee Club. Orrin Clayton Suthern, Director.

Livingstone College Choir. [Spirituals]. Myron Thomas, Director.

Reed, H. Owen. "Spiritual for Band." U. S. Army Band, Capt. Hugh Curry, Conductor.

Shaw University Choir. [Spirituals]. Harry G. Smith, Director.

Still, William Grant. "Africa," Pt. 1 ("Pages from Negro History"). NBC Orchestra, Henri Nosco, Conductor.

Talladega Negro College Choir. [Spirituals]. Frank Harrison, Director.

Tuskegee Institute Choir. [Spirituals]. William Dawson, Director.

Waller, Fats. "Honeysuckle Rose." Johnny Guarnieri Quintet.

———. "The Jitterbug Waltz." Baron Elliot Octet.

Warfield, William (Baritone). [e.g., "The Negro Speaks of Rivers" by Howard Swanson].

Wiley College Choir (Marshall, Texas). [Spirituals]. Gilbert Allen, Director.

Williams, Mary Lou. "Todey Toddle." Roger Renner Trio.

Wings Over Jordan Choir. Rev. Glenn T. Settle, Director.

Xavier University Choir. [Spirituals]. Clifford Richter, Director.

PART II
BIBLIOGRAPHY AND UNION LIST

INTRODUCTION

The purpose of this bibliography is to provide a union list of 1,135 books on Black and African music and musicians in special collections at a selection of Black colleges and universities throughout the United States. Researchers seeking particular publications can readily identify their nearest location since the constituent schools represent a broad geographic area.

Library symbols indicating the source of specific holdings are arranged alphabetically succeeding the bibliographic entry. A parenthetic date following a library symbol is that of a reprint or revised edition by the same publisher. Entries with the same author and title, but a different publisher, are arranged chronologically according to date, so as to facilitate tracing publication history. Unabridged subtitles are provided in every possible instance, thereby annotating the bibliography.

Most entries have been verified for accuracy through the Online Computer Library Center (OCLC). Those volumes not listed in OCLC have been checked with other bibliographic sources. Where verification has been unsuccessful, it has been necessary to rely on the sometimes questionable accuracy of the original bibliographic cards in the catalogs and shelf-listings of the schools visited.

A school not listed as having a particular publication means only that the said volume is not located in its special collection. Several schools, like NCCU and VSU, are therefore underrepresented, when in fact their libraries have significant circulating collectanea on Black music. However, the distinctive importance of this bibliography is in part the fact that books in special collections are typically noncirculatable, therefore increasing the chance that they will always be available to present and future researchers upon need.

The multitudinous countries which have published the books of this bibliography are Liberia, Nigeria, Ghana, Senegal, Cameroon, Congo, Zaire, Kenya, Ethiopia, Sudan, Zambia, South Africa, Lesotho. Virgin Islands, Jamaica, Haiti, Cuba, Argentina, Colombia, United States, Ontario, England, France, Italy, West Germany, Austria, Japan, Switzerland, Sweden, Spain, Netherlands, Belgium, and Denmark. Published in 33 countries and in English, French, German, Italian, and Spanish, the 1,135 volumes of this bibliography are evidence of the world audience and global impact Black and African music have had over the last century.

TABLE OF SYMBOLS

School	Library Division	Code
Atlanta University[1]	Special Collections and Archives	AU
Fisk University	Special Collections	FU
Hampton Institute	Peabody Room	HI
Howard University	Moorland-Spingarn Research Center	HU
Jackson State University	Special Collections	JS
Lincoln University	Langston Hughes Collection Afro-American Collection	LH LU
North Carolina Central University	Treasury Room	NC
Savannah State College	Negro Collection	SS
South Carolina State College	Special Collection	SC
Southern University	Black Heritage Collection Archives	SU SA
Tuskegee Institute	Washington Collection	TI
Virginia State University	Special Collections	VS
Xavier University	Black Collection	XU

[1] Clark, Morehouse, Morris-Brown, and Spelman Colleges are constituents of the Atlanta University center and share its central library facility and Special Collections and Archives.

BIBLIOGRAPHY

1   Aasland, Benny H., ed. *The Wax Works of Duke Ellington*. Danderyd, Sweden: Benny H. Aasland, 1954. HU.

2   ———. *The "Wax Works" of Duke Ellington: The 6th March 1940–30 July 1942 RCA Victor Period*. Jarfalla,Sweden: DEMS, 1978. HU.

3   Abdul, Raoul. *Blacks in Classical Music: A Personal History*. New York: Dodd, Mead, 1977. AU, FU, HU; LU, JS,SC, TI (1978), XU.

4   Accam, T. N. N., ed. *Klama Songs and Chants*. Legon, Ghana: Institute of African Studies, University of Ghana,1967. HU.

5   Adams, Rosemary F. "A Study of Community Services as Professional Laboratory Experiences in Preservice Preparation of Teachers in Music at Knoxville College,Tennessee." Dissertation, New York University, 1960. LU, SS.

6   *African Music: [UNESCO] Meeting in Yaoundé (Cameroon) 23–27 February, 1970*. Paris: La Revue Musicale, 1972. FU, HI, SC.

7   Akpabot, Samuel Ekpe. *Ibibio Music in Nigerian Culture*. East Lansing, Michigan: Michigan State University Press, 1975. FU, HU, LU, SC.

8   Albertson, Chris. *Bessie,* New York: Stein and Day, 1972. FU, JS, LU.

9   ———. *Bessie Smith, Empress of the Blues*. New York: G. Schirmer Books, 1975. SC.

10 ———. *Bessie Smith, Empress of the Blues*. New York: W. Kane, 1975. HU.

11 Albus, Harry J. *The "Deep River" Girl: The Life of Marian Anderson in Story Form*. Grand Rapids: W. B. Eerdmans Publishing Co., 1949. HI, HU, TI.

12 Allen, Stuart. *Stars of Swing*. London: British Yearbook,1946. AU.

13 Allen, Walter C. *Hendersonia, The Music of Fletcher Henderson and His Musicians: A Bio-Discography*. Highland Park, New Jersey: [Walter C. Allen?], 1973. LU.

14 ———, ed. *Studies in Jazz: I*. Westport, Connecticut:Greenwood Press, 1978. HU.

15 ——— and Brian A. L. Rust. *King Joe Oliver.* Belleville, New Jersey: Walter C. Allen, 1955. TI.

16 ——— and Brian A. L. Rust. *King Joe Oliver*. London:Sidgwick and Jackson, 1958. HU.

17 Allen, William Francis, Charles Pickard Ware, and Lucy McKim Garrison. *Slave Songs of the United States*. New York: A. Simpson Co., 1867. FU, NC.

18 ———. *Slave Songs of the United States*. New York: John Ross (Nation Press), 1871. LU.

19 ———. *Slave Songs of the United States*. New York: Peter Smith, 1929. AU, FU, HU, HU (1951), LU (1951), SA(1951), SC (1951), XU.

20 ———. *Slave Songs of the United States*. New York: Oak Publications, 1965. HU.

21 ———. *Slave Songs of the United States*. Freeport, New York: Books for Libraries Press, 1971. FU.

22 *American Folk Songs as Sung by Williams' Colored Singers*. Chicago: Press of the Rosenow, n.d. HU.

23 *American Folk Songs as Sung by Williams' Jubilee Singers*. N.p.: Williams, Johnson, n.d. HU, VS.

24 Ames, David W. and Anthony V. King. *Glossary of Hausa Music and Its Social Contexts*. Evanston: Northwestern University Press, 1971. HI.

25 Anderson, Edison H. "The Historical Development of Music in the Negro Secondary Schools of Oklahoma and at Langston University." Dissertation, State University of Iowa, 1957. HU, LU, SS.

26 Anderson, Marian. *My Lord, What a Morning: An Auto-biography*. New York: Viking, 1956. FU, HU, LU, SC, TI.

27 Aretz, Isabel. *Los Instrumentos Musicales Afroamericanos*. Dakar, Senegal: N. pub., 1974. HU.

28 Armstrong, Louis. *Louis Armstrong: A Self Portrait*. New York: Eakins, 1971. FU, JS, LU.

29 ———. *Satchmo: My Life in New Orleans*. New York: Prentice–Hall, 1954. AU, HU, LH, SC, TI.

30 ———. *Satchmo: My Life in New Orleans*. New York: New American Library, 1955. HU, LU.

31 ———. *Swing that Music*. New York: Longmans Green, 1936. HU, LU, TI.

32 Armstrong, Mary F. M. and Helen Ludlow. *Hampton and Its Students: [With Fifty Cabin and Plantation Songs Arranged by Thomas P. Fenner]*. New York: G. P. Putnam's Sons, 1874. NC.

33   Arnaud, Noel. *Duke Ellington*. Paris: Messager Boiteaux, 1950. HU.

34   Arnaudon, Jean-Claude. *Dictionnaire du Blues*. Paris: Editions Filipacchi, 1977. HU.

35   Arnold, Byron, comp. *Folksongs of Alabama: Includes Biographies of Principal Singers*. University, Alabama:University of Alabama Press, 1950. HU.

36   Arvey, Verna. *Studies of Contemporary American Composers: William Grant Still*. New York: J. Fischer, 1939. HU, SU.

37   *The ASCAP Biographical Dictionary of Composers, Authors and Publishers*. Ed. Lynn Farnol et al., 3rd ed. New York:[ASCAP?], 1966. LH.

38   Attaway, William. *Calypso Song Book*. Ed. Lyle K. Engel. New York: McGraw-Hill, 1957. AU, HI, HU, TI.

39   Ayissi, Leon-Marie. *Contes et Berceuses Beti*. Yaoundé, Cameroon: Editions Cle, 1968. HU.

40   Babalola, Solomon A. *The Content and Form of Yoruba Ijala*. Oxford: Clarendon Press, 1966. HU.

41   Backus, Rob. *Fire Music: A Political History of Jazz,* 2nd ed. Chicago: Vanguard Books, 1976. HU.

42   Bailey, Pearl. *Hurry Up, America, and Spit*. New York: Harcourt, Brace, and Jovanovich, 1976. FU, LU, SC.

43   ———. *The Raw Pearl*. New York: Harcourt, Brace, and World, 1968. AU, FU, HI, HU, JS, LU, SU.

44   ———. *Talking to Myself*. New York: Harcourt, Brace, and Jovanovich, 1971. AU, FU, HU, LU, SC, SS, TI.

45   Baker, David N. et al., eds. *The Black Composer Speaks: A Project of the Afro-American Institute*. Metuchen, New Jersey: Scarecrow Press, 1978. FU, JS, SC, SU.

46   Ballanta-Taylor, Nicholas G. J. *Saint Helena Island Spirituals*. New York: G. Schirmer, 1925. TI.

47   Balliett, Whitney. *Alec Wilder and His Friends: The Words and Sounds of Marian McPartland, Mabel Mercer, Marie Marcus, Bobby Hackett, Tony Bennett, Ruby Braff, Bob and Ray, Blossom Dearie, and Alec Wilder*. Boston: Houghton Mifflin, 1974. HU.

48   ———. *American Singers: A Group of Portraits of Leading Popular and Jazz Singers*. New York: Oxford University Press, 1979. HU.

49   ———. *Dinosaurs in the Morning: 41 Pieces on Jazz*. Philadelphia: Lippincott, 1962. XU.

50   ———. *Dinosaurs in the Morning: 41 Pieces on Jazz*. London: Jazz Book Club, 1965. HU.

51   ———. *Ecstasy at the Onion: Thirty-One Pieces on Jazz*. Indianapolis: Bobbs-Merrill, 1971. HU.

52   ———. *Improvising: Sixteen Jazz Musicians and Their Art*. New York: Oxford University Press, 1977. HU.

53   ———. *Jelly Roll, Jabbo, and Fats: 19 Portraits in Jazz*. New York: Oxford University Press, 1983. HU, JS, LU.

54   ———. *New York Notes: A Journal of Jazz, 1972–1975*. Boston: Houghton Mifflin, 1976. HU, JS, LU.

55   ———. *Night Creatures: A Journal of Jazz, 1975–1980*. New York: Oxford University Press, 1981. HU, JS.

56   ———. *The Sound of Surprise: 46 Pieces on Jazz*. New York: Dutton, 1959. HU.

57   ———. *Such Sweet Thunder: Forty-Nine Pieces on Jazz*. Indianapolis: Bobbs-Merrill, 1966. HU.

58   Barnes, Edwin N. C. *From Plymouth Rock to Tin Pan Alley: [A Lecture on American Music]*. Washington: Music Education Publications, 1936. HU.

59   Barton, William E. *Old Plantation Hymns: A Collection of Hitherto Unpublished Melodies of the Slave and the Freedman, with Historical and Descriptive Notes*. New York: AMS Press, 1972. LU, NC, SC.

60   Basile, Frère. *Aux Rhythmes de Tambours: La Musique chez les Noirs d'Afrique*. Montreal: Les Frères du Sacré-Coeur, 1949. AU.

61   Bebey, Francis. *African Music: A People's Art*. [1st ed.]. New York: Lawrence Hill, 1975. AU, FU, HU.

62   ———. *African Music: A People's Art*. London: Harrap, 1975. SU, TI.

63   ———. *Musique de l'Afrique*. Paris: Horizons de France, 1969. HU.

64   Béchet, Sidney. *Treat It Gentle*. New York: Hill and Wang, 1960. AU, FU, HU, LH, LU, SC.

65   ———. *Treat It Gentle*. New York: Da Capo, 1975. HI, SU, XU.

66   Beckwith, Martha W. *Jamaica Anansi Stories: [With Music Recorded in the Field]*. New York: The American Folk-Lore Society, 1924. NC.

67   Beger, Monroe et al. *Benny Carter: A Life in American Music*. Metuchen, New Jersey: Scarecrow, 1982. JS.

68   Belafonte, Harold. *Songs Belafonte Sings*. New York: Duell, Sloan, and Pearce, 1962. HI, HU, LU.

69   Belinga, Martin Samuel. *Littérature et Musique Populaires en Afrique Noire*. Paris: Editions Cujas, 1965. SU.

70   Belz, Carl. *The Story of Rock*. New York: Oxford University Press, 1969. XU.

71   Berendt, Joachim-Ernst. *Jazz: A Photo History*. New York: Schirmer Books, 1979. HU, JS.

72   ———. *The Jazz Book: From New Orleans to Rock and Free Jazz*. New York: Lawrence Hill, 1975. HU.

73   ———. *The Jazz Book: From Ragtime to Fusion and Beyond*. Westport, Connecticut: Lawrence Hill, 1982. FU.

74   ———. *Jazz Optisch*. München [Munich], West Germany: Nymphenburger Verlagshandlung, 1954. HU.

75   ———. *Das Jazzbuch: Entwicklung and Bedeutung der Jazzmusik*. Frankfurt, West Germany: M. Fischer Bucherei, 1954. HU.

76   ———. *Das Neue Jazzbuch: Entwicklung and Bedeutung der Jazzmusik*. Frankfurt, West Germany: M. Fischer Bücherei, 1959. HU.

77   ———. *The New Jazz Book: A History and Guide*. New York: Hill and Wang, 1962. FU, HU.

78   ———. *The Story of Jazz: From New Orleans to Rock Jazz*. Englewood Cliffs, New Jersey: Prentice-Hall, 1978. JS, SC.

79   ———. *Variationen über Jazz: Aufsätze*. München [Munich], West Germany: Nymphenburger Verlagshandlung, 1956. HU.

80   ——— and William Claxton. *Jazzlife: Auf den Spuren des Jazz*. Baden, Switzerland: Burda Druck und Verlag GMBH Offenburg, 1961. HU, LH.

81   Berlin, Edward A. *Ragtime: A Musical and Cultural History*. Berkeley: University of California Press, 1980. LU.

82   Berliner, Paul. *The Soul of Mbira: Music and Traditions of the Shona People of Zimbabwe*. Berkeley: University of California Press, 1978. HU, LU, TI.

83   Bernhard, Paul. *Jazz, eine Musikalische Zeitfrage: Mit Notenbeigaben*. München [Munich], West Germany: Delphin-Verlag, 1927. AU.

84   Berry, Lemuel, Jr. *Biographical Dictionary of Black Musicians and Music Educators*. N.p.: Educational Book Publishers, 1978. FU, HU, LU.

85   Besmer, Fremont E. *Kídàn Dárán Sállà: Music for the Eve of the Muslim Festivals of Íd Al-Fitr and Íd Al-Kabir in Kano, Nigeria*. Bloomington: African Studies Program,Indiana University, 1974. HU.

86   Bethell, Tom. *George Lewis: A Jazzman from New Orleans*. Berkeley: University of California Press, 1977. HU, JS, LU, SC, SU.

87   Bethune, Thomas Greene. *The Marvelous Musical Prodigy: Blind Tom, the Negro Boy Pianist, Whose Performance at the Great St. James and Egyptian Halls, London, and Salle Hertz, Paris, have Created such a Profound Sensation. Anecdotes, Songs, and Sketches of the Life Testimonials of Musicians and Savans and Opinions of the American and English Press of "Blind Tom."* New York: French and Wheat, [1868?]. HU.

88   Beyer, Jimmy. *Baton Rouge Blues: A Guide to the Baton Rouge Bluesmen and their Music*. Baton Rouge: The Arts and Humanities Council of Greater Baton Rouge, 1980. SU.

89   Bibbs, Hart L. *Poly Rhythms to Freedom*. New York: Mac McNair, 1964. LH.

90   Blacking, John. *Venda Children's Songs: A Study in Ethno-musicological Analysis*. Johannesburg, South Africa: Witwatersrand University Press, 1967. FU, LU, SC.

91   Blackstone, Orin. *Index to Jazz: Jazz Recordings, 1917–1944*. Westport, Connecticut: Greenwood Press, 1978. HU.

92   Blancq, Charles. *Sonny Rollins: The Journey of a Jazzman*. Boston: Twayne, 1983. JS.

93   Bland, James A. *The James A. Bland Album of Outstanding Songs: A Collection for Voice and Piano*. Ed. Charles Haywood. New York: Edward B. Marks Music Corporation, 1946. LH.

94   Blay, J. Bendibengor. *Ghana Sings*. Accra, Ghana: Waterville Publishing House, 1965. LH.

95   Blesh, Rudi. *Classic Piano Rags: Complete Original Music for 81 Rags*. New York: Dover Publications, 1973. FU.

96   ———. *Combo U.S.A.: Eight Lives in Jazz*. Philadelphia: Chilton Book Co., 1971. FU, LU, SC.

97   ———. *Combo U.S.A.: Eight Lives in Jazz*. New York: Da Capo, 1979. HU.

98 ———. *Shining Trumpets: A History of Jazz*. New York: Knopf, 1946. AU, FU, HU, HU (1958), LH, LH (1958), LU (1958), TI.

99 ———. *Shining Trumpets: A History of Jazz*. New York: Da Capo, 1975. SU.

100 ———. *This is Jazz: A Series of Lectures Given at the San Francisco Museum of Art*. San Francisco: [Private Printing], 1943. HU.

101 ——— and Harriet Janis. *They All Played Ragtime: The True Story of an American Music*. New York: Knopf, 1950. HU, LH, TI.

102 ——— and Harriet Janis. *They All Played Ragtime: The True Story of an American Music*. New York: Oak Publications, 1966. FU (1971), LU, SC (1971), XU.

103 Bluestein, Eugene. "The Background and Sources of an American Folksong Tradition." Dissertation, University of Minnesota, Minneapolis, 1960. LU, SS.

104 Boatner, Edward H., ed. *Spirituals Triumphant, Old and New*. Nashville: Sunday School Publishing Board, National Baptist Convention, U.S.A., 1927. AU.

105 ———, ed. *The Story of the Spirituals: 30 Spirituals and their Origins*. New York: McAfee Music Corp., 1973. HU.

106 Boeckman, Charles. *Cool, Hot and Blue: A History of Jazz for Young People*. Washington: R. B. Luce, 1968. HU, JS.

107 ———. *Cool, Hot and Blue: A History of Jazz for Young People*. New York: Washington Square Press, 1970. LU.

108 Boni, Margaret B., ed. *The Fireside Book of Favorite American Songs*. New York: Simon and Schuster, 1952. LH.

109 Boot, Adrian and Vivien Goldman. *Bob Marley, Soul Rebel—Natural Mystic*. New York: St. Martin's Press, 1982. LU, XU.

110 Boot, Adrian and Michael Thomas. *Jamaica: Babylon on a Thin Wire*. New York: Schocken Books, 1977. HU.

111 Bontemps, Arna W. *Chariot in the Sky: A Story of the Jubilee Singers*. Philadelphia: Winston, 1951. XU.

112 Borenstein, Larry and Bill Russell. *Preservation Hall Portraits*. Baton Rouge: Louisiana State University Press, 1969. SU.

113 Bornn, Hugo O., comp. *Virgin Islands Folk Songs*. St. Thomas: Department of Education, U.S. Virgin Islands, 1969. HU.

114 Boulton, David. *Jazz in Britain*. London: W. H. Allen, 1958. HU.

115   Boutney, Charlotte M. *Jazz: An Art Culture*. New Orleans: Clermont Printing and Publishing, 1975. XU.

116   Bowman, Laura and LeRoy Antoine, eds. *The Voice of Haiti: An Unusual Collection of Original Native Ceremonial Songs, Invocations, Voodoo Chants, Drum Beats and Rhythms, Stories of Traditions, etc. of the Haitian People*. New York: Clarence Williams Publishing Co., 1938. HU.

117   Boyce, Carole E. "The Trinidad Calypso: An Analysis of the Functions of an African Oral Tradition in the Caribbean." Thesis, Howard University, 1974. HU.

118   Bradford, Perry. *Born with the Blues: Perry Bradford's Own Story*. New York: Oak Publications, 1965. FU, HI, HU, LU, SC, SU, TI.

119   Brandel, Rose. *The Music of Central Africa: An Ethno-musicological Study*. Hague, Netherlands: M. Nijhoff, 1961. FU, LU.

120   ———. "The Music of Central Africa. An Ethno-Musicological Study: French Equatorial Africa, the Belgian Congo and Ruanda-Urundi, Uganda, Tanganyika." (With Part II: Transcriptions). Dissertation, New York University, 1959. SC, TI.

121   Brask, Ole. *Jazz People*. New York: H. N. Abrams, 1976. LU, SC, SS.

122   Breman, Paul. *Blues: En Andere Wereldlijke Volksmuziekvan de Noordamerikaanse Neger*. Wassenaar, Netherlands: Servire, 1961. HU, LU.

123   ———. *Spirituals*. S. Gravenhage, Netherlands: Servire, 1958. AU.

124   Bricktop with James Haskins. *Bricktop*. New York: Atheneum, 1983. FU, LU.

125   Brooks, Edward. *The Bessie Smith Companion: A Critical and Detailed Appreciation of the Recordings*. New York: Da Capo, 1982. LU.

126   Brooks, Tilford. "A Historical Study of Black Music and Selected Twentieth Century Black Composers: A Source Book for Teachers." Dissertation, Washington University, 1972. FU.

127   Broonzy, William. *Big Bill: Mes Blues, Ma Guitare et Moi: Récits Recueillis par Yannick Bruynoghe*. Bruxelles, Belgium: Editions des Artistes, 1955. HU.

128   ———. *Big Bill Blues: William Broonzy's Story as Told to Yannick Bruynoghe*. London: Cassell, 1955. AU, FU, HU, TI.

129   ———. *Big Bill Blues: William Broonzy's Story as Told to Yannick Bruynoghe*. New York: Oak Publications, 1964. HU.

130 Broven, John. *Rhythm and Blues in New Orleans*. Gretna, Louisiana: Pelican, 1978. FU, HU, LU, SU.

131 Brown, Geoff. *Diana Ross*. New York: St. Martin's Press, 1981. SU.

132 Brown, Rae Linda. *Music, Printed and Manuscript, in the James Weldon Johnson Memorial Collection of Negro Arts and Letters: An Annotated Catalog*. New York: Garland, 1982. FU, HU, SU.

133 Brown, Sandy. *The McJazz Manuscripts: A Collection of Writings of Sandy Brown*. Comp. David Binns. Boston: Faber and Faber, 1979. JS.

134 Brown, William Wells, ed. *The Anti-Slavery Harp: A Collection of Songs for Anti-Slavery Meetings*. Boston: Bela Marsh, 1848. FU, HU, LU.

135 ———, ed. *The Anti-Slavery Harp: A Collection of Songs for Anti-Slavery Meetings*. Philadelphia: Rhistoric Publications, 1969. FU.

136 Browning, Alice C., ed. *Lionel Hampton's Swing Book*. Chicago: Negro Story Press, 1946. LH.

137 Brunn, Harry O. *The Story of the Original Dixieland Jazz Band*. Baton Rouge: Louisiana State University Press, 1960. SU.

138 Bryan, Ashley, ed. *Walk Together Children: Black American Spirituals*. New York: Atheneumn, 1974. FU, HU.

139 Bryant, Lawrence C. *A Study of Music Programs in Private Negro Colleges*. Orangeburg, South Carolina: South Carolina State College, 1962. AU, HU.

140 Budds, Michael J. *Jazz in the Sixties: The Expansion of Musical Resources and Techniques*. Iowa City: University of Iowa Press, 1978. HU.

141 Buerkle, Jack V. and Danny Baker. *Bourbon Street Black: The New Orleans Black Jazzman*. New York: Oxford University Press, 1973. FU, HI, HU, JS, LU, SC, SS, SU, TI, XU.

142 Burleigh, Harry T., ed. *Negro Minstrel Melodies*. New York: G. Schirmer, 1909. HU, SC, XU.

143 ———, ed. *Plantation Melodies Old and New*. New York: G, Schirmer, 1901. HU.

144 Burley, Dan. *Dan Burley's Handbook of Jazz*. N.p.: N.pub., 1944. LH.

145 ———. *Diggeth Thou?* Chicago: Burley, Cross, 1959. LH.

146 Burnett, James. *Bix Beiderbecke*. London: Cassell, 1959. HU.

147 ———. *Bix Beiderbecke*. New York: A. S. Barnes, 1961. TI.

148 Butcher, Veda E. et al. *Development of Materials for a One Year Course in African Music for the General Undergraduate Student.* Washington: Office of Education, 1970. XU.

149 Cable, George W. *The Dance in Place Congo & Creole Slave Songs.* New Orleans: Faruk von Turk, 1974. XU.

150 Cain, George. *Blueschild.* New York: Dell Publishing Co., 1972. HU.

151 ———. *Blueschild Baby.* New York: McGraw-Hill, 1970. AU, HU.

152 Calloway, Cab and Bryant Rollins. *Of Minnie the Moocher and Me.* New York: Thomas Y. Crowell, 1976. FU, HU, LU, SC, TI.

153 Camara, Sory. *Gens de la Parole: Essai sur la Condition et le Rôle des Griots dans la Société Malinké.* Paris: Mouton, 1976. HU.

154 Carawan, Guy and Candie Carawan, eds. *Freedom is a Constant Struggle: Songs of the Freedom Movement, With Documentary Photographs.* New York: Oak Publications, 1968. LU.

155 ———, eds. *We Shall Overcome: Songs of the Southern Freedom Movement.* New York: Oak Publications, 1963. LH, LU, SC.

156 Carey, David and Albert J. McCarthy, comps. *The Directory of Recorded Jazz and Swing (Including Gospel and Blues Records),* vols. 1–3. London: Cassell, 1949–53. HU.

157 Charles, Philippe and Jean-Louis Comolli. *Free Jazz, Black Power.* Paris: Union Générale d'Editions, 1972. HU.

158 Carr, Ian. *Miles Davis: A Biography.* New York: William Morrow, 1982. FU, HU, JS, SC.

159 Carrington, John F. *Talking Drums of Africa.* London: Carey Kingsgate Press, 1949. HU, TI.

160 ———. *Talking Drums of Africa.* New York: Negro Universities Press, 1969. FU, HI, LU, SC.

161 Carter, Lawrence T. *Eubie Blake: Keys of Memory.* Detroit: Balamp, 1979. HU, SC, SU.

162 Case, Brian and Stan Britt, eds. *The Illustrated Encyclopedia of Jazz.* New York: Harmony Books, 1978. HU, LU, TI.

163 Casey, Mary E. D. "The Contributions of the Reverend James Cleveland to Gospel Music and Its Implications for Music Education." Thesis, Howard University, 1980. HU.

164 Castilla, Willenham C. "The Life and Music of Charles Price Jones Revisited." Thesis, Fisk University, 1974. FU.

165 *Catalog of the E. Azalia Hackley Memorial Collection of Negro Music, Dance, and Drama.* Boston: G. K. Hall, 1979. HU.

166 *Catalog of Music, from the House of Handy.* New York: Handy Brothers Music Co., 1948. AU, HU.

167 *A Catalog of Phonorecordings of Music and Oral Data Held by the Archives of Traditional Music.* [Bloomington: Archives of Traditional Music, Folklore Institute, Indiana University]. Boston: G. K. Hall, 1975. HU.

168 Cazort, Jean E. and Constance T. Hobson. *Born to Play: The Life and Career of Hazel Harrison.* Westport, Connecticut: Greenwood Press, 1983. FU, JS.

169 Cerulli, Dom et al. *The Jazz Word.* New York: Ballantine Books, 1960. HU, TI.

170 Chambers, Herbert A., ed. *The Treasury of Negro Spirituals.* London: Blandford Press, 1953. HU.

171 ———, ed. *The Treasury of Negro Spirituals.* New York: Emerson Books, 1963. FU, HU, LU, SC.

172 Chambers, Jack. *Milestones.* Toronto: University of Toronto Press, 1983. LU.

173 Charles, Norman. "Social Values in American Popular Songs (1890–1950)." Dissertation, University of Pennsylvania, Philadelphia, 1958. LU, SS.

174 Charles, Ray and David Ritz. *Brother Ray: Ray Charles' Own Story.* New York: Dial Press, 1978. AU, FU, HU, LU, SC, SU.

175 ———. *Brother Ray: Ray Charles' Own Story.* New York: Warner Books, 1978. TI.

176 Charters, Ann, ed. *The Ragtime Songbook: Songs of the Ragtime Era by Scott Joplin, Hughie Cannon, Ben Harney, Will Marion Cook, Alex Rogers and Others.* New York: Oak Publications, 1965. HU.

177 Charters, Samuel Barclay. *The Bluesmen: The Story and the Music of the Men Who Made the Blues.* New York: Oak Publications, 1967. AU, HU, LU (1977), SC, SS, TI.

178 ———. *The Country Blues.* New York: Rinehart, 1959. HU, LH, TI.

179 ———. *The Country Blues.* London: Michael Joseph, 1960. LU.

180 ———. *Jazz, New Orleans, 1885–1957: An Index to the Negro Musicians of New Orleans.* Belleville, New Jersey: Walter C. Allen, 1958. HU, LH.

181   ———. *Jazz, New Orleans, 1885–1963: An Index to the Negro Musicians of New Orleans*. New York: Oak Publications, 1963. HI, JS, TI.

182   ———. *Jazz, New Orleans, 1885–1963: An Index to the Negro Musicians of New Orleans*. New York: Da Capo, 1983. FU, HU, SU.

183   ———. *The Legacy of the Blues: A Glimpse into the Art and the Lives of Twelve Great Bluesmen*. New York: Da Capo, 1977. HU, JS, SU.

184   ———. *The Poetry of the Blues*. New York: Oak Publications, 1963. LH.

185   ———. *The Roots of the Blues: An African Search*. Boston: M. Boyars, 1981. HU, JS, LU.

186   ———. *The Roots of the Blues: An African Search*. New York: Putnam, 1982. TI.

187   ———. *Sweet as the Showers of Rain*. New York: Oak Publications, 1977. HU.

188   ——— and Leonard Kunstadt. *Jazz: A History of the New York Scene*. Garden City, New York: Doubleday, 1962. HU, TI, XU.

189   ———. *Jazz: A History of the New York Scene*. New York: Da Capo, 1981. FU.

190   Chauvet, Stephen. *Musique Negrè*. Paris: Société d'Editions Géographiques, Maritimes et Coloniales, 1929. AU, HI, HU, TI, XU.

191   Chernoff, John M. *African Rhythm and African Sensibility: Aesthetics and Social Action in African Musical Idioms*. Chicago: University of Chicago Press, 1979. HU, SC.

192   Chilton, John. *Billie's Blues: A Survey of Billie Holiday's Career, 1933–1959*. New York: Stein and Day, 1975. FU, JS, LU, SC.

193   ———. *Who's Who of Jazz: Storyville to Swing Street*. Philadelphia: Chilton Book Co., 1972. HU, TI.

194   Christy, Edwin P. *Christy's Plantation Melodies*. Philadelphia: J. Fischer, 1851. NC.

195   Claghorn, Charles E. *Biographical Dictionary of Jazz*. Englewood Cliffs, New Jersey: Prentice-Hall, 1982. HU, JS.

196   Clark, Edgar R., comp. *Moment Musical: Ten Selected Newspaper Articles*. Fort Valley, Georgia: Department of Music, Fort Valley State College, 1940. AU, FU.

197   Clark, Francis A. *The Black Music Master: A Facinating but Truthful Setting Forth of Facts, Giving Indisputable Evidence that the Primitive*

Black Peoples were the First Natural Musicians! Who, in Unconscious Obedience to Great Natural Laws within Them, Did Crudely and Awkwardly, but None the Less Certainly Give to the World, the Earliest Practical Demonstration of Making Music! Philadelphia: F. A. Clark, 1923. HU.

198 Clark, George W. *The Liberty Minstrel*. New York: Leavitt and Alden, 1845. HU.

199 Clarke, Bonna M. P., ed. *A Collection of Negro Spirituals for Mixed Voices*. New York: Handy Brothers Music Co. 1939. XU.

200 Clarke, Sebastian. *Jah Music: The Evolution of the Popular Jamaican Song*. London: Heinemann Educational Publications, 1980. HU (1981), LU.

201 Closson, David L. "One Life in Black Music: An Ethnography of a Black Jazz Musician." Dissertation, University of Pennsylvania, Philadelphia, 1980. LU.

202 Cohen, Lily Y. *Lost Spirituals*. New York: Walter Neale, 1928. AU, HU, NC, SU, XU.

203 ———. *Lost Spirituals*. Freeport, New York: Books for Libraries Press, 1972. SS.

204 Cohen, Norm. *Long Steel Rail: The Railroad in American Folksong*. Urbana: University of Illinois Press, 1981. FU.

205 Cole, Bill. *John Coltrane*. New York: Schirmer Books, 1976. FU, HU, SC, TI.

206 ———. *Miles Davis: A Musical Biography*. New York: William Morrow, 1974. FU, HU, HU (1980), LU, SC, TI.

207 Cole, Bob and J. Rosamond Johnson. *Cole and Johnson Vocal Folio: A Superior Collection of Quaint and Classic Negro Songs*. New York: Jos. W. Stern and Co., 1904. HU.

208 Cole, Maria. *Nat King Cole: An Intimate Biography*. New York: William Morrow, 1971. FU, LU.

209 Coleman, Satis N. B. and Adolph Bregman, eds. *Songs of American Folks*. Freeport, New York: Books for Libraries Press, 1968. FU, LU.

210 Coleridge-Taylor, Avril G. *The Heritage of Samuel Coleridge-Taylor*. London: Dobson, 1979. LU.

211 Coleridge-Taylor, Samuel. *Scenes from the Song of Hiawatha by Longfellow*. London: Novello, 1900. NC.

212   ———, ed. *Twenty-Four Negro Melodies*. Boston: Oliver Ditson; New York: C. H. Ditson, 1905. FU, HU, LU.

213   Collier, Graham, ed. *Cleo and John: A Biography of the Dankworths*. London: Quartet Books, 1976. JS.

214   Collier, James L. *The Great Jazz Artists*. New York: Four Winds Press, 1977. HU.

215   ———. *Inside Jazz*. London: Quartet Books, 1973. HU, JS.

216   ———. *Inside Jazz*. New York: Four Winds Press, 1973. HU.

217   ———. *Louis Armstrong, An American Genius*. New York: Oxford University Press, 1983. FU, JS, TI, XU.

218   ———. *The Making of Jazz: A Comprehensive History*. Boston: Houghton Mifflin, 1978. HU, JS.

219   Collins, Lee. *Oh, Didn't He Ramble: The Life Story of Lee Collins as Told to Mary Collins*. Urbana: University of Illinois Press, 1974. FU, HU, SC.

220   *Columbia Clef Series Records, Up to and Including February 1959*. London: E. M. I. Records, 1959. HU.

221   Como, Frank. *The Music A B C's of Black History*. Tannersville, Pennsylvania: Tandem Press, 1974. FU, HU, SC.

222   Condon, Eddie. *We Call It Music: A Generation of Jazz*. New York: H. Holt, 1947. HU.

223   ——— and Richard Gehman, eds. *Treasury of Jazz*. New York: Dial Press, HU, TI.

224   Cone, James H. *The Spirituals and the Blues: An Interpretation*. New York: Seabury Press, 1972. FU, HU, LU, SC, SS, TI, XU.

225   ———. *The Spirituals and the Blues: An Interpretation*. Westport, Connecticut: Greenwood Press, 1980. FU.

226   Cook, Bruce. *Listen to the Blues*. New York: C. Scribner's Sons, 1973. HU, JS, LU, SC, SS, XU.

227   Cornell, Jean G. *Louis Armstrong, Ambassador Satchmo*. New York: Dell Publishing Co., 1977.

228   Coryell, Julie and Laura Friedman. *Jazz-Rock Fusion: The People, the Music*. New York: Dell Publishing Co., 1978. HU, JS.

229   Courlander, Harold. *The Drum and the Hoe: Life and Lore of the Haitian People*. Berkeley: University of California Press, 1960. HU.

230 ———. *Haiti Singing*. Chapel Hill: University of North Carolina Press, 1939. FU, HU, LH, SC, SS, VS, XU.

231 ———. *Negro Folk Music, U.S.A.* New York: Columbia University Press, 1963. FU, HI, HU, LH, LU, SC (1966), SS, TI, XU.

232 ———. *Negro Songs from Alabama*. New York: Wenner-Gren Foundation for Anthropological Research, 1960. HU, LU.

233 ———. *Negro Songs from Alabama*. New York: Oak Publications, 1963. LU, SS.

234 Cox, John H., ed. *Folk-Songs of the South: Collected Under the Auspices of the West Virginia Folk-Lore Society*. Cambridge: Harvard University Press, 1925. HU.

235 Crite, Allan R. *Three Spirituals from Earth to Heaven*. Cambridge: Harvard University Press, 1944. XU.

236 ———. *Were You There When They Crucified My Lord: A Negro Spiritual in Illustrations*. Cambridge: Harvard University Press, 1936. VS, XU.

237 Cummins, Willis. *Calypso: Symphonies and Incest*. Toronto: Arawak Publishing House, 1974. HU.

238 Cuney-Hare, Maud. *Negro Musicians and Their Music*. Washington: The Associated Publishers, 1936. AU, FU, HI, HU, JS, LU, NC, TI, VS, XU.

239 ———. *Negro Musicians and Their Music*. New York: Da Capo, 1974. AU, FU, SS.

240 ———. *Six Creole Folk-Songs with Original Creole and Translated English Text*. New York: Carl Fischer, 1921. HU.

241 Curtis-Burlin, Natalie. *Hampton Series Negro Folk-Songs*. New York: G. Schirmer, 1918. VS, XU (4 vols. 1918–19).

242 ———. *Songs and Tales from the Dark Continent: Recorded from the Singing and Sayings of C. Kamba Simango and Madikane Cele*. New York: G. Schirmer, 1920. HU, NC, XU.

243 Cyovo, Katende. *Viola la Nouvelle Lune! Dansons!: Chansons Populaires de la Zone Gandajika (Rep. du Zaire)*. Bandundu, République du Zaire: GEEBA Publications, 1977. HU.

244 Dahl, Linda. *Stormy Weather: The Music and Lives of a Century of Jazzwomen*. New York: Pantheon Books, 1984. XU.

245 Dain, Bernice and David Nevin, eds. *The Blake Record: A Selective Discography of Afro-Americana on Audio Discs Held by the Audio/Visual*

Department, John M. Olin Library [Washington University]. St. Louis: Washington University Library Studies, 1973. SU.

246 Daly, John J. *A Song in His Heart*. Philadelphia: Winston, 1951. FU, LH, LU, SC, XU.

247 Damas, Leon G. *African Songs of Love, War, Grief, and Abuse*. Ibadan, Nigeria: Mbari Publications, 1961. LH, LU.

248 Dance, Stanley et al. *Jazz Era: The Forties*. London: MacGibbon and Kee, 1961. HU.

249 ———. *The World of Count Basie*. New York: C. Scribner's Sons, 1980. FU, JS, LU, TI.

250 ———. *The World of Duke Ellington*. New York: C. Scribner's Sons, 1970. FU, HU, LU, TI.

251 ———. *The World of Earl Hines*. New York: C. Scribner's Sons, 1977. FU, HU, JS, LU, SU, TI, XU.

252 ———. *The World of Swing*. New York: C. Scribner's Sons, 1974. HU, SC.

253 Dankworth, Avril. *Jazz: An Introduction to Its Musical Basis*. London: Oxford University Press, 1968, HU.

254 Dann, Hollis, ed. *Fifty-Eight Spirituals for Choral Use*. Boston: C. C. Birchard, 1924. TI.

255 ———. *Hollis Dann Song Series*. New York: American Book Co., 1935. SA.

256 Daughtry, Willia E. "Sissieretta Jones: A Study of the Negro's Contribution to Nineteenth Century American Concert and Theatrical Life." Dissertation, Syracuse University, 1967. HI.

257 Davenport, M. Marguerite. *Azalia: The Life of Madame E. Azalia Hackley*. Boston: Chapman and Grimes, 1947. FU (1949), HU, LU.

258 Davidson, Celia E. "Operas by Afro-American Composers: A Critical Survey and Analysis of Selected Works." Dissertation, Catholic University, 1967. LU.

259 Davidson, Frank C. "The Rise, Development, Decline and Influence of the American Minstrel Show." Dissertation, New York University, 1952. SS.

260 Davis, Arthur K., Jr. *Folk-Songs of Virginia: A Descriptive Index and Classification of Materials Collected Under the Auspices of the Virginia Folklore Society*. Durham, North Carolina: Duke University Press, 1949. HU.

261 Davis, Robert B. *An Introductory Survey of the Development of Music in the West on Tape.* Tuskegee, Alabama: Community Education Program, Tuskegee Institute, n.d. TI.

262 Davis, Stephen. *Reggae Bloodlines: In Search of the Music and Culture of Jamaica.* Garden City, New York: Doubleday, Anchor, 1977. FU, LU, SU.

263 DeCarava, Roy. *The Sound I Saw: The Jazz Photographs of Roy De-Carava, January 20 to March 20, 1983.* New York: Studio Museum in Harlem, 1983. LU.

264 Delaunay, Charles. *Hot Discography.* New York: Commodore Record Co., 1943. HU.

265 ———. *New Hot Discography: The Standard Directory of Recorded Jazz.* New York: Criterion, 1948. HU.

266 De Lerma, Dominique-René. *Bibliography of Black Music*, Vols. 1–4. Westport, Connecticut: Greenwood Press, 1981–84. FU, HI, HU, JS, LU.

267 ———, ed. *Black Music in Our Culture: Curriculum Ideas on the Subjects, Materials and Problems.* Kent, Ohio: Kent State University Press, 1970. AU, FU, HI, HU, LU, SC, SS, TI, XU.

268 ———. *A Discography of Concert Music by Black Composers.* Minneapolis: The AAMOA Press, 1973. LU.

269 ———, ed. *Explorations in Black Music: Black Music Center Seminar.* Bloomington: The Black Music Center, Indiana University. 1971. FU, LU.

270 ———, ed. *Reflections on Afro-American Music.* Kent, Ohio: Kent State University Press, 1973. FU, HU, LU, SC, SS, XU.

271 DeLong, Thomas A. *Pops: Paul Whiteman, King of Jazz.* Piscataway, New Jersey: New Century Publishers, 1983. JS.

272 Demervé, Etienne C. E. M. *Histoire de la Musique en Haïti.* Port-au-Prince, Haiti: Imprimerie des Antilles, 1968. HU.

273 Deng, Francis M. *The Dinka Songs.* Washington: Embassy of the Democratic Republic of the Sudan, [197?]. HU.

274 Delphin, Wilfred J. "A Comparative Analysis of Two Sonatas by George Walker: Sonata No. 1 and Sonata No. 2." Dissertation, University of Southern Mississippi, 1976. FU.

275 Denis, Lorimer and Emmanuel C. Paul. *Essai d'Organographie Haïtienne,* Port-au-Prince: Imprimerie V. Valcin, 1947. HU.

276   Dennison, Sam. *Scandalize My Name: Black Imagery in American Popular Music*. New York: Garland, 1982. FU, HU, LU, SC, SU, XU.

277   Dennison, Tim. *The American Negro and His Amazing Music*. New York: Vantage, 1963. HU, SC, SS, TI.

278   Derek, Jewell. *Duke: A Portrait of Duke Ellington*. New York: Norton, 1977. AU.

279   DeToledano, Ralph. *Frontiers of Jazz*. New York: O. Durrell, 1947. AU, TI.

280   Dett, Robert Nathaniel. *The Collected Piano Works of R. Nathaniel Dett*. Intro., Dominique-René de Lerma and Vivian Flagg McBrier. Evanston, Illinois: Summy-Birchard, 1973. FU, SC.

281   ————, ed. *The Dett Collection of Negro Spirituals*, 4 vols. Chicago: Hall and McCreary, 1936. HU, TI.

282   ————, ed. *Negro Spirituals*. London: Blandford, 1959. XU.

283   ————, ed. *Religious Folk-Songs of the Negro as Sung at Hampton Institute*. Hampton, Virginia: Hampton Institute Press, 1927. LH, LU, SA, XU.

284   ————, ed. *Religious Folk-Songs of the Negro as Sung at Hampton Institute*. New York: AMS Press, 1972. FU, SC.

285   DeVeaux, Alexis. *Don't Explain: A Song of Billie Holiday*. New York: Harper and Row, 1980. LU, SS, SU.

286   Dexter, Dave, Jr. *Jazz Cavalcade: The Inside Story of Jazz*. New York: Criterion, 1946. FU, HU, TI.

287   ————. *The Jazz Story, From the '90s to the '60s*. Englewood Cliffs, New Jersey: Prentice-Hall, 1964. HU.

288   Dietz, Elisabeth H. W. and Michael B. Olatunji. *Musical Instruments of Africa: Their Nature, Use, and Place in the Life of a Deeply Musical People*. New York: John Day, 1965. FU, HI, HU, LU, XU.

289   Diton, Carl, ed. *Thirty-Six South Carolina Spirituals*. New York: G. Schirmer, 1928. AU, HU.

290   Dixon, Christa K. *Negro Spirituals: From Bible to Folk Song*. Philadelphia: Fortress Press, 1976. HU.

291   Dixon, Robert M. W. and John Godrich. *Recording the Blues*. New York: Stein and Day, 1970. HU, LU.

292   Djedje, Jacqueline C. *American Black Spiritual and Gospel Songs from Southwest Georgia: A Comparative Study*. Los Angeles: Center for Afro-American Studies, 1978. HU.

293 Dobrin, Arnold. *Voices of Joy, Voices of Freedom: Ethel Waters, Sammy Davis, Jr., Marian Anderson, Paul Robeson, Lena Horne*. New York: Coward, McCann and Geoghegan, 1972. FU, HU, LU.

294 Docks, L. R. *1915–1965 American Premium Record Guide: Identification and Values 78's, 45's and LP's*. San Antonio, Texas: L. R. Docks, 1980. HU.

295 Dodds, Warren. *The Baby Dodds Story as Told to Larry Gara*. Los Angeles: Contemporary Press, 1959. TI.

296 Dragonwagon, Crescent. *Stevie Wonder*. New York: Flash Books, 1977. HU, SC.

297 Driggs, Frank and Harris Lewine. *Black Beauty, White Heat: A Pictorial History of Classic Jazz, 1920–1950*. New York: William Morrow, 1982. JS, TI.

298 Dunson, Josh. *Freedom in the Air: Song Movements of the Sixties*. New York: International Publishers, 1965. HU, LH.

299 Eaton, Jeanette. *Trumpeter's Tale: The Story of Young Louis Armstrong*. New York: William Morrow, 1965. LH, SU.

300 Edet, Edna S., ed. *The Griot Sings: Songs from the Black World*. New York: Medgar Evers College Press, 1978. HU, SC.

301 Edrei, Mary J., ed. *The Magic of Michael Jackson*. Cresskill, New Jersey: Starbooks, 1984. LU.

302 Edwards, Audrey and Gary Wohl. *The Picture Life of Stevie Wonder*. New York: F. Watts, 1977. HU, SC.

303 Edwards, Charles L. *Bahama Songs and Stories: A Contribution to Folk-Lore*. Boston: Houghton Mifflin, 1895. NC.

304 ———. *Bahama Songs and Stories: A Contribution to Folk-Lore*. New York: G. E. Stechert, 1942. XU.

305 Ellington, Duke. *The Great Music of Duke Ellington*. Melville, New York: Belwin Mills, 1973. HU, SU.

306 ———. *Music is My Mistress*. Garden City, New York: Doubleday, 1973. FU, HI, HU, JS, LU, SU, TI.

307 ———. *Music is My Mistress*. New York: Da Capo, 1976. HU, LU.

308 Ellington, Mercer. *Duke Ellington in Person: An Intimate Memoir*. Boston: Houghton Mifflin, 1978. AU, FU, HU, JS, LU, SC, SU, TI.

309 Emerson, William C. *Stories and Spirituals of the Negro Slave*. Boston: Richard G. Badger, 1930. HU, VS.

310   Ennett, Dorothy M. "An Analysis and Comparison of Selected Piano Sonatas by Three Contemporary Black Composers: George Walker, Howard Swanson, and Roque Cordero." Dissertation, New York University, 1973. FU.

311   Eno-Belinga, Martin S. *Ballades et Chansons Camerounaises*. Yaoundé, Cameroon: Editions CLE, 1974. HU.

312   ———. *Découverte des Chantefables, Beti-Bulu-Fang du Cameroun*. Paris: Klincksieck, 1970. HU.

313   ———. *Littérature et Musique Populaires en Afrique Noire*. Paris: Editions Cujas, 1965. HU.

314   Epstein, Dena J. *Sinful Tunes and Spirituals: Black Folk Music to the Civil War*. Urbana: University of Illinois Press, 1977. AU, FU, HU, LU, SC, SS, SU, TI, XU.

315   Erlich, Lillian. *What Jazz is All About*. New York: J. Messner, 1962. HU.

316   *Esquire's Jazz Book*. New York: A. S. Barnes, 1944. FU, HI, HU, TI, VS.

317   *Esquire's 1945 Jazz Book*. New York: A. S. Barnes. 1945. HU.

318   *Esquire's World of Jazz*. New York: Grossett and Dunlap, 1962. HU, XU.

319   *Esquire's World of Jazz*. New York: Thomas Y. Crowell, 1975. JS.

320   Evans, David. *Big Road Blues: Tradition and Creativity in the Folk Blues*. Berkeley: University of California Press, 1982. HU, SC.

321   Ewen, David. *All the Years of American Popular Music*. Englewood Cliffs, New Jersey: Prentice-Hall, 1977. FU.

322   ———. *Men of Popular Music*. Chicago: Ziff Davis, 1944, HI.

323   Fahey, John A. *Charley Patton*. London: Studio Vista, 1970. HU.

324   Feather, Leonard G. *The Book of Jazz*. New York: Meridian Books, 1960. HU.

325   ———. *The Book of Jazz: A Guide to the Entire Field*. New York: Horizon Press, 1957. AU, LH.

326   ———. *The Book of Jazz, From Then till Now: A Guide to the Entire Field*. New York: Bonanza Books, 1965. HU, SU.

327   ———, ed. *The Encyclopedia of Jazz*. New York: Horizon Press, 1955. HU, TI.

328 ———, ed. *The Encyclopedia of Jazz in the Sixties*. New York: Horizon Press, 1966. FU, HU.

329 ———. *The Encyclopedia Yearbook of Jazz*. New York: Horizon Press, 1956. HU.

330 ———. *From Satchmo to Miles*. New York: Stein and Day, 1972. FU, HU, SC, TI.

331 ———. *Inside Be-bop*. New York: J. J. Robbins, 1949. HU, TI.

332 ———. *Inside Jazz*. New York: Da Capo, 1977. XU.

333 ———. *The New Yearbook of Jazz*. New York: Horizon Press, 1958. AU.

334 ———. *The Passion for Jazz*. New York: Horizon Press, 1980. HU, JS.

335 ———. *The Pleasures of Jazz: Leading Performers on Their Lives, Their Music, Their Contemporaries*. New York: Horizon Press, 1976. HU, LU, SC.

336 ———, ed. *[Two Hundred] 200 Omnibus of Jazz: A Unique Collection of Jazz Themes by the World's Greatest Jazz Instrumentalists and Artists*. N.p.: Hansen House, 1975. HU.

337 ——— and Ira Gitler. *The Encyclopedia of Jazz in the Seventies*. New York: Horizon Press, 1976. FU, HU.

338 Fenner, Thomas P., Frederic G. Rathbun, and Bessie Cleaveland, eds. *Cabin and Plantation Songs as Sung by the Hampton Students*. New York: G. P. Putnam's Sons, 1890. VS (1901), XU.

339 Fenner. Thomas P., ed. *Religious Folk Songs of the Negroes Sung on the Plantations*. Hampton, Virginia: Hampton Institute Press, 1909. LU, LU (1920), NC, VS.

340 ———, ed. *Religious Folk Songs of the Negroes Sung on the Plantations*. New York: AMS Press, 1973. SC.

341 Fernández, Fernando Ortiz. *La Africanía de la Música Folklórica de Cuba*. Habana, Cuba: Dirección de Cultura del Ministerio de Educación, 1950. HU, TI.

342 ———. *Los Instrumentos de la Música Afrocubana*. Habana, Cuba: Dirección de Cultura del Ministerio de Educación, 1952. HU.

343 Fernett, Gene. *Swing Out: Great Negro Dance Bands*. Midland, Michigan: Pendell Publishing Co., 1970. FU, HU, LU, SS.

344 Ferris, William R., Jr. *Blues from the Delta*. London: Studio Vista, 1970. HU, JS.

345   ———. *Blues from the Delta*. New York: Anchor, Doubleday, 1978.
       AU, FU, HU, JS, XU (1979).

346   ———. *Blues from the Delta*. New York: Da Capo, 1984. SU.

347   ———. *Mississippi Black Folklore: A Research Bibliography and Dis-
       cography*. Hattiesburg: University and College Press of Mississippi, 1971.
       AU, HU, TI.

348   Finklestein, Sidney W. *Jazz: A People's Music*. New York: Citadel Press,
       1948. AU, FU, HU, LH, LU, TI.

349   ———. *Jazz: A People's Music*. New York: Da Capo, 1975. AU, FU,
       HU.

350   Fisher, Miles Mark. *Negro Slave Songs in the United States*. Ithaca, New
       York: Cornell University Press (for the American Historical Association),
       1953. FU, LU, XU.

351   ———. *Negro Slave Songs in the United States*. New York: Citadel Press,
       1963. SC.

352   ———. *Negro Slave Songs in the United States*. New York: Russell and
       Russell, 1968. HU, JS, LU, SC, SS, SU, TI.

353   Fischer, Williams Arms, ed. *Seventy Negro Spirituals*. Boston: AMS
       Press, 1974. SC.

354   Flender, Harold. *Paris Blues*. New York: Ballantine Books, 1957. AU,
       TI.

355   Fléouter, Claude. *La Mémoire du Peuple Noir*. Paris: A. Michel, 1979.
       HU.

356   Fletcher, Tom. *100 Years of the Negro in Show Business: The Tom Fletcher
       Story*. New York: Burdge, 1954. FU, JS, LU.

357   ———. *100 Years of the Negro in Show Business: The Tom Fletcher
       Story*. New York: Da Capo, 1984. SS, SU.

358   Floyd, Samuel A. and Marsha J. Reisser. *Black Music in the United
       States: An Annotated Bibliography of Selected Reference and Research
       Materials*. Millwood, New York: Kraus International, 1983. FU, HU,
       JS, LU (1984), TI, XU.

359   *Folk Songs to Sing*. [Richmond?]: Virginia Writers Project, Virginia
       State Board of Education, 1942. VS.

360   Foster, Pops [George M.]. *Pops Foster: An Autobiography of a New
       Orleans Jazzman as Told to Tom Stoddard*. Berkeley: University of Cal-
       ifornia Press, 1971. HU, LU, SC.

361 Foster, Stephen C. *Old Folks at Home: "Way Down Upon the Swanee Ribber."* Boston: Ticknor, 1889. XU.

362 Foster, William P. *Band Pagentry: A Guide for the Marching Band.* Winona, Minnesota: Hal Leonard, 1968. SS.

363 Fox, Charles. *Fats Waller.* London: Cassell, 1960. HU, LH.

364 ———. *Fats Waller.* New York: A. S. Barnes, 1961. HU, SU, TI.

365 ———. *The Jazz Scene.* London: Hamlyn, 1972. HU.

366 ———, Peter Gammond, Alun Morgan, and Alexis Korner. *Jazz On Record: A Critical Guide.* Westport, Connecticut: Greenwood Press, 1978. FU, HU.

367 Fox, Ted. *Showtime at the Apollo.* New York: Holt, Rinehart and Winston, 1983. HU.

368 Francis, André. *Jazz.* New York: Grove Press, 1960. HU, TI.

369 *The Free Soil Minstrel.* New York: Martyn and Ely, 1848. NC.

370 Frey, Hugo. *A Collection of 25 Selected Famous Negro Spirituals.* New York: Robbins-Engel, 1924. TI.

371 Friedel, L. M. *The Bible and the Negro Spirituals.* Bay St. Louis, Mississippi: St. Augustine Seminary, 1947. XU.

372 Friedman, Carol. *A Moment's Notice: Portraits of American Jazz Musicians.* New York: Schirmer Books, 1983. FU.

373 Furguson, Norma Jean. "A Profile Study of the Learning Experiences of Ten Professional Jazz Musicians Currently Performing in the Washington, D.C. Area." Thesis, Howard University, 1977. HU.

374 Futrell, Jon et al, eds. *The Illustrated Encyclopedia of Black Music.* New York: Harmony Books, 1982. FU, HU, JS, LU, TI, XU.

375 Gammond, Peter, ed. *Duke Ellington: His Life and Music.* London: Roy Publishers, 1958. LU, SC.

376 ———, ed. *Duke Ellington: His Life and Music.* New York: Da Capo, 1977. FU.

377 ———. *Fourteen Miles on a Clear Night: An Irreverent, Skeptical, Affectionate Book About Jazz Records.* Westport, Connecticut: Greenwood Press, 1978. HU.

378 ———. *Scott Joplin and the Ragtime Era.* New York: St. Martin's Press, 1975. FU, SC.

379 Garcia, William B. "The Life and Choral Music of John Wesley Work (1901–1967)." Dissertation, University of Iowa, Iowa City, 1973. FU.

380 Garland, Phyl. *The Sound of Soul*. Chicago: H. Regnery Co., 1969. FU, HI, HU, LU, SS, TI.

381 Garnett, Thomas C. "A Comparative Study of Ancient Hebrew and American Negro Folk–Songs." Thesis, Howard University, 1937. HU.

382 Garon, Paul. *Blues and the Poetic Spirit*. New York: Da Capo, 1978. FU, HU, SU.

383 Garvin, Richard M. and Edmond G. Addeo. *The Midnight Special: The Legend of Leadbelly*. New York: B. Geis Associates, 1971. FU, HU, LU, SC.

384 Garwood, Donald. *Masters of Instrumental Blues Guitar*. New York: Oak Publications, 1968. SU.

385 Gaskin, L. J. P. *A Select Bibliography of Music in Africa: Compiled at the International African Institute*. London: [International African Institute?], 1965. HU, TI.

386 Gellert, Lawrence, comp. *"Me and My Captain" (Chain Gangs): Negro Songs of Protest from the Collection of Lawrence Gellert*. Arr. [Voice and Piano] Lan Adomian. New York: Hours Press, 1939. FU, HU, LH, XU.

387 ——, comp. *Negro Songs of Protest, Collected by Lawrence Gellert*. Arr. [Voice and Piano] Elie Siegmeister. New York: American Music League, 1936. HU.

388 Geoffrey, César. *Dix Negro Spirituals*. Paris: Bordas, 1946. XU.

389 George, Don R. *Sweet Man, The Real Duke Ellington*. New York: Putnam, 1981. HU.

390 George, Nelson. *The Michael Jackson Story*. New York: Dell Publishing Co., 1984. SS.

391 George, Zelma Watson. "A Guide to Negro Music: An Annotated Bibliography of Negro Folk Music, and Art Music by Negro Composers or Based on Negro Thematic Material." Dissertation, New York University, 1953. HU, LU, SS, TI.

392 Gibbs, John A. *The Unit Steel Band*. Hicksville, New York: Exposition Press, 1978. HU.

393 Giddins, Gary. *Riding on a Blue Note: Jazz and American Pop*. New York: Oxford University Press, 1981. HU, LU.

394 Gillespie, Dizzy. *To Be, Or Not...To Bop: Memoirs, Dizzy Gillespie*. Garden Gity, New York: Doubleday, 1979. FU, HU, JS, LU, SU.

395   Gillett, Charlie. *The Sound of the City: The Rise of Rock and Roll*. New York: Outerbridge and Dienstfrey, 1970. LU.

396   Gillis, Frank and Alan P. Merriam. *Ethnomusicology and Folk Music: An International Bibliography of Dissertations and Theses*. Middleton, Connecticut: Wesleyan University Press (for the Society for Ethnomusicology), 1966. FU.

397   Gitler, Ira. *Jazz Masters of the Forties*. New York: Macmillan, 1966. HU, SC, TI.

398   ———. *Jazz Masters of the Forties*. New York: Da Capo, 1983. FU.

399   Glass, Paul, ed. *Songs and Stories of Afro-Americans*. New York: Grossett and Dunlap, 1971. FU.

400   Glazer, Tom, comp. *Songs of Peace, Freedom, and Protest*. New York: D. McKay Co., 1970. FU, LU, SC.

401   Gleason, Ralph J. *Celebrating the Duke, and Louis, Bessie, Billie, Bird, Carmen, Miles, Dizzy, and Other Heroes*. Boston: Little, Brown, 1975. AU, FU, HU, JS, SS, TI.

402   ———. *Celebrating the Duke, and Louis, Bessie, Billie, Bird, Carmen, Miles, Dizzy, and Other Heroes*. New York: Dell Publishing Co., 1976. SC.

403   ———, ed. *Jam Session: An Anthology of Jazz*. New York: Putnam, 1958. HU, TI.

404   *A Glimmer of Their Own Beauty: Black Sounds of the Twenties*. Washington: National Portrait Gallery of the Smithsonian Institute, 1971. AU, FU.

405   Glover, Tony. *Blues Harp Songbook*. New York: Oak Publications, 1975. HU.

406   Goddard, Chris. *Jazz Away from Home*. New York: Paddington Press, 1979. JS.

407   Godrich, John and Robert M. W. Dixon. *Blues and Gospel Records, 1902–1942*. London: Storyville Publications, 1969. FU.

408   Goffin, Robert. *Aux Frontières du Jazz*. Paris: Editions du Sagittaire, 1932. HU.

409   ———. *Histoire du Jazz*. Montreal: Lucien Parizeau, 1945. HU.

410   ———. *Horn of Plenty: The Story of Louis Armstrong*. New York: Allen, Towne, and Heath, 1947. AU, HU, LH, LU, SC, TI.

411   ———. *Horn of Plenty: The Story of Louis Armstrong*. New York: Da Capo, 1977. FU, SU.

412 ———. *Horn of Plenty: The Story of Louis Armstrong*. Westport, Connecticut: Greenwood Press, 1978. HU.

413 ———. *Jazz, From the Congo to the Metropolitan*. Garden City, New York: Doubleday, Doran, 1944. HI, HU, LH (1945), LU, TI, XU.

414 ———. *Jazz, From the Congo to the Metropolitan*. New York: Da Capo, 1975. AU, FU.

415 Goines, Leonard. "Music and Music Education in Predominantly Negro Colleges and Universities: Offering a Four-Year Program of Music Study Terminating in a Degree." Dissertation, Columbia University, 1964. HU.

416 Gold, Robert S. *A Jazz Lexicon*. New York: Knopf, 1964. HU.

417 ———. *Jazz Talk: A Dictionary of the Colorful Language that has Emerged from America's Own Music*. Indianapolis: Bobbs–Merrill, 1975. JS.

418 Goldberg, Isaac. *Tin Pan Alley: A Chronicle of the American Popular Music Racket*. New York: John Day Co., 1930. AU, FU, HI, HU, NC.

419 Goldberg, Joe. *Jazz Masters of the Fifties*. New York: Macmillan, 1965. HU, SC, TI.

420 ———. *Jazz Masters of the Fifties*. New York: Da Capo, 1980. LU.

421 ———. *Jazz Masters of the Forties*. New York: Macmillan, 1966. TI.

422 Goldblatt, Burt. *Newport Jazz Festival: The Illustrated History*. New York: Dial Press, 1977. HU, JS, SC.

423 Goldstein, Richard. *Goldstein's Greatest Hits: A Book Mostly About Rock 'n' Roll*. Englewood Cliffs, New Jersey: Prentice-Hall, 1970. SS.

424 Gonzales, Babs. *I Paid My Dues: Good Times, No Bread*. East Orange, New Jersey: Expubidence Publishing Corp., 1967. HU.

425 Goreau, Laurraine R. *Just Mahalia Baby*. Waco, Texas: Word Books, 1975. FU, LU, SC.

426 Gottlieb, William P. *The Golden Age of Jazz: On-Location Portraits, Words and Pictures of More than 200 Outstanding Musicians from the Late '30s through the '40s*. New York: Simon and Schuster, 1979. JS, LU, SC.

427 Gourse, Leslie. *Louis' Children: American Jazz Singers*. New York: William Morrow, 1984. JS.

428 Graham, Alberta P. *Strike Up the Band!: Bandleaders of Today*. New York: Nelson, 1949. HU.

429 Graham, Shirley. *Paul Robeson, Citizen of the World*. New York: J. Messner, 1946. FU, LH.

430 Grant, Harrison. "The Broadway Revue." Thesis, Howard University, 1973. HU.

431 Green, Archie. *Only a Miner: Studies in Recorded Coal-Mining Songs*. Urbana: University of Illinois Press, 1972. FU.

432 Green, Benny. *Drums in My Ears*. London: Davis-Poynter, 1973. HU.

433 ———. *Drums in My Ears*. New York: Horizon, 1973. JS.

434 Green, Jeffrey P. *Edmund Thornton Jenkins: The Life and Times of an American Black Composer, 1894–1926*. Westport, Connecticut: Greenwood Press, 1982. JS.

435 Green, Mildred D. *Black Women Composers: A Genesis*. Boston: Twayne Publishers, 1983. JS, LU, XU.

436 Gregg, Dianne and Carol Comer, eds. *National Directory of Female Jazz Performers*. Kansas City, Missouri: Women's Jazz Festival, 1980. HU.

437 Gridley, Mark C. *Jazz Styles*. Englewood Cliffs, New Jersey: Prentice-Hall, 1978. FU, HU, JS, LU.

438 Grissom, Mary A. *The Negro Sings a New Heaven*. Chapel Hill: University of North Carolina Press, 1930. HU, LU, SU.

439 ———. *The Negro Sings a New Heaven*. Durham, North Carolina: Seeman Printery, 1930. FU.

440 ———. *The Negro Sings a New Heaven*. New York: Dover Publications, 1969. HU, LU, SC.

441 Groia, Philip. *They All Sang on the Corner: New York City's Rhythm and Blues Vocal Groups of the 1950's*. Setauket, New York: Edmond Publishing Co., 1973. HI (1974), HU.

442 Grossman, Stefan. *Delta Blues Guitar*. New York: Oak Publications, 1969. JS.

443 Grossman, William L. and Jack W. Farrell. *The Heart of Jazz*. New York: New York University Press, 1956. HU, LU, TI.

444 Guralnick, Peter. *Feel Like Going Home: Portraits in Blues and Rock 'n' Roll*. New York: Outerbridge and Dienstfrey, 1971. AU, SC.

445 ———. *The Listener's Guide to the Blues*. N.p.: Facts on File, 1982. HU, JS.

446 Gutman, Bill. *Duke: The Musical Life of Duke Ellington*. New York: Random House, 1977. AU, JS.

447   Haas, Robert B., ed. *William Grant Still and the Fusion of Cultures in American Music.* Los Angeles: Black Sparrow, 1972. LU, SC, SU, XU.

448   Hadley, Richard T. "The Published Choral Music of Ulysses Simpson Kay, 1943–1968." Dissertation, University of Iowa, 1972. FU.

449   Hadlock, Richard. *Jazz Masters of the Twenties.* New York: Macmillan, 1965. HU, LU, SC, TI.

450   Hamlin, Lydia. *Musical Culture in Negro Schools and Colleges.* N.p.: M.T.N.A. Proceedings, 1916. AU.

451   Hammond, John. *John Hammond on Record: An Autobiography.* New York: Ridge Press, 1977. HU, JS.

452   Hampton, Lionel. *Lionel Hampton's Swing Book.* Ed. Alice C. Browning. Chicago: Lionel Hampton and Negro Story Press, 1946. TI.

453   Handy, D. Antoinette. *Black Music: Opinions and Reviews.* Ettrick, Virginia: BM & M, 1974. FU, HU, VS.

454   ———. *Black Women in American Bands and Orchestras.* Metuchen, New Jersey: Scarecrow, 1981. FU, JS, LU, SC, SU, VS, XU.

455   Handy, William Christopher, ed. *Blues; An Anthology: Complete Words and Music of 53 Great Songs.* New York: Albert and Charles Boni, 1926. HU, LU, VS.

456   ———, ed. *Blues; An Anthology: Complete Words and Music of 53 Great Songs.* New York: Macmillan, 1972. FU, HU, SC, SS, TI.

457   ———. *Father of the Blues: An Autobiography.* Ed. Arna Bontemps. New York: Macmillan, 1941. AU, HI, HU, LH, SU (1942), TI (1942).

458   ———. *Father of the Blues: An Autobiography.* Ed. Arna Bontemps. London: Sidgwick and Jackson, 1957. LU.

459   ———. *Father of the Blues: An Autobiography.* Ed. Arna Bontemps. New York: Collier, 1970. SC.

460   ———. *Negro Authors and Composers of the United States.* New York: Handy Brothers Music Co., 1937. FU (1938), HU.

461   ———. *Negro Authors and Composers of the United States.* New York: AMS Press, 1976. HU, LU, SC, SS.

462   ———. *A Treasury of the Blues: Complete Words and Music of 67 Great Songs from Memphis Blues to the Present Day.* New York: Charles Boni, 1949. HI, HU, LH, LU, TI, XU.

463   ———, ed. *Unsung Americans Sung.* New York: Handy Brothers Music Co., 1944. LU, SS, SU, XU.

464 Hansen, Chadwick C. "The Ages of Jazz: A Study of Jazz in its Cultural Context." Dissertation, University of Minnesota, 1956. HU, LU.

465 Harlambos, Michael. *Right On: From Blues to Soul in Black America.* New York: Drake Publishers, 1975. AU, HU, LU, TI.

466 ———. *Right On: From Blues to Soul in Black America.* New York: Da Capo, 1979. FU, SS.

467 Harris, Carl G. "A Study of the Characteristic Stylistic Trends Found in the Choral Works of a Selected Group of Afro-American Composers and Arrangers." Dissertation, University of Missouri, Kansas City, 1973. FU.

468 Harris, Charles J. *Reminiscences of My Days with Roland Hayes.* Orangeburg, South Carolina: N.pub., 1944. FU, HI, HU, LH.

469 Harris, Joel C. *Uncle Remus and His Friends: Old Plantation Stories, Songs, and Ballads with Sketches of Negro Character.* Boston: Houghton, Mifflin, 1892. NC.

470 ———. *Uncle Remus, His Songs and His Sayings: The Folk-Lore of the Old Plantation.* New York: D. Appleton, 1890. NC, NC (1897).

471 Harris, Rex. *Jazz.* Baltimore: Penguin Books, 1952. HU, HU (1958), LH, TI.

472 ——— and Brian Rust. *Recorded Jazz: A Critical Guide.* Baltimore: Penguin Books, 1958. AU.

473 Harris, Sheldon. *Blues Who's Who: A Biographical Dictionary of Blues Singers.* New Rochelle, New York: Arlington House, 1979. FU, HU.

474 Harris, Tesfa. *The Politics of Caribbean Music.* N.p.: n.pub., n.d. HU.

475 Harrison, Max. *Charlie Parker.* London: Cassell, 1960. HU.

476 ———. *Charlie Parker.* New York: A. S. Barnes, 1961. HU, LU, TI.

477 ———. *A Jazz Retrospect.* New York: Crescendo, 1977. HU.

478 Hasegawa, Sam. *Stevie Wonder.* Mankata, Minnesota: Creative Education, 1975. SU.

479 Haskins, James. *The Cotton Club.* New York: Random House, 1977. AU, HU, JS, LU, SU, TI, VS.

480 ———. *I'm Gonna Make You Love Me: The Story of Diana Ross.* New York: Dial Press, 1980.

481 ———. *Nat King Cole.* New York: Stein and Day, 1984. LU.

482 ———. *The Story of Stevie Wonder.* New York: Lothrup and Shepard, 1976. FU, HU.

483 —— and Kathleen Benson. *Lena: A Personal and Professional Biography of Lena Horne.* New York: Stein and Day, 1984. FU, HU, JS, LU.

484 —— and Kathleen Benson. *Scott Joplin.* Garden City, New York: Doubleday, 1978. FU, HU, LU, SC.

485 Hatfield, Edwin Francis, comp. *Freedom's Lyre: Or, Psalms, Hymns, and Sacred Songs, for the Slave and His Friends.* New York: S. W. Benedict, 1840. FU, HU, NC.

486 ——, comp. *Freedom's Lyre: Or, Psalms, Hymns, and Sacred Songs, for the Slave and His Friends.* Miami: Mnemosyne Publishing Co., 1969. HU.

487 Hawes, Hampton and Don Asher. *Raise Up Off Me: A Portrait of Hampton Hawes.* New York: Da Capo, 1979. HU.

488 Hawkins, John D. *Daily Food in Negro Spirituals.* Henderson, North Carolina: J. D. Hawkins, 1943. HU.

489 Hayes, Laurence M. "The Music of Ulysses Kay, 1939–1963." Dissertation, University of Wisconsin, Madison, 1971. FU.

490 Hayes, Roland. *God Sings Thru Me.* New York: Guideposts Associates, n.d. HU.

491 ——. *My Songs: Aframerican Religious Folk Songs Arranged and Interpreted by Roland Hayes.* Boston: Little, Brown, 1948. HU, SS, XU.

492 Haywood, Charles. *James A. Bland: "Prince of the Colored Songwriters."* Flushing, New York: Flushing Historical Society, 1944. HU.

493 Heaton, Peter. *Jazz.* London: Burke, 1964. HU.

494 Hefele, Bernhard. *Jazz-Bibliographie: International Literature on Jazz, Blues, Spirituals, Gospel and Ragtime Music with a Selected List of Works on the Social and Cultural Background from the Beginning to the Present.* Munchen, New York: K. G. Saur, 1981. HU, JS, LU.

495 Heide, Karl G. Zur. *Deep South Piano: The Story of Little Brother Montgomery.* London: Studio Vista, 1970. HU.

496 Heilbut, Tony. *The Gospel Sound: Good News and Bad Times.* New York: Simon and Schuster, 1971. FU, HU, LU, SC, SS, TI.

497 ——. *The Gospel Sound: Good News and Bad Times.* Garden City, New York: Anchor Press, 1975. XU.

498 Helm, MacKinley. *Angel Mo' and Her Son, Roland Hayes.* Boston: Little, Brown, 1942. FU, LU (1945), SU (1943).

499 ———. *Angel Mo' and Her Son, Roland Hayes*. New York: Greenwood Press, 1969. SC.

500 Henderson, David. *Jimi Hendrix: Voodoo Child of the Aquarian Age*. Garden City, New York: Doubleday, 1978. LU, SU.

501 Hennessey, Thomas J. "From Jazz to Swing: Black Jazz Musicians and Their Music, 1917–1935." Dissertation, Northwestern University, 1973. HU.

502 Henry, Robert E. *The Jazz Ensemble: A Guide to Technique*. Englewood Cliffs, New Jersey: Prentice-Hall, 1981. JS.

503 Hentoff, Nat. *Jazz Is*. New York: Random House, 1976. HU, JS.

504 ———. *The Jazz Life*. New York: Dial Press, 1961. HU, SU, TI.

505 ———. *The Jazz Life*. New York: Da Capo, 1975. AU, FU, HU.

506 ———. *Journey Into Jazz*. New York: Coward-McCann, 1968. HU.

507 ——— and Albert J. McCarthy, eds. *Jazz: New Perspectives on the History of Jazz by Twelve of the World's Foremost Jazz Critics and Scholars*. New York: Rinehart, 1959. HU, LH, LU, TI.

508 Herskovits, Melville J. *Musica de Culto Afrobahiana Mendoza*. Argentina: Departamento de Musicologia, Universidad Nacional de Cuto, 1946. AU.

509 ——— and Frances S. Herskovits. *Suriname Folk-Lore: [With Transcriptions of Suriname Songs and Musicological Analysis by Dr. M. Kolinski]*. New York: Columbia University Press, 1936. HU.

510 Hildreth, John Wesley. "Keyboard Works of Selected Black Composers." Dissertation, Northwestern University, 1979. FU.

511 Hill, Edwin. *A Brief Sketch of the Career of Edwin Hill: As a Composer and Publisher of Music with Catalogue*. Philadelphia: A.M.E. Book Concern, n.d. HU.

512 Himes, Chester B. *The Real Cool Killers*. Chatham, New Jersey: The Chatham Bookseller, 1973. SU.

513 Hirshey, Gerri. *Nowhere to Run: The Story of Soul Music*. New York: Times Books, 1984. LU, XU.

514 Hoare, Ian et al, eds. *The Soul Book*. London: E. Methuen, 1975. HU.

515 Hobson, Anne. *In Old Alabama: Being the Chronicles of Miss Mouse, The Little Black Merchant [With Plantation Song Lyrics]*. New York: Doubleday, Page, 1903. NC.

516   Hobson, Wilder. *American Jazz Music*. New York: W. W. Norton, 1939. HU, SC.

517   ———. *American Jazz Music*. New York: Da Capo, 1976. JS, LU.

518   Hodeir, André. *Jazz: Its Evolution and Essence*. New York: Grove Press, 1956. FU, HU, TI.

519   ———. *Jazz: Its Evolution and Essence*. New York: Da Capo, 1975. LU.

520   ———. *Toward Jazz*. New York: Grove Press, 1962. HU.

521   ———. *The Worlds of Jazz*. New York: Grove Press, 1972. HU.

522   Hodes, Art and Chadwick Hansen, eds. *Selections from the Gutter: Jazz Portraits from "The Jazz Record."* Berkeley: University of California Press, 1977. HU, JS, SC.

523   Hodges, Fletcher. *Swanee Ribber and a Biographical Sketch of Stephen Collins Foster*. Orlando, Florida: Robinsons Inc., 1958. LU.

524   Holiday, Billie with William Dufty. *Lady Sings the Blues*. Garden City, New York: Doubleday, 1956. FU, HU.

525   ———. *Lady Sings the Blues*. New York: Popular Library, 1958. HU.

526   ———. *Lady Sings the Blues*. New York: Lancer Books, 1965. LH, LU (1972).

527   ———. *Lady Sings the Blues*. New York: Avon, 1976. HI, HU, SC.

528   Hopkins, Jerry. *Hit and Run: The Jimi Hendrix Story*. New York: Putnam, 1983. FU.

529   Hornbostel, Erich M. von. *African Negro Music*. London: Oxford University Press, 1928. AU, HI, HU.

530   Horne, Lena. *In Person, Lena Horne: As Told to Helen Artstein and Carlton Moss*. New York: Greenberg, 1950. AU, HI, HU, LH, TI.

531   ———with Richard Schickel. *Lena*. Garden City, New York: Doubleday, 1965. FU, HI, HU, LH, LU, SC, TI.

532   Horricks, Raymond. *Count Basie and His Orchestra: Its Music and Its Musicians*. London: Gollancz, 1957. LU.

533   ———. *Count Basie and His Orchestra: Its Music and Its Musicians*. New York: Citadel Press, 1957. AU, HU, SU, TI.

534   ———. *Count Basie and His Orchestra: Its Music and Its Musicians*. Westport, Connecticut: Negro Universities Press, 1971. SC, TI.

535 Horton, Christian D. "The Suitability of the Indigenous Music of Sierra Leone for Use in the Public Schools." Thesis, Howard University, 1967. HU.

536 Hoskins, Robert. *Louis Armstrong: Biography of a Musician*. Los Angeles: Holloway House, 1979. JS, SC.

537 Hoyt, Edwin P. *Paul Robeson: The American Othello*. Cleveland: World Publishing Co., 1967. FU, LU, SC.

538 Huff, William H. *Jehovah Locked the Lion's Jaw and Other Songs*. Chicago: H & H Music, 1954. AU.

539 Hughes, Langston. *Ask Your Mama: 12 Moods for Jazz*. New York: Knopf, 1961. LH.

540 ———. *Famous Negro Music Makers*. New York: Dodd, Mead, 1955. HU, JS, LH, LU (1957), SU.

541 ———. *The First Book of Jazz*. New York: F. Watts, 1955. HU, JS, LH, LU, SC.

542 ———. *The First Book of Rhythms*. New York: F. Watts, 1954. LH.

543 ———. *Jazz [The First Book of Jazz]*. New York: F. Watts, 1982. HU, SU, TI.

544 ———. *Simply Heavenly: A Comedy with Music*. [Music by David Martin]. New York: Dramatists Play Service, 1959. LH, LU.

545 Hurok, Solomon. *Impresario: A Memoir*. New York: Random House, 1946. HI.

546 Hyslop, Graham. *Musical Instruments of East Africa*. Nairobi, Kenya: Nelson Africa Ltd., 1975. HU.

547 Irvine, Betty Jo and Jane A. McCabe, eds. *Fine Arts and the Black American, and Music and the Black American: [A Bibliography]*. Bloomington: Indiana University Libraries, 1969. HU.

548 Jackson, Bruce, ed. *Wake Up Dead Man: Afro-American Worksongs from Texas Prisons*. Cambridge: Harvard University Press, 1972. FU, JS, LU (1974), SC, SU, XU.

549 Jackson, Clyde O. *Come Like the Benediction: A Tribute to Tuskegee Institute and Other Essays*. Smithtown, New York: Exposition Press, 1981. SC.

550 ———. *The Songs of Our Years: A Study of Negro Folk Music*. New York: Exposition Press, 1968. AU, FU, HI, HU, LU.

551   Jackson, George Pullen, ed. *Spiritual Folk-Songs of Early America: Two Hundred and Fifty Tunes and Texts, With an Introduction and Notes.* New York: J. J. Augustin, 1937. AU, HU (1953).

552   ———. *White and Negro Spirituals: Their Life Span and Kinship, Tracing 200 Years of Untrammeled Song Making and Singing Among Our Country Folk, With 116 Songs as Sung by Both Races.* New York: J. J. Augustin, 1944. FU, HU, LU, SC, XU.

553   ———. *White and Negro Spirituals: Their Life Span and Kinship, Tracing 200 Years of Untrammeled Song Making and Singing Among Our Country Folk, With 116 Songs as Sung by Both Races.* New York: Da Capo, 1975. SC.

554   Jackson, Irene V. *Afro-American Religious Music: A Bibliography and a Catalogue of Gospel Music.* Westport, Connecticut: Greenwood Press, 1979. FU, HU, LU, SC, SU, TI.

555   Jackson, Jesse. *Make a Joyful Noise Unto the Lord: The Life of Mahalia Jackson, Queen of Gospel Singers.* New York: Thomas Y. Crowell, 1974. SC.

556   Jackson, Mahalia. *Movin' On Up.* New York: Hawthorn Books, 1966. AU, HI, HU, LU, SC, TI, XU.

557   Jaegerhuber, Werner A., ed. *Chansons Folkloriques d'Haïti.* Port-au-Prince, Haiti: Valerio Canez, 1945. FU, HU.

558   James, Burnett. *Billie Holiday.* New York: Hippocrene Books, 1984. LU.

559   ———. *Essays on Jazz.* London: Sidgwick and Jackson, 1962. LU.

560   James, Michael. *Dizzy Gillespie.* London: Cassell, 1959. HU, LH.

561   ———. *Dizzy Gillespie.* New York: A. S. Barnes, 1961. TI.

562   ———. *Miles Davis.* New York: A. S. Barnes, 1961. TI.

563   ———. *Miles Davis.* London: Cassell, 1961. HU.

564   Jasen, David A. *Recorded Ragtime, 1897–1958.* Hamden, Connecticut: Archon Books, 1973. FU.

565   ——— and Trebor J. Tichenor. *Rags and Ragtime: A Musical History.* New York: Seabury Press, 1978. JS.

566   *Jazz in [Fifty-Nine] '59.* New York: Program Publishing Co., n.d. HU.

567   *Jazz in Music Education.* Los Angeles: Children's Music Center, 1956. LH.

568   *Jazz on LP's: A Collector's Guide to Jazz on Decca, Brunswick, London, Felsted, Ducretet-Thomson, Vogue Coral, Telefunken, and Durium Long Playing Records.* Westport, Connecticut: Greenwood Press, 1978. HU.

569 *Jazz on [Seventy-Eights] 78's: A Guide to Many Examples of Classic Jazz on Decca, Brunswick, Vocalion, and London, 78 R.P.M. Records.* London: Decca Record Co., 1954. HU.

570 Jekyll, Walter, ed. *Jamaican Song and Story: Annancy Stories, Digging Songs, Ring Tunes, and Dancing Tunes.* London: David Nutt, 1907. NC, VS.

571 ———, ed. *Jamaican Song and Story: Annancy Stories, Digging Songs, Ring Tunes, and Dancing Tunes.* New York: Dover Publications, 1966. HU.

572 Jelliffe, Rowena W. *Here's Zelma: Zelma Watson George.* Cleveland: The Biography Committee for Dr. Zelma Watson George Appreciation Dinner, 1971. FU.

573 Jepsen, Jorgen G. *Discography of Duke Ellington.* Brande, Denmark: Debut Records, 1959. HU.

574 ———. *Discography of Louis Armstrong.* Brande, Denmark: Debut Records, 1959. HU.

575 ———. *Jazz Records: A Discography.* Hoete, Denmark: Karl Emil Knudsen, 1963. HU.

576 Jessye, Eva A. *My Spirituals.* New York: Robbins-Engel, 1927. FU, NC, VS.

577 Jewell, Derek. *Duke: A Portrait of Duke Ellington.* New York: W. W. Norton, 1977. HU, JS, LU, SU, TI, XU.

578 Johnson, Guy B. *John Henry: Tracking Down a Negro Legend.* Chapel Hill: University of North Carolina Press, 1929. SU.

579 Johnson, J. Rosamond, ed. *Rolling Along in Song: Chronological Survey of American Negro Music.* New York: Viking Press, 1937. LU, NC, SC, XU.

580 ———, arr. *Sixteen New Negro Spirituals.* New York: Handy Brothers Music Co., 1939. FU, HU, TI.

581 ———. *Utica Jubilee Singers Spirituals as Sung at the Utica Normal and Industrial Institute of Mississippi.* Boston: Oliver Ditson, 1930. HU.

582 Johnson, James P. *Bibliographic Guide to the Study of Afro-American Music.* Washington: Consciousness IV, Howard University Libraries, 1973. HU.

583 Johnson, James Weldon and J. Rosamond Johnson, eds. *The Book of American Negro Spirituals.* New York: Viking Press, 1925. FU, HU, LU, NC.

584   ———, eds. *The Books of American Negro Spirituals*. New York: Viking Press, 1940. HU, LH (1961), LU (1962), SC (1969), SU (1969), TI, VS, XU.

585   ———. *Lift Every Voice and Sing: [Illustrated by Mozell Thompson]*. New York: Hawthorn Books, 1970. FU, LU, SU.

586   ———. *Lift Ev'ry Voice: NAACP Song Book*. New York: NAACP [Song Book Committee], 1972. LU.

587   ———, eds. *The Second Book of American Negro Spirituals*. New York: Viking Press, 1926. HU, LU, NC, SA, XU.

588   Joplin, Scott. *The Collected Works of Scott Joplin*. Ed. Vera Brodsky Lawrence. New York: The New York Public Library, 1971. FU, LU, SC, SU.

589   ———. *The Complete Works of Scott Joplin*, vol 2. Ed. Vera Brodsky Lawrence. New York: The New York Public Library, 1981. SU.

590   ———. *Scott Joplin Collected Piano Works*. Ed. Vera Brodsky Lawrence. New York: The New York Public Library, 1972. SU.

591   ———. *Scott Joplin Ragtime Piano Selections*. Eds. Takako Nagase and J. Young. Tokyo, Japan: Rittor Music, 1981. LU.

592   Jones, A. M. *African Drumming: A Study in the Combination of Rhythms in African Music*. Johannesburg, South Africa: University of Witwatersrand Press, 1934. LU.

593   ———. *Africa and Indonesia: The Evidence of the Xylophone and Other Musical and Cultural Factors*. Leiden, Netherlands: E, J. Brill, 1964. HU.

594   ———. *African Music*. Livingstone, Northern Rhodesia: The Rhodes-Livingstone Institute, 1943. HU, TI.

595   ———. *African Music in Northern Rhodesia and Some Other Places*. Livingstone, Northern Rhodesia: The Rhodes-Livingstone Institute, 1949. AU, LH.

596   ———. *African Rhythm*. London: Stone and Cox, 1965. LU.

597   ———. *African Rhythm*. London: International African Institute, 1972. FU.

598   ———. *Studies in African Music*. London: Oxford University Press, 1959. AU, FU, HI, HU, LU (1961), SC, TI, XU.

599   Jones, Anthony M. *Steelband: A History: The Winston "Spree" Simon Story*. Port of Spain, Trinidad: Educo Press, 1975.

600 Jones, Bessie. *For the Ancestors: Autobiographical Memoirs*. Ed, John Stewart. Urbana: University of Illinois Press, 1983. FU, HU, JS, LU.

601 Jones, Hettie. *Big Star Fallin' Mama: Five Women in Black Music*. New York: Dell Publishing Co., 1974. SC.

602 ———. *Big Star Fallin' Mama: Five Women in Black Music*. New York: Viking Press, 1974. HU, JS, LU.

603 Jones, LeRoi. *Black Music*. New York: William Morrow, 1967. AU, FU, HI, HU, HU (1980), JS, LU, TI, XU.

604 ———. *Blues People: Negro Music in White America*. New York: William Morrow: 1963. AU, FU, HI, HU, LH, LU (1970), SC, SS, SS (1967), SU, TI, XU.

605 ———. *Blues People: Negro Music in White America*. Westport, Connecticut: Greenwood Press, 1980. JS.

606 Jones, Max and Albert McCarthy, eds. *Jazz Music: A Tribute to Huddie Ledbetter*. London: Jazz Music Books, 1946. TI.

607 ———, eds. *Jazz Review: A Selection of Notes and Essays on Live and Recorded Jazz, Most of Which were Written in the U.S.A. Before the End of the War*. London: Jazz Music Books, 1945. HU.

608 Jones, Max and John Chilton. *Louis: The Louis Armstrong Story, 1900–1971*. Boston: Little, Brown, 1971. FU, LU.

609 Jost, Ekkehard. *Free Jazz*. New York: Da Capo, 1981. FU.

610 Joyner, Charles W. *Folk Song in South Carolina*. Columbia: University of South Carolina Press, 1971. HU.

611 *Jubilee and Plantation Songs: Characteristic Favorites, As Sung by the Hampton Students, Jubilee Singers, Fisk University Students, and Other Concert Companies*. Boston: Oliver Ditson, 1915. FU.

612 *Jubilee Songs as Sung by the Jubilee Singers of Fisk University*. New York: Biglow and Main, n.d. XU.

613 Kaminsky, Max. *My Life in Jazz*. New York: Harper and Row, 1963. HU.

614 Kane, Henry. *How to Write a Song: As Told to Henry Kane by Duke Ellington*. New York: Macmillan, 1962. LH.

615 Katz, Bernard, ed. *The Social Implications of Early Negro Music in the United States: With Over 150 of the Songs, Many of them with their Music*. New York: Arno Press, 1969. FU, HU, LU, NC, SC, XU.

616 Kaufman, Fredrick and John P. Guckin. *The African Roots of Jazz*. Sherman Oaks, California: Alfred, 1979. HU, SC.

617 Kay, Shirley, ed. *The Book of the Blues*. New York: Leeds Music Corp., 1963. HU.

618 Kebede, Ashenafi. "The Music of Ethiopia: Its Development and Cultural Setting." Dissertation, Wesleyan University, 1971. HU.

619 ———. *Roots of Black Music: The Vocal, Instrumental, and Dance Heritage of Africa and Black America*. Englewood Cliffs, New Jersey: Prentice-Hall, 1982. FU, HU, JS.

620 Keepnews, Orrin and Bill Grauer, Jr., eds. *A Pictorial History of Jazz: People and Places from New Orleans to Modern Jazz*. New York: Crown, 1955. FU (1966), HU, LH, LU (1966), SC (1971), TI (1966), XU.

621 Keil, Charles. *Tiv Song*. Chicago: University of Chicago Press, 1979. FU, HU, SC.

622 ———. *Urban Blues*. Chicago: University of Chicago Press, 1966. FU, HI, HU, LU, SU, TI, XU.

623 Kennedy, Robert E. *Black Cameos: [Negro Songs and Stories]*. New York: Albert and Charles Boni, 1924. NC.

624 ———. *Mellows: A Chronicle of Unknown Singers*. New York: Albert and Charles Boni, 1925. SC, VS, XU.

625 ———. *More Mellows*. New York: Dodd, Mead, 1931. FU, VS, XU.

626 Kennington, David. *The Literature of Jazz: A Critical Guide*. Chicago: American Library Association, 1971. AU (1980), HU, HU (1980).

627 Kimball, Robert and William Bolcom. *Reminiscing with Sissle and Blake*. New York: Viking Press, 1973. FU, HU, LU, NC, SC.

628 King, Anthony. *Yoruba Sacred Music from Ekiti*. Ibadan, Nigeria: Ibadan University Press, 1961. HU.

629 Kirby, Percival R. *The Musical Instruments of the Native Races of South Africa*. London: Oxford University Press, 1934. HI, HU, XU.

630 ———. *The Musical Instruments of the Native Races of South Africa*. Johannesburg, South Africa: Witwatersrand University Press, 1965. LU.

631 ———. *Wits End: An Unconventional Autobiography*. Cape Town, South Africa: Timmins, 1967. HU.

632 Kirkeby, W. T., ed. *Ain't Misbehavin': The Story of Fats Waller*. New York: Dodd, Mead, 1966. FU, HU, LU.

633 ———, ed. *Ain't Misbehavin': The Story of Fats Waller*. New York: Da Capo, 1975. SU.

634 Kitt, Eartha. *Alone with Me: A New Autobiography*. Chicago: H. Regnery Co., 1975. FU, HU, LU (1976), SC, TI.

635 ———. *Thursday's Child*. New York: Duell, Sloan and Pearce, 1956. HI, LU, TI.

636 Kmen, Henry A. *Music in New Orleans: The Formative Years, 1791–1841*. Baton Rouge: Louisiana State University Press, 1966. SU.

637 Knaack, Twila. *Ethel Waters, I Touched a Sparrow*. Waco, Texas: Word Books, 1978. SC.

638 Knight, Curtis. *Jimi: An Intimate Biography of Jimi Hendrix*. New York: Praeger, 1974. SC.

639 Kofsky, Frank. *Black Nationalism and the Revolution in Music*. New York: Pathfinder, 1970. FU, HU, LU, SC, SS, SU (1972), TI, XU.

640 Krehbiel, Henry E. *Afro-American Folksongs: A Study in Racial and National Music*. New York: G. Schirmer, 1914. LU, NC, SU, VS, XU.

641 ———. *Afro-American Folksongs: A Study in Racial and National Music*. New York: Frederick Unger, 1962. FU, HU, SC, SU.

642 ———. *Afro-American Folksongs: A Study in Racial and National Music*. Portland, Maine: Longwood, 1976. SS.

643 Kubik, Gerhard. *The Kachamba Brothers' Band: A Study of Neo-Traditional Music in Malawi*. Manchester, England: University Press for University of Zambia Institute for African Studies, 1975. HU.

644 Kyagambiddwa, Joseph. *African Music from the Source of the Nile*. New York: Praeger, 1955. AU, HI, HU, SC, TI, XU.

645 Kynaston, Trent P. and Robert J. Ricci. *Jazz Improvisation*. Englewood Cliffs, New Jersey: Prentice-Hall, 1978. HU.

646 Laade, Wolfgang et al. *Jazz-Lexikon*. Stuttgart: G. Hatje, 1953. HU.

647 LaBrew, Arthur R. *The Black Swan: Elizabeth T. Greenfield, Songstress*. Detroit: Arthur R. LaBrew, 1969. SU.

648 ———. *Studies in 19th Century Afro-American Music*. Baton Rouge: Arthur R. LaBrew, 1974. SU.

649 Ladipo, Duro. *Selection from Oba Ko' So (The King Did Not Hang): [Opera]*. Ibadan, Nigeria: Gaxton, 1966. LU.

650 Lambert, George E. *Duke Ellington*. London: Cassell, 1959. LH, LU, HU.

651 ———. *Duke Ellington*. New York: A. S. Barnes, 1961. TI, XU.

652 ———. *Johnny Dodds*. London: Cassell, 1961. HU.

653 ———. *Johnny Dodds*. New York: A. S. Barnes, 1961. LU, TI.

654 Landeck, Beatrice. *Echoes of Africa in Folk Songs of the Americas*. New York: D. McKay, 1961. AU (1969), FU (1969), HU, HU (1969), LH (1969), LU (1969), SC (1969), SU, SU (1969), TI, TI (1969).

655 Laubich, Arnold and Ray Spencer. *Art Tatum: A Guide to His Recorded Music*. Newark, New Jersey: Institute of Jazz Studies, Rutgers University; Metuchen, New Jersey: Scarecrow, 1982. HU, JS.

656 Lawless, Ray M. *Folksingers and Folksongs in America: A Handbook of Biography, Bibliography, and Discography*. Westport, Connecticut: Greenwood Press, 1965. FU.

657 Leaf, Earl. *Isles of Rhythm*. New York: A. S. Barnes, 1948. LH.

658 Leadbetter, Huddie. *The Leadbelly Songbook*. Ed. Moses Asch and Alan Lomax. New York: Oak Publications, 1962. HU, JS.

659 Leadbitter, Mike and Neil Slaven. *Blues Records, January 1943 to December 1966*. London: Hanover Books, 1968. HU.

660 Lee, Edward. *Jazz: An Introduction*. New York: Crescendo, 1977. JS.

661 Lehmann, Theo. *Negro Spirituals: Geschichte und Theologie*. Berlin, West Germany: Eskart-Verlag, 1965. HU.

662 Leisy, James F. *Songs for Pickin' and Singin'*. Greenwich, Connecticut: Fawcett, 1963. LH.

663 Lems-Dworkin, Carol. *World Music Center: African and New World Black Music Bibliography*. Evanston: Program of African Studies, Northwestern University, 1976. HU.

664 Leonard, Neil. *Jazz and the White Americans: The Acceptance of a New Art Form*. Chicago: University of Chicago Press, 1962. HU, TI.

665 Lewis, Ellistine P. "The E. Azalia Hackley Memorial Collection of Negro Music, Dance, and Drama: A Catalogue of Selected Afro-American Materials." Dissertation, University of Michigan, 1978. LU.

666 Lieb, Sandra R. *Mother of the Blues: A Study of Ma Rainey*. Amherst: University of Massachusetts Press, 1981. JS, LU.

667 Litchfield, Jack. *The Canadian Jazz Discography*. Toronto: University of Toronto Press, 1982. HU.

668 Litweiler, John. *The Freedom Principle: Jazz After 1958*. New York: William Morrow, 1984. HU.

669 Locke, Alain L. *The Negro and His Music.* Washington: The Associates in Negro Folk Education, 1936. AU, FU, HI, HU, LH, LU, XU.

670 ———. *The Negro and His Music.* New York: Arno, 1969. HI, HU, SC.

671 Logan, William A., ed. *Road to Heaven: Twenty-Eight Negro Spirituals.* University, Alabama: University of Alabama Press, 1955. HU.

672 Lomax, Alan. *The Folk Songs of North America.* Garden City, New York: Doubleday, 1960. FU.

673 ———, ed. *Hard Hitting Songs for Hard-Hit People: American Folk Songs of the Depression and Labor Movement of the 1930's.* New York: Oak Publications, 1967. LH.

674 ———. *Mister Jelly Roll: The Fortunes of Jelly Roll Morton, New Orleans Creole and "Inventor of Jazz."* New York: Duell, Sloan and Pearce, 1950. AU, FU, HU, LH, SU, TI.

675 ———. *Mister Jelly Roll: Den Märklinga Historien om Jelly Roll Morton en Kreol fran New Orleans och "Jazzens Uppfinnare."* Orebro: Rabén and Sjögren, 1954. HU.

676 ———. *Mister Jelly Roll: The Fortunes of Jelly Roll Morton, New Orleans Creole and "Inventor of Jazz."* London: Jazz Book Club, 1956. LU.

677 ———. *Mister Jelly Roll: The Fortunes of Jelly Roll Morton, New Orleans Creole and "Inventor of Jazz."* New York: Grove Press, 1956. LU.

678 ———. *Mister Jelly Roll: The Fortunes of Jelly Roll Morton, New Orleans Creole and "Inventor of Jazz."* Berkeley: University of California Press, 1973. SU.

679 ———. *The Rainbow Sign: A Southern Documentary.* New York: Duell, Sloan and Pearce, 1959. HU.

680 Lomax, John and Alan Lomax, eds. *American Ballads and Folk Songs.* New York: Macmillan, 1934. FU, HU, LU, XU.

681 ———, eds. *Folk Song U.S.A.* New York: Duell, Sloan and Pearce, 1947. HU, XU.

682 ———, eds. *Negro Folk Songs as Sung by Lead Belly.* New York: Macmillan, 1936. FU, LU, XU.

683 ———, eds. *Our Singing Country: A Second Volume of American Ballads and Folk Songs.* New York: Macmillan, 1941. HU, XU.

684 Longstreet, Stephen. *The Real Jazz, Old and New.* Baton Rouge: Louisiana State University Press, 1956. SU.

685 ———. *The Real Jazz, Old and New.* New York: Greenwood Press, 1969. LU, SC, XU.

686 ———. *Sportin' House: A History of the New Orleans Sinners and the Birth of Jazz.* Los Angeles: Sherbourne Press, 1965. HU.

687 Lonoh, Michel. *Négritude et Musique: Regards sur les Origines et l'Evolution de la Musique Négro-Africaine de Conception Congolaise.* N.p.: République Démocratique de Congo, 1971. HU.

688 Lovell, John. *Black Song, The Forge and the Flame: The Story of How the Afro-American Spiritual was Hammered Out.* New York: Macmillan, 1972. FU, HU, LU, SC, SS, XU.

689 Lovinggood, Penman. *Famous Modern Negro Musicians.* New York: Da Capo, 1978. FU, HU, XU.

690 Lucas, John. *Basic Jazz on Long Play.* Northfield, Minnesota: Carleton Jazz Club, Carleton College, 1954. TI.

691 ———. *The Great Revival on Long Play.* Northfield, Minnesota: Carleton Jazz Club, Carleton College, 1957. TI.

692 Lydon, Michael. *Boogie Lightning: How Music Became Electric.* New York: Dial Press, 1974. FU.

693 ———. *Boogie Lightning: How Music Became Electric.* New York: Da Capo, 1980. HU.

694 Lyon, Hugh L. *Leontyne Price: Highlights of a Prima Donna.* New York: Vantage, 1973. FU, JS, LU, SC, XU.

695 Lyons, Leonard, ed. *The Great Jazz Pianists: Speaking of Their Lives and Music.* New York: William Morrow, 1983. JS.

696 ———. *The [One Hundred and One] 101 Best Jazz Albums: A History of Jazz on Records.* New York: William Morrow, 1980. FU, HU, JS.

697 Lyttleton, Humphrey. *The Best of Jazz, Basin Street to Harlem: Jazz Masters and Masterpieces, 1917–1930.* New York: Taplinger, 1979. HU, JS, LU.

698 ———. *Enter the Giants, 1931–1944.* New York: Taplinger, 1982. HU.

699 McBrier, Vivian Flagg. "The Life and Works of Robert Nathaniel Dett." Dissertation, Catholic University, 1967. FU.

700 ———. *R. Nathaniel Dett: His Life and Works, 1882–1943.* Washington: The Associated Publishers, 1977. LU, SC.

701 McCalla, James. *Jazz: A Listener's Guide.* Englewood Cliffs, New Jersey: Prentice-Hall, 1982. JS.

702 McCarthy, Albert J. *Coleman Hawkins*. London: Cassell, 1963. HU.

703 ———. *Louis Armstrong*. London: Cassell, 1960. HU, LH, LU.

704 ———. *Louis Armstrong*. New York: A. S. Barnes, 1961. AU, SC, XU.

705 ———. *The Trumpet in Jazz*. London: The Citizen Press, 1945. HU.

706 ——— and Charles Fox, eds. *Jazz On Record: A Critical Guide to the First 50 Years, 1917–1967*. London: Hanover Books, 1968. HU.

707 McCoy, Frank M. *Black Tomorrow*. New York: Vantage Press, 1976. HU.

708 McIlhenny, Edward A., ed. *Befo' de War Spirituals: Words and Melodies*. Boston: Christopher Publishing House, 1933. HU, TI.

709 ———, ed. *Befo' de War Spirituals: Words and Melodies*. New York: AMS Press, 1973. SC, SU.

710 McKay, Claude. *Songs from Jamaica*. London: Augener Ltd., 1912. HU.

711 McKee, Margaret and Fred Chisenhall. *Beale Black and Blue: Life and Music on America's Main Street*. Baton Rouge: Louisiana State University Press, 1981. HU, JS, SC, SS, SU, XU.

712 McLaughlin, Roberta, ed. *Folk Songs of Africa*. Hollywood: Highland Music Company, 1963. LU.

713 McRae, Barry. *The Jazz Cataclysm*. South Brunswick, New York: A. S. Barnes, 1967. HU.

714 Macon, J. A. *Uncle Gabe Tucker: Or, Reflection, Song, and Sentiment in the Quarters*. Philadelphia: J. B. Lippincott, 1883. NC.

715 Mainé, Marie-Collette. *Jeune Afrique, Chante!: Adaptation du Célèbre Abécédaire Musical de Maurice Chevais pour la Jeunesse Africaine Francophone*. Paris: Editions Musicales Alphonse Leduc, 1965. HU.

716 Makeba, Miriam, ed. *The World of African Song*. Chicago: Quadrangle Books, 1971. FU, HU, SC.

717 Malson, Lucien. *Les Maitres du Jazz*. Paris: Universitaires de France, 1958. HU.

718 *Mamie Smith, First Race Woman to Make Phonograph Records: A Sketch*. N.p.: N.pub., n.d. HU.

719 Mann, Woody, ed. *Six Black Blues Guitarists*. New York: Oak Publications, 1973. FU, HU.

720 Manone, Wingy and Paul Vandervoort. *Trumpet on the Wing*. Garden City, New York: Doubleday, 1948. HU.

721   Mansangaza, Kanza M. *Musique Zairoise Moderne*. Kinshasa, Zaire: Publications du C.N.M.A., 1972. HU.

722   Marfurt, Luitfrid. *Musik in Africa*. München [Munich], West Germany: Nymphenburger Verlagshandlung, 1957. HU.

723   Marquis, Donald M. *In Search of Buddy Bolden, First Man of Jazz*. Baton Rouge: Louisiana State University Press, 1978. FU, HU. JS, SC.

724   Marsh, J. B. T. *De Geschiedenis van de Jubilee-Zangers met Hunne Liederen*. Vertaald door C. S. Adama Van Scheltema. Amsterdam, Netherlands: Het Evangelisch Verbond, 1877. FU.

725   ———. *The Story of the Jubilee Singers; With Their Songs*. London: Hodder and Stoughton, 1876. FU, XU (1877).

726   ———. *The Story of the Jubilee Singers; With Their Songs*. Boston: Houghton Mifflin, 1880. FU, HU, LU. VS.

727   ———. *The Story of the Jubilee Singers; With Their Songs*. New York: Negro Universities Press, 1969. HU, SC.

728   ———. *The Story of the Jubilee Singers; With Their Songs*. New York: AMS Press, 1971. SC, SU.

729   Martin, Carol E. "Analytical Comments on the Literature Selected for a Master's Piano Recital Performed on July 21, 1974." Thesis, Fisk University, 1974. FU.

730   Massagli, Luciana, Liborio Pusateri, and Giovanni M. Volonte. *Duke Ellington's Story on Records: 1946–*. Milan, Italy: Musica Jazz, 1971. HU.

731   Matshikiza, Todd. *King Kong: An African Jazz Opera*. London: Collins, 1961. FU.

732   Mbabi-Katana, Solomon. "An Introduction to East African Music for Schools." Thesis, Washington State University, 1966. HU.

733   Meadows, Eddie S. *Jazz Reference and Research Materials: A Bibliography*. New York: Garland, 1981. FU, HU.

734   Meeker, David. *Jazz in the Movies: A Tentative Index to the Works of Jazz Musicians for the Cinema*. London: British Film Institute, 1972. JS.

735   ———. *Jazz in the Movies: A Guide to Jazz Musicians, 1917–1977*. New Rochelle, New York: Arlington House, 1977. LU.

736   Merriam, Alan P. *African Music in LP: An Annotated Discography*. Evanston: Northwestern University Press, 1970. FU, HI, HU.

737   ———. *African Music in Perspective*. New York: Garland, 1982. HI, HU, LU, XU.

738 ———. *A Bibliography of Jazz*. Philadelphia: American Folk-Lore Society, 1954. HU, SC.

739 ———. *A Bibliography of Jazz*. New York: Da Capo, 1970. SC.

740 Merritt, Nancy G. "Negro Spirituals in American Collections." Thesis, Howard University, 1940. HU.

741 Metfessel, Milton F. *Phonophotography in Folk Music: American Negro Songs in New Notation*. Chapel Hill: University of North Carolina Press, 1928. HU.

742 Mezzrow, Milton and Bernard Wolfe. *Really the Blues*. New York: Random House, 1946. AU, FU, HI, HU, LH, TI.

743 ———. *Really the Blues*. New York: New American Library, 1964. LU.

744 Middleton, Richard. *Pop Music and the Blues: A Study of the Relationship and its Significance*. London: Collencz, 1972. JS.

745 Millar, Bill. *The Drifters: The Rise and Fall of the Black Vocal Group*. London: Studio Vista, 1971. FU, LU.

746 ———. *The Drifters: The Rise and Fall of the Black Vocal Group*. New York: Macmillan, 1971. SC.

747 Miller, Mark. *Jazz in Canada: Fourteen Lives*. Toronto: University of Toronto Press, 1982. JS.

748 Miller, Paul E. *Down Beat's Yearbook of Swing*. Westport, Connecticut: Greenwood Press, 1978. HU.

749 ———. *Miller's Yearbook of Popular Music and Jazz*. Chicago: PEM Publications, 1943. HU.

750 Miller, William R. *The World of Pop Music and Jazz*. St. Louis: Concordia Publishing House, 1965. HU.

751 Mingus, Charles. *Beneath the Underdog: His World as Composed by Mingus*. New York: Knopf, 1971. FU, HU, LU.

752 *Minstrel Songs, Old and New: A Collection of World-Wide, Famous Minstrel and Plantation Songs, Including the Most Popular of the Celebrated Foster Melodies*. Boston: Oliver Ditson, 1882. LU.

753 Mitchell, George. *Blow My Blues Away*. Baton Rouge: Louisiana State University Press, 1971. FU, HU, LU, SC, SU, XU.

754 Mixter, Keith E. *General Bibliography for Music Research*. Detroit: Information Service, 1962. HU.

755 Mokhali, A. G. *Basotho Music and Dancing*. Roma, Lesotho, South Africa: St. Michael's Mission, 1966. LU.

756 Molitor, Henri. *La Musique chez les Nègres du Tanganika*. Vienna, Austria: "Anthropos"-Administration, 1913. HU.

757 Mordden, Ethan. *The Jazz!: An Idiosyncratic Social History of the American Twenties*. New York: Putnam, 1978. HU.

758 Morgan, Alun and Raymond Horricks. *Modern Jazz: A Survey of Developments Since 1939*. Westport, Connecticut: Greenwood Press, 1977. JS.

759 Moore, Bai T. *Categories of Traditional Liberian Songs*. Monrovia, Liberia: N.pub., n.d. FU.

760 Moore, Carmen. *Somebody's Angel Child: The Story of Bessie Smith*. New York: Thomas Y. Crowell, 1969. JS, LU.

761 Morris, Ronald L. *Wait Until Dark: Jazz and the Underworld, 1880–1940*. Bowling Green, Ohio: Bowling Green University Popular Press, 1980. HU, JS.

762 Morse, David. *Motown and the Arrival of Black Music*. New York: Bantam Books, 1958. NC.

763 Morton, Jelly Roll. *Ferdinand "Jelly Roll" Morton: The Collected Piano Music*, ed. James Dapogny. Washington: Smithsonian Institution Press, 1982. FU, HU.

764 Most, Marty. *New Orleans Blues*. New Orleans: Marty Most, 1964. LH.

765 Murray, Albert. *Stomping the Blues*. New York: McGraw-Hill, 1976. FU, HU, LU, NC, TI.

766 Murray, Tom, ed. *Folk Songs of Jamaica*. London: Oxford University Press, 1966. HU.

767 *Music of Our Land and Our Traditional Dances*. Lagos, Nigeria: Federal Ministry of Information, 1966. FU.

768 Myers, James G., arr. "God's Trombones." Dissertation, Columbia University, 1965. HU, LU, SS.

769 Myrus, Donald. *I Like Jazz*. New York: Macmillan, 1964. HU, TI.

770 Nagashima, Yoshiko S. *Rastafarian Music: A Study of Socioreligious Music of the Rastafarian Movement in Jamaica*. Tokyo, Japan: Institute for the Study of Languages and Cultures of Asia and Africa, 1984. LU.

771 Nanry, Charles, ed. *American Music: From Storyville to Woodstock*. New Brunswick, New Jersey: Transaction Books, 1972. HU.

772 ———— and Edward Berger. *The Jazz Text*. New York: Van Nostrand Reinhold Co., 1979. HU.

773   Nathan, Hans. *Dan Emmett and the Rise of Early Negro Minstrelsy.* Norman: University of Oklahoma Press, 1962. FU, HU, LU, SC, SS, XU.

774   Nathan, Mary E. "Concert Overture for Full Orchestra." Thesis, Fisk University, 1942. FU.

775   Neff, Robert and Anthony Connor. *Blues.* Boston: D. R. Godine, 1975. HU, JS, LU, XU.

776   Nelson, Rose K. and Dorothy L. Cole. *The Negro's Contribution to Music in America.* New York: Service Bureau for Intercultural Education, 1941. AU.

777   Newman, Shirlee P. *Marian Anderson: Lady from Philadelphia.* Philadelphia: Westminster Press, 1966. SC.

778   Newson, Roosevelt. "A Style Analysis of Three Piano Sonatas (1953, 1957, 1976) of George Theophilus Walker." Dissertation, Peabody Conservatory, 1977. FU.

779   Newton, Francis J. *The Jazz Scene.* New York: Monthly Press, 1960. LH, TI.

780   ———. *The Jazz Scene.* New York: Da Capo, 1975. AU.

781   Nicholas, A. X. *The Poetry of the Soul.* New York: Bantam Books, 1971. SC.

782   Niles, John J. *Singing Soldiers.* New York: C. Scribner's Sons, 1927. FU, LU, NC, SC, VS, XU.

783   Nisenson, Eric. *Round About Midnight: A Portrait of Miles Davis.* New York: Dial Press, 1982. HU, JS.

784   Nketia, J. H. Kwabena. *African Music in Ghana: A Survey of Traditional Forms.* Accra, Ghana: Longmans, 1962. HU, SU.

785   ———. *African Music in Ghana: A Survey of Traditional Forms.* Evanston: Northwestern University Press, 1963. FU, HI, SC, TI.

786   ———. *Drumming in Akan Communities of Ghana.* Edinburgh, Scotland: T. Nelson [for the University of Ghana], 1963. FU, HU, LU, TI.

787   ———, ed. *Folk Songs of Ghana.* Legon, Ghana: University of Ghana, 1963. HU.

788   ———. *History and the Organisation of Music in West Africa.* Legon, Ghana: Institute of African Studies, University of Ghana, 196?. FU.

789   ———. *Music in African Cultures: A Review of the Meaning and Significance of Traditional African Music.* Legon, Ghana: Institute of African Studies, University of Ghana, 1966. FU.

790 ———. *The Music of Africa*. New York: W. W. Norton, 1974. FU, HU, SU, TI, XU.

791 ———. *Our Drums and Drummers*. Accra, Ghana: Ghana Publishing House, 1968. FU, LU.

792 ———. *Prepatory Exercises in African Rhythm*. Legon, Ghana: Institute of African Studies, University of Ghana, 1970. LU.

793 Nohavec, Hazel B. *Dusky Clouds: A Complete Minstrel Show*. Cincinnati: Willis Music, n.d. TI.

794 *Notes on Education and Research in African Music, No. 2*. Legon, Ghana: Institute of African Studies, University of Ghana, 1975. HU.

795 Oakley, Giles. *The Devil's Music: A History of the Blues*. New York: Harcourt, Brace, Jovanovich, 1976. FU.

796 ———. *The Devil's Music: A History of the Blues*. New York: Taplinger, 1977. HU, JS, LU, SC, TI.

797 Obojski, Robert. *Prodigy at the Piano: The Amazing Story of Frank "Sugarchile" Robinson*. Parma, Ohio: N.pub., 1962. FU, HU, SC.

798 Oderigo, Néstor R. O. *Diccionario del Jazz*. Buenos Aires, Colombia: Ricordi Americana, 1959. HU.

799 ———. *Estetica del Jazz*. Buenos Aires, Colombia: Ricordi Americana, 1951. HU.

800 ———. *Historia del Jazz*. Buenos Aires, Colombia: Ricordi Americana, 1952. HU.

801 ———. *Origenes y Esencia del Jazz*. [Buenos Aires?], Colombia: Editorial Colombia, 1959. HU.

802 ———. *Panorama de la Música Afroamericana*. Buenos Aires, Colombia: Editorial Claridad, 1944. AU, HU, TI.

803 ———. *Perfiles del Jazz*. Buenos Aires, Colombia: Ricordi Americana, 1960. HU.

804 Odum, Howard W. and Guy B. Johnson. *The Negro and His Songs: A Study of a Typical of Negro Songs in the South*. Chapel Hill: University of North Carolina Press, 1925. LH, LU, NC (1926), XU.

805 ———. *The Negro and His Songs: A Study of a Typical of Negro Songs in the South*. Westport, Connecticut: Negro Universities Press, 1968. SU, SS.

806 ———. *The Negro and His Songs: A Study of a Typical of Negro Songs in the South*. New York: New American Library, 1969. LU, SC.

807 ———. *Negro Workaday Songs*. Chapel Hill: University of North Carolina Press; London: H. Milford, Oxford University Press, 1926. FU, LU, NC, SS, VS, XU.

808 ———. *Negro Workaday Songs*. New York: Negro Universities Press, 1969. FU, SC, SS, SU (1977).

809 Offei, William E. *20 Melodies, English and Twi: Tonic Solfa and Staff Notation*. Accra, Ghana: Multipress Services, 1969. HU.

810 Ogunbowale, P. O. *Akojopo Orin Ibile Yoruba [Yoruba Traditional Folk Songs]*. London: Evans Brothers, 1961. HU.

811 Ojehomon, Agnes A. *Catalog of Recorded Sound*. Ibadan, Nigeria: Institute of African Studies, University of Ibadan, 1969. FU.

812 Oliver, Paul. *Aspects of the Blues Tradition*. New York: Oak Publications, 1970. JS.

813 ———. *Bessie Smith*. London: Cassell, 1959. HU, LH.

814 ———. *Bessie Smith*. New York: A. S. Barnes, 1961. AU, FU, LU, TI.

815 ———. *Blues Fell this Morning: The Meaning of the Blues*. London: Cassell, 1960. HU, LH, TI.

816 ———. *Blues Fell this Morning: The Meaning of the Blues*. New York: Horizon Press, 1965. HU, SU.

817 ———. *Conversation with the Blues*. New York: Horizon Press, 1965. HU, LU, SS.

818 ———. *The Meaning of the Blues*. New York: Collier, 1969. HU, LU, SC (1972).

819 ———. *The Meaning of the Blues*. Philadelphia: Chilton Book Co., 1969. LU.

820 ———. *Savannah Syncopators: African Retentions in the Blues*. London: Studio Vista, 1970. HU.

821 ———. *The Story of the Blues*. Philadelphia: Chilton Book Co., 1969. HU.

822 Olsson, Bengt. *Memphis Blues and Jug Bands*. London: Studio Vista, 1970. HU.

823 Osborne, Jerry and Bruce Hamilton. *Blues, Rhythm and Blues, Soul*. Pheonix: O'Sullivan Woodside, 1980. HU.

824 Osei, Gabriel K. *The Story of the Blackman in Radio: (WLIB)*. London: Afrikan Publication Society, 1976. HU.

825 Osgood, Henry O. *So This Is Jazz*. Boston: Little, Brown, 1926. HU, LH, TI.

826 Oster, Harry. *Living the Country Blues*. Detroit: Folklore Associates, 1969. FU, HU, LU, SC, TI, XU.

827 Ostransky, LeRoy. *The Anatomy of Jazz*. Seattle: University of Washington Press, 1960. HU.

828 ———. *The Anatomy of Jazz*. Westport, Connecticut: Greenwood Press, 1973. HU, LU.

829 ———. *Jazz City: The Impact of Our Cities on the Development of Jazz*. Englewood Clifs, New Jersey: Prentice-Hall, 1978. HU, SC.

830 Otis, Johnny. *Listen to the Lambs*. New York: W. W. Norton, 1968. HI, LU, SC.

831 Owens, James G. *All God's Chillun: Meditations on Negro Spirituals*. Nashville: Abingdon Press, 1971. HU.

832 Pack, Louise H. "The Status of Music in Negro Secondary Schools of Washington, D.C." Thesis, Howard University, 1945. HU.

833 Page, Drew, *Drew's Blues: A Sideman's Life with Big Bands*. Baton Rouge: Louisiana State University Press, 1980. JS.

834 Paget, Michael, ed. *Spirituals Reborn: Melody and Guitar Edition*. New York: Cambridge University Press, 1976. SC.

835 Palmer, Robert. *Deep Blues*. New York: Viking Press, 1981. HU, JS.

836 ———. *Deep Blues*. New York: Penguin Books, 1982. FU.

837 Palmer, Tony. *All You Need Is Love: The Story of Popular Music*. New York: Penguin Books, 1977. LU.

838 Panassié, Hugues. *Douze Anneés de Jazz (1927–1938)*. Paris: Editions R.-A. Corrêa, 1946. TI.

839 ———. *Hot Jazz: The Guide to Swing Music*. New York: M. Witmark, 1936. HU.

840 ———. *Hot Jazz: The Guide to Swing Music*. Westport, Connecticut: Negro Universities Press, 1970. LU, SC.

841 ———. *Le Jazz Hot*. Paris: Editions R.-A. Corrêa, 1934. HU.

842 ———. *Louis Armstrong*. New York: C. Scribner's Sons, 1971. FU, JS, SC.

843 ———. *Louis Armstrong*. New York: Da Capo, 1979. HU, LU, SU.

844 ———. *The Real Jazz*. New York: Smith and Durell, 1942. FU (1943), HU, LU, TI.

845 ———. *The Real Jazz*. New York: A. S. Barnes, 1960. AU, HU.

846 ———. *The Real Jazz*. Westport, Connecticut: Greenwood Press, 1973. HU.

847 ——— and Madeleine Gautier. *Guide to Jazz*. Boston: Houghton Mifflin, 1956. AU, TI.

848 ———. *Guide to Jazz*. Westport, Connecticut: Greenwood Press, 1973. HU, JS.

849 Parrish, Lydia A., ed. *Slave Songs of the Georgia Sea Islands*. New York: Creative Age Press, 1942. AU, FU, HI, HU, SU, TI, VS, XU.

850 ———, ed. *Slave Songs of the Georgia Sea Islands*. Hatboro, Pennsylvania: Folklore Associates, 1965. LU, SC, SS, SU.

851 *Patterns of Progress: Music, Dance, and Drama in Ethiopia, Book IX*. Addis Ababa, Ethiopia: Ministry of Information, Publications and Foreign Languages Press Department, 1968. HU.

852 Patterson, Cecil L. "A Different Drum: The Image of the Negro in the Nineteenth Century Popular Song Book." Dissertation, University of Pennsylvania, Philadelphia, 1961. HU, LU, SS.

853 Patterson, Lindsay, ed. *The Afro-American in Music and Art*. Cornwells Heights, Pennsylvania: Publishers Agency, 1978. SS.

854 ———, ed. *The Negro in Music and Art*. New York: Publishers Co., 1967. FU, HI, HU, LU, SS, TI, XU.

855 Paul, Elliot H. *That Crazy American Music: [Jazz]*. Indianapolis: Bobbs-Merrill, 1957. HU.

856 Paul, Emmanuel C. *Notes sur la Folk-Lore d'Haïti: Proverbes et Chansons*. Port-au-Prince, Haïti: Imprimerie Télhomme, 1946. HU.

857 Paul, Jane B. "Music in Culture: Black Sacred Song Style, in Slidell, Louisiana and Chicago, Illinois." Dissertation, Northwestern University, 1973. HU.

858 Pearson, Barry L. *"Sounds So Good to Me": The Bluesman's Story*. Philadelphia: University of Pennsylvania Press, 1984. LU.

859 Peek, Philip M., ed. *Catalog of Afroamerican Music and Oral Data Holdings*. Bloomington: Archives of Traditional Music, Indiana University, 1970. LU.

860 Pepper, Herbert. *Musique Centre-Africaine: Extrait du Volume "Afrique Equatoriale Francaise" de l'Encyclopédie Coloniale et Maritime*. Paris:

Edité par le Gouvernement Général de l'Afrique Equatoriale Francaise, n.d. HU.

861 Petrie, Gavin, ed. *Black Music*. London: Hamlyn, 1974. XU.

862 Pevar, Susan G. *Teach-in: The Gambian Kora*. N.p.: N.pub., 1977. LU.

863 Phillips, Ekundayo. *Yoruba Music (Africa): Fusion of Speech and Music*. Johannesburg, South Africa: Music Society, 1953. AU.

864 Pike, Gustavus D. *The Jubilee Singers, and Their Campaign for Twenty Thousand Dollars*. Boston: Lee and Shepard; New York: Lee, Shepard,and Dillingham, 1873. FU, HU, LU, NC, XU.

865 ———. *The Jubilee Singers, and Their Campaign for Twenty Thousand Dollars*. New York: AMS Press, 1974. SC, SU.

866 ———. *The Singing Campaign for Ten Thousand Pounds: Or, The Jubilee Singers in Great Britain*. London: Hodder and Stoughton; Boston: Lee and Shepard, 1874. FU.

867 ———. *The Singing Campaign for Ten Thousand Pounds: Or, The Jubilee Singers in Great Britain*. New York: American Missionary Society, 1875. LU, NC.

868 ———. *The Singing Campaign for Ten Thousand Pounds: Or, The Jubilee Singers in Great Britain*. Freeport, New York: Books for Libraries Press, 1971. SC.

869 Pinkston, Alfred A. "Lined Hymns, Spirituals, and the Associated Lifestyle of Rural Black People in the United States." Dissertation, University of Miami, 1975. HU.

870 Pittman, Evelyn L. *Rich Heritage: Songs About American Negro Heroes*. Oklahoma City: Harlow Publishing Corp., 1944. HU.

871 *The PL Yearbook of Jazz*. London: Editions Poetry, 1946. TI.

872 Placksin, Sally. *American Women in Jazz, 1900 to the Present: Their Words, Lives, and Music*. New York: Seaview, 1982. JS.

873 Pleasants, Henry. *The Great American Popular Singers*. New York: Simon and Schuster, 1974. LU.

874 ———. *Serious Music, and All That Jazz: An Adventure in Music Criticism*. New York: Simon and Schuster, 1969. HU.

875 Powne, Michael. *Ethiopian Music, An Introduction: A Survey of Ecclesiastical and Secular Ethiopian Music and Instruments*. London: Oxford University Press, 1968. FU, HI, HU, LU, SC, XU.

876 Priestly, Brian. *Charlie Parker*. New York: Hippocrene Books, 1984. LU.

877   ———. *Mingus: A Critical Biography*. New York: Da Capo, 1982. FU.

878   *Racial and Ethnic Directions in American Music: Report of the College Music Society*. Boulder, Colorado: Committee on the Status of Minorities in the Profession, College Music Society, 1982. LU.

879   Ramon y Rivera, Lius F. *La Música Afroamericana*. Dakar, Senegal: N.pub., 1974. HU.

880   Ramsey, Frederic. *Been Here and Gone*. New Brunswick, New Jersey: Rutgers University Press, 1960. AU, HI, HU, JS, LH, LU, SC, SS, TI, XU.

881   ———. *A Guide to Longplay Records*. New York: Long Player Publications, 1954. HU.

882   ———. *Where the Music Started: A Photographic Essay*. New Brunswick, New Jersey: Rutgers University Press, 1970. LU.

883   ——— and Charles E. Smith, eds. *Jazzmen*. New York: Harcourt, Brace, 1939. AU, HU, LH, SC, TI.

884   ———, eds. *Jazzmen*. St. Clair Shores, Michigan: Scholarly Press, 1972. HU, LU.

885   Redd, Lawrence N. *Rock is Rhythm and Blues: The Impact of Mass Media*. East Lansing: Michigan State University Press, 1974. FU, HU, LU.

886   Reisner, Robert G. *Bird: The Legend of Charlie Parker*. New York: Citadel Press, 1962. FU, HU, LU.

887   ———. *The Jazz Titans, Including "The Parlance of Hip" : With Short Biographical Sketches and Brief Discographies*. Garden City, New York: Doubleday, 1960. HU.

888   ———. *The Legend of Charlie Parker*. New York: Da Capo, 1975. SU.

889   ———. *The Literature of Jazz: A Selective Bibliography*. New York: New York Public Library, 1959. HU, LU, TI.

890   Rhea, La Julia. *America's First Black Artist to Star with a Major Opera Company, Chicago, 1937: But Still Excluded from Black Musical History, Why?* Blue Island, Illinois: L. Rhea, 197? FU.

891   Rich, Alan. *The Simon and Schuster Listener's Guide to Jazz*. New York: Simon and Schuster, 1980. JS.

892   Ricks, George R. "Some Aspects of the Religious Music of the United States Negro: An Ethnomusicological Study with Special Emphasis on the Gospel Tradition." Dissertation, Northwestern University, 1960. FU, HU, LU, SS.

893 ———. *Some Aspects of the Religious Music of the United States Negro: An Ethnomusicological Study with Special Emphasis on the Gospel Tradition*. New York: Arno Press, 1977. HU, JS, XU.

894 Riedel, Johannes. *Soul Music, Black and White: The Influence of Black Music on the Churches*. Minneapolis: Augsburg, 1975. FU, HU, SC, SS.

895 Rive, Richard. *African Songs*. Berlin: Seven Seas, 1963. LH.

896 Rivelli, Pauline and Robert Levin, eds. *The Black Giants*. New York: World Publishing Co., 1970. AU, FU, HU.

897 ———, eds. *Giants of Black Music*. New York: Da Capo, 1980. HU.

898 Roach, Hildred. *Black American Music: Past and Present*. Boston: Crescendo, 1973. FU, HU, NC, XU.

899 Roberts, John S. *Black Music of Two Worlds*. New York: Praeger, 1972. AU, FU, HI, HU, JS, LU, SS, TI, XU.

900 Robeson, Eslanda G. *Paul Robeson, Negro*. New York: Harper, 1930. NC.

901 Rockmore, Noel. *Preservation Hall Portraits*. Baton Rouge: Louisiana State University Press, 1968. HU, XU.

902 Rodeheaver, Homer A. *Negro Spirituals*. Chicago: Rodeheaver, n.d. XU.

903 ———. *Southland Spirituals*. Chicago: Rodeheaver, Hall-Mack, 1936. XU.

904 Rogers, James O. *Blues and Ballads of a Black Yankee: A Journey with Sad Sam*. New York: Exposition Press, 1965. HU, LH, TI.

905 Rollins, Charlemae, ed. *Christmas Gif': An Anthology of Christmas Poems, Songs, and Stories, Written By and About Negroes*. Chicago: Follett, 1963. LH.

906 Rooney, James. *Bossmen: Bill Monroe and Muddy Waters*. New York: Dial Press, 1971. HU, JS, SC.

907 Rose, Al. *Eubie Blake*. New York: Schirmer, 1979. FU, HU, LU, SC, TI.

908 ——— and Edmond Souchon. *New Orleans Jazz: A Family Album*. Baton Rouge: Louisiana State University Press, 1967. AU, HU, HU (1978), JS, JS (1977), JS (1978), LU, SU, TI.

909 Rosenthal, George S., Frank Zachary, Frederic Ramsey, Jr., and Rudi Blesh, eds. *Jazzways*. New York: Greenberg, 1946. HU.

910   Rowe, Mike. *Chicago Blues: The City and the Music.* New York: Da Capo, 1981. HU.

911   ———. *Chicago Breakdown.* New York: Drake Publishers, 1975. FU, HU, LU, SC.

912   Rublowsky, John. *Black Music in America.* New York: Basic Books, 1971. FU, LU, SC, SS.

913   Ruppli, Michel. *Atlantic Records: A Discography.* Westport, Connecticut: Greenwood Press, 1979. HU.

914   ——— and Bob Porter. *The Prestige Label: A Discography.* Westport, Connecticut: Greenwood Press, 1980. HU.

915   ——— and Bob Porter. *The Savoy Label: A Discography.* Westport, Connecticut: Greenwood Press, 1980. HU.

916   Rusch, Robert D. *JazzTalk: The Cadence Interviews.* Secaucus, New Jersey: Lyle Stuart, 1984. HU, LU.

917   Ruspoli, Mario, ed. *Blues: Poesie de l'Amerique Noire.* Paris: Publications Techniques et Artistiques, 1947. HU.

918   Russell, Ross. *Bird Lives: The High Life and Hard Times of Charlie (Yardbird) Parker.* New York: Charter House, 1973. FU, SU (1976), XU.

919   ———. *Jazz Style in Kansas City and the Southwest.* Berkeley: University of California Press, 1971. HU.

920   Russell, Tony. *Blacks, Whites, and Blues.* New York: Stein and Day, 1970. AU, FU, HI, HU, LU, SC, SS, TI.

921   Russo, William. *Jazz Composition and Orchestra.* Chicago: University of Chicago Press, 1968. FU.

922   Rust, Brian A. L. *Jazz Records, 1897–1942.* New Rochelle, New York: Arlington House, 1978. HU.

923   Ryder, Noah Francis, ed. *Modern Spirituals.* New York: Handy Brothers Music Co., 1938. XU.

924   Sackheim, Eric, ed. *The Blues Line: A Collection of Blues Lyrics.* New York: Grossman Publishers, 1969. HU, TI.

925   Sainte-Croix, Basile. *Blues.* Kbehavn, Virgin Islands: Privat Tryk, 1935. HU.

926   Sampson, Henry T. *Blacks in Blackface: A Source Book on Early Black Musical Shows.* Metuchen, New Jersey: Scarecrow, 1980. HI, HU, JS, LU, SC, TI, XU.

927   Sancho, Ignatius. *Ignatius Sancho (1729–1780), An Early African Composer in England: The Collected Editions of His Music in Facsimile*, ed. Josephine R. B. Wright. New York: Garland, 1981. SC.

928   Sandilands, Alexander, ed. *A Hundred and Twenty Negro Spirituals, Selected by Alexander Sandilands Particularly for Use in Africa.* Morija, Basutoland: Marija Sesuto Books Depot, 1964. HU.

929   Sargeant, Winthrop. *Jazz, Hot and Hybrid.* New York: E. P. Dutton, 1946. HU, LH, TI.

930   ———. *Jazz, Hot and Hybrid.* New York: Da Capo, 1975. FU, HU.

931   Sawyer, Charles. *The Arrival of B. B. King: The Authorized Biography.* Garden City, New York: Doubleday, 1980. FU, HU, JS, LU, SC, SU.

932   Sayers, William C. B. *Samuel Coleridge-Taylor, Musician: His Life and Letters.* London: Cassell, 1915. HU, SC.

933   ———. *Samuel Coleridge-Taylor, Musician: His Life and Letters.* Chicago: Afro-American Press, 1969. LU, SC.

934   Scarborough, Dorothy. *On the Trail of Negro Folk-Songs.* Cambridge: Harvard University Press, 1925. LU, SC, VS, XU.

935   ———. *On the Trail of Negro Folk-Songs.* Hatboro, Pennsylvania: Folklore Associates, 1963. LU, SS.

936   Schaeffner, André. *Les Kissi: Une Societe Noire et ses Instruments de Musique.* Paris: Hermann, 1951. HU, TI.

937   Schafer, William J. and Johannes Riedel. *The Art of Ragtime: Form and Meaning of an Original Black American Art.* Baton Rouge: Louisiana State University Press, 1973. FU, HU, LU, SC, XU.

938   ———. *The Art of Ragtime: Form and Meaning of an Original Black American Art.* New York: Da Capo, 1977. LU.

939   ——— and Richard B. Allen. *Brass Bands and New Orleans Jazz.* Baton Rouge: Louisiana State University Press, 1977. FU, HU, JS, LU, SS, SU, TI, XU.

940   Schiedt, Duncan P. *The Jazz State of Indiana.* Pittsboro, Indiana: Schiedt, 1977. HU.

941   Schiesel, Jane. *The Otis Redding Story.* Garden City, New York: Doubleday, 1973. XU.

942   Schiffman, Jack. *Uptown: The Story of Harlem's Apollo Theatre.* New York: Cowles, 1971. FU, HU, LU.

943   Schuller, Gunther. *The History of Jazz.* New York: Oxford University Press, 1968. FU, HU, LU.

944 Schuyler, Josephine. *Philippa, The Beautiful American: The Traveled History of a Troubadour.* New York: Philippa Schuyler Memorial Foundation, 1969. LU.

945 Schuyler, Philippa D. *Adventures in Black and White.* New York: Robert Speller and Sons, 1960. LU, SU.

946 Schwerke, Irving. *Kings Jazz and David.* Paris: Les Presses Modernes, 1927. HU.

947 Scott, Allen. *Jazz Educated Man: A Sound Foundation.* Washington: American International Publishers, 1973. HU.

948 Scott, Thomas J. *Sing of America.* New York: Thomas Y. Crowell, 1947. XU.

949 *Selected Items from the George Gershwin Memorial Collection of Music and Musical Literature, Founded by Carl van Vechten.* Nashville: N.pub., 1947. HU, TI.

950 Seton, Marie. *Paul Robeson.* London: D. Dobson, 1958. LH, LU.

951 Seward, Theodore F. *Jubilee Songs: Complete as Sung by the Jubilee Singers of Fisk University.* New York: Biglow and Main, 1872. FU.

952 ———. *Jubilee Songs: Complete as Sung by the Jubilee Singers of Fisk University.* New York: Taylor and Barwood, n.d. HU.

953 Shaner, Dolph. *The Story of Joplin.* New York: Stratford House, 1948. LH.

954 Shapiro, Nat and Nat Hentoff, eds. *Hear Me Talkin' To Ya: The Story of Jazz by the Men Who Made It.* New York: Rinehart, 1955. AU, LH, SC, SU, TI.

955 ———, eds. *Hear Me Talkin' To Ya: The Story of Jazz by the Men Who Made It.* New York: Dover Publications, 1966. HU, LU.

956 ———, eds. *The Jazz Makers.* New York: Rinehart, 1957. FU, HU, SU, TI.

957 ———, eds. *The Jazz Makers.* Westport, Connecticut: Greenwood Press, 1975. LU.

958 Shaw, Arnold. *Belafonte: An Unauthorized Biography.* Philadelphia: Chilton Book Co., 1960. LU.

959 ———. *Honkers and Shouters: The Golden Years of Rhythm and Blues.* New York: Macmillan, 1978. AU, FU, HU, JS, LU, SC.

960 ———. *The Rock Revolution.* New York: Paperback Library, 1971. LU.

961   ———. *The World of Soul: Black America's Contribution to the Pop Music Scene.* New York: Cowles Book Co., 1970. FU, HI, HU, LU, SC, SS, TI.

962   Shepperd, Eli. *Plantation Songs for My Lady's Banjo and Other Negro Lyrics and Monologues.* New York: R. H. Russell, 1901. HU.

963   Shirley, Kay, ed. *The Book of Blues.* New York: Leeds Music Corp., 1963. SS.

964   Short, Bobby. *Black and White Baby.* New York: Dodd, Mead, 1971. AU, FU, HU, LU, SC, SU.

965   *Short Talks on Music.* Nashville: National Baptist Publishing Board, 1903. AU.

966   Sidran, Ben. *Black Talk.* New York: Holt, Rinehart and Winston, 1971. FU, HU, LU, SC, SS.

967   ———. *Black Talk.* New York: Da Capo, 1981. SU.

968   Silber, Irwin, ed. *Lift Every Voice: The Second People's Song Book.* New York: Oak Publications, 1957. SC.

969   Sill, Harold D., Jr. *Misbehavin' with Fats: A Toby Bradley Adventure.* Reading, Massachusetts: Addison-Wesley, 1978. HU.

970   Silverman, Jerry, ed. *Folk Blues: 110 American Folk Blues.* New York: Macmillan, 1958. HU.

971   ———, ed. *Folk Blues: 110 American Folk Blues.* New York: Oak Publications, 1968. FU, LU.

972   Simmons, Homer. *Music Conversation.* Berkeley, Virginia: H. Simmons, 1903. AU.

973   Simon, George T. *The Big Bands.* New York: Schirmer Books, 1981. FU.

974   ———. *The Feeling of Jazz.* New York: Simon and Schuster, 1961. HU, TI.

975   Simosko, Vladimir and Barry Tepperman. *Eric Dolphy: A Musical Bibliography and Discography.* Washington: Smithsonain Institution Press, 1974. FU, JS, LU.

976   ———. *Eric Dolphy: A Musical Bibliography and Discography.* New York: Da Capo, 1979. HU.

977   Simpkins, Cuthbert O. *Coltrane: A Biography.* New York: Herdon House, 1975. LU.

978 Simpson, Ralph R. "William Grant Still, The Man and His Music." Dissertation, Michigan State University, 1964. FU, VS.

979 Sims, Janet. *Marian Anderson: An Annotated Bibliography and Discography*. Westport, Connecticut: Greenwood Press, 1981. LU, SC.

980 Skowronski, JoAnn. *Black Music in America: A Bibliography*. Metuchen, New Jersey: Scarecrow, 1981. AU, HU, JS, LU, SC, TI.

981 Slonimsky, Nicholas. *Music of Latin America*. New York: Da Capo, 1972. JS.

982 Smith, Charles E., Frederick Ramsey, Jr., Charles P. Rogers, and William Russell. *The Jazz Record Book*. New York: Smith and Durrell, 1942. FU, HU, LU (1946).

983 Smith, Willie L. and George Hoefer. *Music On My Mind: The Memoirs of an American Pianist*. Garden City, New York: Doubleday, 1964. HU, LU, TI.

984 ———. *Music On My Mind: The Memoirs of an American Pianist*. New York: Da Capo, 1975. FU, HI.

985 Snyder, Jack, ed. *Synder's Collection of Favorite American Negro Spirituals*. New York: Jack Snyder Publishing Co., 1926. HU.

986 *Songs and Spirituals of Negro Composition, Also Patriotic Songs, Songs of Colleges and College Fraternities and Sororities*. Chicago: Progressive Book Co., n.d. HU.

987 *Songs and Spirituals of Negro Composition for Revivals and Congregational Singing*. Chicago: Overton-Hygenic Co., 1921. HU.

988 *Songs of the South: Words and Music of 17 Favorite Negro Spirituals*. Atlanta: Conference on Education and Race Relations, n.d. HU.

989 Sonnier, Austin M., Jr. *Willie Geary "Bunk" Johnson: The New Iberia Years*. New York: Crescendo, 1977. HU.

990 Southern, Eileen. *Biographical Dictionary of Afro-American and African Musicians*. Westport, Connecticut: Greenwood Press, 1982. FU, HI, HU, JS, LU.

991 ———. *The Music of Black Americans: A History*. New York: W. W. Norton, 1971. FU, HI, HU, JS (1983), LU, LU (1983), SS, SS (1983), TI, TI (1983).

992 ———, ed. *Readings in Black American Music*. New York: W. W. Norton, 1971. FU (1972), HU, LU, XU (1972).

993 Southall, Geneva. *Blind Tom: The Post-Civil War Enslavement of Black Musical Genius*. Minneapolis: Challenge Productions, 1979. FU, LU.

994   Spady, James G., ed. *William L. Dawson: A Umum Tribute and a Marvelous Journey.* Philadelphia: Creative Artists' Workshop, 1981. SC.

995   Spaeth, Sigmund G. *A History of Popular Music in America.* New York: Random House, 1948. TI.

996   Spellman, A. B. *Black Music: Four Lives.* New York: Schocken Books, 1970. AU, FU, TI, XU.

997   ———. *Four Lives in the Bebop Business.* New York: Pantheon Books, 1966. HU, LU.

998   ———. *Four Lives in the Bebop Business.* New York: Schocken Books, 1970. LU.

999   Stambler, Irwin. *Encyclopedia of Pop, Rock and Soul.* New York: St. Martin's Press, 1975. HU.

1000 Standifer, James A. and Barbara Reeder. *Source Book of African and Afro-American Materials for Music Educators.* Washington: Contemporary Music Project, 1972. FU, SC, SU.

1001 Stanton, Frank L. *Songs from Dixie Land.* Indianapolis: Bowen-Merrill, 1900. NC.

1002 Starr, S. Frederick. *Red and Hot: The Fate of Jazz in the Soviet Union, 1917–1980.* New York: Oxford University Press, 1983. HU, JS.

1003 Stearns, Marshall W. *The Story of Jazz.* New York: Oxford University Press, 1956. HU, HU (1958), LU (1972), TI, TI (1970), XU.

1004 Stewart, Charles E. "The African Roots of the Spiritual: An Historical and Musical Study." Thesis, Fisk University, 1876. FU.

1005 Stewart, Rex W. *Jazz Masters of the Thirties.* New York: Macmillan, 1972. HU, LU, SC.

1006 Stewart-Baxter, Derrick. *Ma Rainey and the Classic Blues Singers.* London: Studio Vista, 1970. HU.

1007 ———. *Ma Rainey and the Classic Blues Singers.* New York: Stein and Day, 1970. FU, HU, LU, SC, TI.

1008 Still, William Grant, ed. *Twelve Negro Spirituals.* New York: Handy Brothers Music Co., 1937. AU, LU, TI.

1009 Stock, Dennis. *Jazz Street: Photos.* Garden City, New York: Doubleday, 1960. HU, LH, TI.

1010 Stoddard, Tom. *Pops Foster: The Autobiography of a New Orleans Jazzman.* Berkeley: University of California Press, 1971. SU.

1011   Stone, Ruth M. and Frank J. Gillis. *African Music and Oral Data: A Catalog of Field Recordings, 1902–1975*. Bloomington: Indiana University Press, 1976. HU, SC.

1012   *The Story of Music at Fisk University*. Nashville: Fisk University Press, 1936. FU.

1013   Strider, Rutherford H. "Music in the General College Program: A Plan for Morgan State College." Dissertation, New York University, 1955. HU, LU, SS.

1014   ———. "Overture for Full Orchestra." Thesis, Fisk University, 1935. FU.

1015   Strumpf, Mitchel. *Ghanian Xylophone Studies*. Legon, Ghana: Institute of African Studies, University of Ghana, 1970. FU.

1016   Surge, Frank. *Singers of the Blues*. Minneapolis: Lerner, 1969. LU.

1017   Taft, Michael. *Blues Lyric Poetry*. New York: Garland, 1983. TI.

1018   Talley, Thomas W. *Negro Folk Rhymes, Wise and Otherwise, With a Study*. Port Washington, New York: Kennikat Press, 1922. NC.

1019   Tallmadge, William. *Afro-American Music*. N.p.: NEA, 1962. SU.

1020   Tanner, Paul O. W. and Maurice Gerow. *A Study of Jazz*. Dubuque, Iowa: William C. Brown, 1973. FU, HU, JS, LU (1981).

1021   Tarse, Jean. *Le Jazz: De la Bamboula au Be-Bop*. Verviers, Belgium: Marabout Flash, 1959. LH.

1022   Taylor, Arthur R. *Notes and Tones: Musician to Musician Interviews*. New York: Coward, McCann and Geoghegan, 1982. JS.

1023   Taylor, Billy. *Jazz Piano: A History*. Dubuque, Iowa: William C. Brown, 1982. HU, JS (1983), VS.

1024   Taylor, Marshall W. *A Collection of Revival Hymns and Plantation Melodies*. Cinncinati: Marshall W. Taylor and W. C. Echols, 1882. FU.

1025   Terkel, Louis Studs and Milly Hawk Daniel. *Giants of Jazz*. New York: Crowell, 1957. HI, HU, HU (1975).

1026   Thieme, Darius L., ed. *African Music: A Briefly Annotated Bibliography*. Washington: Music Division, Library of Congress, 1964. FU, HU.

1027   Thomas, J. C. *Chasin' the Trane: The Music and Mystique of John Coltrane*. Garden City, New York: Doubleday, 1975. XU.

1028   ———. *Chasin' the Trane: The Music and Mistique of John Coltrane*. New York: Da Capo, 1976. FU, HU, LU.

1029   Thomas, Will H. *Some Current Folk-Songs of the Negro*. Austin: Folk-Lore Society of Texas, 1936. HU, SU.

1030   Thompson, Bruce A. "Musical Style and Compositional Techniques in Selected Works of T. J. Anderson." Dissertation, Indiana University, 1978. LU.

1031   Thurman, Howard. *Deep River and The Negro Speaks of Life and Death*. Richmond, Indiana: Friends United Press, 1975. FU, HU.

1032   ———. *Deep River: Reflections on the Religious Insight of Certain of the Negro Spirituals*. New York: Harper, 1955. HU, SC, XU.

1033   ———. *Deep River: Reflections on the Religious Insight of Certain of the Negro Spirituals*. Port Washington, New York: Kennikat, 1969. LU.

1034   ———. *The Negro Speaks of Life and Death*. New York: Harper, 1947. HU, LU.

1035   Tirro, Frank. *Jazz: A History*. New York: W. W. Norton, 1977. FU, HU, JS, LU, SC.

1036   Tischler, Alice. *Fifteen Black American Composers: A Bibliography of Their Works*. Detroit: Information Coordinators, 1981. FU, LU.

1037   Titon, Jeff T., ed. *Downhome Blues Lyrics: An Anthology from the Post-World War II Era*. Boston: Twayne Publishers, 1981. HU, XU.

1038   ———, ed. *Early Downhome Blues: A Musical and Cultural Analysis*. Urbana: University of Illinois Press, 1977. AU, FU, HU, LU (1979), SC.

1039   Toll, Robert C. *Blacking Up: The Minstrel Show in Nineteenth Century America*. New York: Oxford University Press, 1974. AU, FU, HI, HU, JS, LU, SC, SS, TI, XU.

1040   Torrend, J. *Specimens of Bantu Folk-Lore from Northern Rhodesia*. London: K. Paul, Trench, Truber and Co.; New York: E. P. Dutton, 1921. HU.

1041   Tortolano, William. *Samuel Coleridge-Taylor: Anglo-Black Composer, 1875–1912*. Metuchen, New Jersey: Scarecrow, 1977. FU, JS, SC.

1042   Tracey, Hugh. *Chopi Musicians: Their Music, Poetry, and Instruments*. New York: Oxford University Press, 1948. FU (1970), HU.

1043   ———. *The Evolution of African Music and Its Function in the Present Day*. Johannesburg, South Africa: Institute for the Study of Man in Africa, 1962. HU, LU.

1044   ———. *"Lalela Zulu": 100 Zulu Lyrics*. Johannesburg, South Africa: African Music Society, 1948. HU.

1045 ———. *Ngoma: An Introduction to Music for Southern Africans.* London: Longmans, Green, 1948. HU.

1046 Traill, Sinclair, ed. *Concerning Jazz.* London: Faber and Faber, 1957. TI.

1047 Travis, Dempsey. *An Autobiography of Black Jazz.* Chicago: Urban Research Institute, 1983. LU, XU.

1048 Trent-Johns, Altona. *Play Songs of the Deep South.* Washington: The Associated Publishers, 1944. HU, SA, SU, VS.

1049 Trotter, James M. *Music and Some Highly Musical People: Containing Brief Chapters on I. A Description of Music. II. The Music of Nature. III. A Glance at the History of Music. Following which are Given Sketches of the Lives of Remarkable Musicians of the Colored Race. With Portraits, Composed by Colored Men.* Boston: Lee and Shepard; New York: Charles T. Dillingham, 1878. FU, HI, HU, HU (1881), LU, LU (1881), NC, SC (1881), SS, TI, VS (1881), XU.

1050 ———. *Music and Some Highly Musical People: Containing Brief Chapters on I. A Description of Music. II. The Music of Nature. III. A Glance at the History of Music. Following which are Given Sketches of the Lives of Remarkable Musicians of the Colored Race. With Portraits, Composed by Colored Men.* Chicago: Afro-American Press, 1969. SU, XU.

1051 Tucker, Archibald N. *Tribal Music and Dancing in Southern Sudan (Africa), at Social and Ceremonial Gatherings.* London: William Reeves Book Seller, 1933. HI, LU, SU.

1052 Tucker, John T. *Drums in Darkness.* New York: George H. Doran, 1927. NC.

1053 Tudor, Dean and Nancy Tudor. *Black Music.* Littleton, Colorado: Libraries Unlimited, 1979. FU, HI, HU, SC.

1054 Turner, Frederick. *Remembering Song: Encounters with the New Orleans Jazz Tradition.* New York: Viking Press, 1982. HU, JS.

1055 Turner, Patricia. *Afro-American Singers: An Index and Preliminary Discography of Long-Playing Recordings of Opera, Choral Music, and Song.* Minneapolis: Patricia Turner, 1976. TI.

1056 ———. *Afro-American Singers: An Index and Preliminary Discography of Long-Playing Recordings of Opera, Choral Music, and Song.* Minneapolis: Challenge Productions, 1977. FU, SC.

1057 Ulanov, Barry. *Duke Ellington.* New York: Creative Age Press, 1946. LH, SC.

1058   ———. *Duke Ellington.* New York: Da Capo, 1975. JS, LU.

1059   ———. *A Handbook of Jazz.* New York: Viking Press, 1957. HU.

1060   ———. *A History of Jazz in America.* New York: Viking Press, 1952. HU, TI.

1061   ———. *A History of Jazz in America.* New York: Da Capo, 1972. FU, LU, TI.

1062   Ullman, Michael. *Jazz Lives: Portraits in Words and Pictures.* Washington: New Republic Books, 1980. HU, JS.

1063   Unterbrink, Mary. *Jazz Women at the Keyboard.* Jefferson, North Carolina: McFarland, 1983. JS.

1064   Vance, Joel. *Fats Waller: His Life and Times.* Chicago: Contemporary Books, 1977. FU, HU, JS, LU.

1065   Varley, Douglas H. *African Music: An Annotated Bibliography.* Folkstone, England: Dawsons, 1970. HI, HU, SC.

1066   ———. *African Native Music: An Annotated Bibliography.* London: The Royal Empire Society, 1936. HU, TI.

1067   Vehanen, Kosti. *Marian Anderson: A Portrait.* New York: McGraw-Hill, 1941. FU, LU, SC.

1068   Victor, Rene. *Les Voix de Nos Rues.* Port-au-Prince, Haiti: N.pub., 1949. HU.

1069   Wachsmann, Klaus, ed. *Essays on Music and Music History in Africa.* Evanston: Northwestern University Press, 1971. FU, HI.

1070   Wahome, John K. *Traditional Music and Songs for Adult Education: Kikuyu.* Kampala, Nairobi: East African Literature Bureau, 1974. HU.

1071   Walcott, Derek. *Ione: A Play with Music.* Mona, Jamaica: Extra-Mural Department, University College of the West Indies, [1957?]. LH.

1072   Waldo, Terri. *This is Ragtime.* New York: Hawthorn Books, 1976. FU.

1073   Walker, Maurice and Anthony Calabrese. *Fats Waller.* New York: Schirmer Books, 1977. FU, HU, LU, TI (1979).

1074   Walker, Wyatt T. *"Somebody's Calling My Name": Black Sacred Music and Social Change.* Valley Forge, Pennsylvania: Judson Press, 1979. SC, SS, TI, XU.

1075   Walton, Ortiz. *Music; Black, White and Blue: A Sociological Survey of the Use and Misuse of Afro-American Music.* New York: William Morrow, 1972. AU, FU, HI, HU, JS, LU, SC, SS, TI.

1076   Warner, Keith Q. *Kaiso! The Trinidad Calypso: A Study of the Calypso as Oral Literature.* Washington: Three Continents Press, 1982. JS, LU.

1077   Warren, Fred and Lee Warren. *The Music of Africa: An Introduction.* Englewood Cliffs, New Jersey: Prentice-Hall, 1970. FU, HI, HU, LU, XU.

1078   Warrick, Mancel, Joan R. Hillsman, and Anthony Manno. *The Progress of Gospel Music: Spirituals to Contemporary Gospel.* New York: Vantage Press, 1977. HU, LU, SS, XU.

1079   Waters, Ethel. *His Eye is on the Sparrow: An Autobiography.* Garden City, New York: Doubleday, 1951. AU, FU, HI, LH, LU, NC, TI.

1080   ———. *His Eye is on the Sparrow: An Autobiography.* New York: Bantam Books, 1952. HU.

1081   ———. *His Eye is on the Sparrow: An Autobiography.* Westport, Connecticut: Greenwood Press, 1978. SU.

1082   ———. *To Me It's Wonderful.* New York: Harper and Row, 1972. FU, LU, SC.

1083   Watkins, Clifford E. "The Works of Three Selected Band Directors in Predominantly-Black American Colleges and Universities." Dissertation, Southern Illinois University at Carbondale, 1975. HU, SC.

1084   Welch, Chris. *Hendrix: Biography.* New York: Flash Books, 1973. FU.

1085   Wells, Dicky. *The Night People: Reminiscences of a Jazzman.* Boston: Crescendo, 1971. FU, SC, SU.

1086   Wells, Lewis G., ed. *Social, Love-Feast, Class, Prayer, and Camp Meeting Songs and Hymns.* Baltimore: Lewis G. Wells, 1827. HU.

1087   Weman, Henry. *African Music and the Church in Africa.* Uppsala, Sweden: Lundequistska Bokhandeln, 1960. HU.

1088   Westlake, Neda M. and Otto E. Albrecht. *Marian Anderson: A Catalog of the Collection at the University of Pennsylvania Library.* Philadelphia: University of Pennsylvania Press, 1981. HI, HU, SC, SU.

1089   Wheeler, Mary. *Steamboatin' Days: Folk Songs of the River Packet Era.* Baton Rouge: Louisiana State University Press, 1944. LU, XU.

1090   ———. *Steamboatin' Days: Folk Songs of the River Packet Era.* Freeport, New York: Books for Libraries Press, 1969. FU, SC.

1091   White, Clarence Cameron, ed. *Forty Negro Spirituals.* Philadelphia: Theodore Presser, 1927. TI, VS.

1092 White, Evelyn D. *Choral Music by Afro-American Composers: A Selected, Annotated Bibliography*. Metuchen, New Jersey: Scarecrow, 1981. FU, HU, LU, SC.

1093 White, Josh. *The Josh White Song Book*, ed. Walter Raim. Chicago: Quadrangle Books, 1963. HU, LH, SC, XU.

1094 White, Mark. *The Observer's Book of Big Bands*. London: F. Warner, 1978. HU.

1095 White, Newman I. *American Negro Folk-Songs*. Cambridge: Harvard University Press, 1928. LU.

1096 ———. *American Negro Folk-Songs*. Hatboro, Pennsylvania: Folklore Associates, 1965. XU.

1097 White, Timothy. *Catch a Fire: The Life of Bob Marley*. New York: Holt, Rinehart, Winston, 1983. LU.

1098 Whiting, Helen A. J. *Negro Art, Music and Rhyme, for Young Folks*, Book II. Washington: The Associated Publishers, 1938. LH, SA (1967).

1099 Whittke, Carl F. *Tambo and Bones: A History of the American Minstrel Stage*. Durham, North Carolina: Duke University Press, 1930. XU.

1100 ———. *Tambo and Bones: A History of the American Minstrel Stage*. New York: Greenwood Press, 1968. SS.

1101 Wier, Albert E. *Songs of the Sunny South*. New York: D. Appleton, 1929. LU.

1102 Williams, H. C. N. and J. N. Maselwa, eds. *African Folk Songs*. East London, South Africa: St. Matthew's College, 1947. HU, TI.

1103 Williams, Martin T., ed. *The Arts of Jazz: Essays on the Nature and Development of Jazz*. New York: Oxford University Press, 1959. AU, FU, HU, LH, LU, SU.

1104 ———, ed. *The Art of Jazz: Ragtime to Bebop*. New York: Da Capo, 1980. FU.

1105 ———. *Jazz Masters of New Orleans*. New York: Macmillan, 1967. HU, SS.

1106 ———. *Jazz Masters of New Orleans*. New York: Da Capo, 1978. LU.

1107 ———. *Jazz Masters in Transition, 1957–69*. New York: Macmillan, 1970. FU, HU, JS, TI.

1108 ———, ed. *Jazz Panorama: From the Pages of the Jazz Review*. New York: Collier, 1962. HU, HU (1964), HU (1967), LU (1967), XU (1964).

1109 ———. *The Jazz Tradition*. New York: Oxford University Press, 1970. FU (1983), HU, HU (1983), JS (1983), LU, TI.

1110 ———. *Jelly Roll Morton*. London: Cassell, 1962. FU, HU.

1111 ———. *Jelly Roll Morton*. New York: A. S. Barnes, 1963. LU, TI.

1112 ———. *King Oliver*. London: Cassell, 1960. HU, LH.

1113 ———. *Where's the Melody?: A Listener's Introduction to Jazz*. New York: Minerva Press, 1966. HU.

1114 Williams, Robert. "Preservation of the Oral Tradition of Singing Hymns in Negro Religious Music." Dissertation, Florida State University, 1973. HU.

1115 Williams, Willie L. "Curriculum for Teaching the Black Experience through Music and Dramatic History." Dissertation, University of Massachusetts, Amherst, 1972. HU.

1116 Wilmer, Valerie. *As Serious as Your Life: The Story of the New Jazz*. London: Allison and Busby, 1977. HU.

1117 ———. *As Serious as Your Life: The Story of the New Jazz*. London: Quartet Books, 1977. JS.

1118 ———. *As Serious as Your Life: The Story of the New Jazz*. Westport, Connecticut: Lawrence Hill, 1980. SU.

1119 ———. *The Face of Black Music: Photographs*. New York: Da Capo, 1976. FU, HU, LU, SC, SS.

1120 ———. *Jazz People*. Indianapolis: Bobbs-Merrill, 1971. SC.

1121 Wilson, Beth P. *Stevie Wonder*. New York: Putnam, 1979. HU.

1122 Wilson, John S. *The Collector's Jazz: Modern*. Philadelphia: J. B. Lippincott, 1959. HU, TI.

1123 ———. *The Collector's Jazz: Traditional to Swing*. Philadelphia: J. B. Lippincott, 1958. AU, HU.

1124 ———. *Jazz: The Transition Years, 1940–1960*. New York: Appleton-Century-Crofts, 1966. HU.

1125 Witmark, Isidore and Isaac Goldberg. *The Story of the House of Witmark: From Ragtime to Swingtime*. New York: L. Furman, 1939. HU.

1126 Wood, Adolf, ed. *Songs of Southern Africa: A Collection of 100 Songs*. London: Essex Music, 1968. LU.

1127 Woodward, Woody. *Jazz Americana: The Story of Jazz and All-Time Greats from Basin Street to Carnegie Hall*. Los Angeles: Trend Books, 1956. HU.

1128   Work, Frederick J., ed. *Folk Songs of the American Negro*. Nashville: Work Brothers and Hart, 1907. FU, HU, XU.

1129   Work, John Wesley, ed. *American Negro Songs: A Comprehensive Collection of 230 Folk Songs, Religious and Secular*. New York: Crown, 1940. SS.

1130   ———, ed. *American Negro Songs: A Comprehensive Collection of 230 Folk Songs, Religious and Secular*. New York: Howell, Soskin, 1940. FU, LU, VS, XU.

1131   ———. *Folk Song of the American Negro*. Nashville: Fisk University Press, 1915. FU, HU, LU, NC, VS.

1132   ———. *Folk Song of the American Negro*. New York: Negro Universities Press, 1969. SU.

1133   Wright, Jeremiah A. "The Treatment of Biblical Passages in Negro Spirituals." Thesis, Howard University, 1976. HU.

1134   Young, Fredricka R. "An Investigation of the Current State of Music Education in Relation to the Performance-Based Teacher Education Movement." Dissertation, Catholic University, 1975. FU.

1135   Zinsser, William. *Willie and Dwike: An American Profile*. Philadelphia: Harper and Row, 1984. LU.

INDEX

Collections within a school's archives are italicized. Boldface numerals refer to entries in the Bibliography and Union List. Authors in the Union List are not indexed.

A

Aaronson, Lazarus A., 20
Abbot, Francis H., 20
Abolitionist songs, **134, 135, 485, 486**
Abrams, Muhal Richard, 19
Adams, Eldridge L., 13
Adams, Leslie, 3
Adams, Stephen R., 78
Adams, Wellington A., 20, 50
Adderley, Julian "Cannonball," 4
Adkins, Aldrich, 5
African Jazz Opera, An, **731**
African Mass (Luboff), 75
African Methodist Episcopal Church, 5
   hymnals, 67–68
African Music, 15, 71, 90, **4, 6, 39, 60, 61,**
   63, 69, 242, 247, 300, 313, 529, 594,
   598, 619, 644, 712, 715, 716, 722, 737,
   789, 790, 809, 895, 1043, 1069, 1077,
   1087, 1102
   of Basotho, **755**
   bibliographies, **385, 663, 1026, 1065, 1066**
   of Cameroon, **311, 312**
   of Central Africa, 15, **119, 120, 860**
   of the Chopi, **1042**
   clippings about, 57
   concert programs of, 20
   of the Congo, **687**
   in curriculums, 7, 94, **148, 535, 732, 794,**
   1000
   of the Dinka, **273**

discographies, **736, 811, 1011**
drumming in, 13, 14, 47, **159, 160, 592,**
   786, 791
of Ethiopia, **618, 851, 875**
of Gambia, **862**
of Ghana, **94, 784, 785, 786, 787**
of the Hausa, **24**
instruments, **288, 546, 593, 629, 630, 875,**
   936, 1015, 1042
lectures on, 94
of Liberia, 56, **759**
of Malawi, **643**
of the Malinké, **153**
of Nigeria, **7, 85, 767**
of Northern Rhodesia, **595, 1040**
photographs of, 56
recordings of, 34, 40, 94
rhythm in, **191, 596, 597, 792**
of South Africa, **1045, 1126**
of Sudan, **1051**
of Tanganika, **756**
of the Tiv, **621**
of the Venda, **90**
of West Africa, **788**
of the Yoruba, 15, **40, 628, 810, 863**
of Zaire, **243, 721**
of Zimbabwe, **82**
of the Zulu, 40, **1044**
African Music Society, 57
Alabama State Arts Council, 3
Alabama State University, 2, 7, 10, 61
Aldridge, Amanda Ira, 54, 55

ABOUT THE AUTHOR

Jon Michael Spencer was born in Amherst, Massachusetts in 1957. He received his B.A. (1978) in music from Hampton Institute and his M.A. (1980) and Ph.D. (1982) in music composition from Washington University, St. Louis. Formerly an Assistant Professor of Music Composition and Theory at North Carolina Central University (1982–86), he is currently a Visiting Postdoctoral Scholar in the Department of Music at Duke University. He is founder (1986) and editor of *The Journal of Black Sacred Music*.